Also by Jim Lynch

# BEFORE THE WIND

# BEFORE
# THE WIND

## Jim Lynch

Alfred A. Knopf   New York   2016

THIS IS A BORZOI BOOK
PUBLISHED BY ALFRED A. KNOPF

Copyright © 2016 by Jim Lynch

All rights reserved. Published in the United States by Alfred A. Knopf,
a division of Penguin Random House LLC, New York.

www.aaknopf.com

Knopf, Borzoi Books, and the colophon are registered trademarks of
Penguin Random House LLC.

Library of Congress Cataloging-in-Publication Data
Lynch, Jim, [date]
Before the wind / Jim Lynch. — First edition.
pages ; cm
ISBN 978-0-307-95898-3 (hardcover) — ISBN 978-0-307-95899-0 (eBook)
I. Title.
PS3612.Y542B44 2016   813'.6—dc23   2015018848

Jacket photograph © Image Source / Alamy Stock
Jacket design by Chip Kidd

Manufactured in the United States of America
First Edition

TO MY FATHER

# BEFORE THE WIND

# SAILING LIKE EINSTEIN

Einstein wasn't a great sailor, probably not even a mediocre one. He didn't race or cruise, but he understood the pleasing mix of action and inaction and the thrill of a sunset sail into the spangled bliss. Many of us have fallen hard for all of this. On water, we feel competent and exalted, the glory lingering until we step ashore and trip on the curb and can't find our keys and remember our yard is overgrown and the roof moss is two inches deep and the smoke detectors need fresh batteries and some rat died in the wall and our mothers sure wish we lived closer. At least somebody wants more of us. But the *us* we want more of is on a sleek boat with a clean bottom and crisp sails with wind on the beam.

Am I comparing us to Einstein? Yes. Sailboats attract the loons and geniuses among us, the romantics whose boats represent some outlaw image of themselves. We fall for these things, but what we're slow to grasp is that it's not the boats but rather those inexplicable moments on the water when time slows. The entire industry is built on a feeling, an emotion. It's rarely the thing—or is it?

Regardless, boaters are suckers. They'll pay more in moorage and repairs than their vessels are worth and rarely understand how swiftly rain and salt water conspire to corrode and rot, costs soaring as values spiral. And don't get me started on racers who blow thousands to make their sloops go half a smidge faster so they can finish eighth instead of eleventh in regattas so obscure they don't make the tiniest print in the sports section. One local fanatic spent eleven grand on a carbon-fiber toilet to save seventeen pounds. There are plaques on the walls at Capital City Boatworks from skippers thanking us for overpriced paint jobs they're convinced helped them win. It's all in their heads. So yes, there's a special wing of any boaters' asylum for racers, but they're *all* nuts. Myself included. Sinners too. Wrath began on boats, my grandfather told me, insisting Noah himself was a notorious cusser. But sloth, envy, lust, pride, greed and gluttony thrive here, too, as do naïveté, belligerence and other second-tier failings. Consider the new owner of that gutted twenty-one-foot speedboat against the fence there. He rammed the gas dock so hard last week that he tore a hole in the bow because he couldn't find *the brake*. Or pull up a lawn chair and watch public ramps on any sunny Saturday and let the blooper reels begin. As the saying goes, all you need to become a boater is money, though you don't necessarily need even that. Wait long enough, and somebody will pay you to haul theirs away.

Then, of course, there are those who refuse to ever let go. That gashed Pearson 36 peeking out of the first work bay hit a rock in a freak squall in March and lost its keel and rudder. Yet the owner insisted—before going under for three heart stents—to *do whatever it took* to get *Sophia* ready for the summer races.

Mr. Stanton, we gently counseled, fixing her may cost far more than you could sell her for.

"Who said anything about selling?" he asked, choking on his words. "I. Want. To. Sail. *Sophia*. Again."

Do boats have souls? Apparently. At least their essence mingles with their owners'. And just as people start to look like their dogs, they eventually begin to resemble their boats. I could stroll through the marinas and boatyards of the world and pick out the owners from lineups, then straighten their masts, rewire their engines, paint their bottoms and set them free again, until something else dripped, jammed or snapped. Like most boat doctors, I try not to get too close to my customers, but while they begin as strangers I get to know them soon enough. Many become friends; some are family.

This morning it was my father waking me to announce he'd be bringing me a boat to *fix*. He didn't say what that involved, nor ask if I had time or room in the yard. Just that he'd be bringing it all the way down from Seattle and might not arrive till five, so I'd better make damn certain the lift bastard waited for him. That was all. My father used the phone like a bullhorn, to make announcements and dispatch orders.

Bracing for his arrival, I made my final rounds as smitten boaters ogled the naked hulls propped on blocks and stands, the boatyard brimming, as usual, with everything from abandoned wrecks to gleaming yachts worth between nothing and a million. See that faded tub with its snapped lifelines and waterline beard of sea slime? Catalina 27s are as common as gulls around here, but in the moony vision of Rex and Marcy, that neglected waif is an exotic, ocean-ready sailboat.

Barely in their twenties, they moved here from St. Louis to work on an organic chicken farm south of town and discovered their spiritual elixir when their hippie boss took them sailing just once. The next weekend they began scouring marinas for orphaned boats such as this worn-out twenty-seven-footer they snatched at auction for $875.

"Gonna fix her up and sail the islands this summer?" I asked, scanning the harbor for incoming masts.

Smiling too hard to speak, they were glancing at each other to see who'd admit what.

"We're quitting in May and heading out," Rex finally volunteered.

"For how long?"

"Indefinitely."

I laughed before I could stop myself. "Sailed her yet?"

"Nope." He grinned. "Can't wait."

"Spent a night on her?"

"Just in the lot here." Marcy's thick glasses made her eyes too big for her head. Now her teeth wouldn't fit in her mouth either. "It's totally comfortable," she said.

While offering my most reassuring nod, I noticed a tall black mast rounding the marina entrance buoy and storming toward us along the dredged channel.

"Heading to Alaska first," she told me, eyeing Rex to make sure she wasn't oversharing.

"Cool," I said. You're batshit crazy, I thought.

Running a boatyard is like working in a dementia clinic. We commiserate with comforting nods and winces. We play cameos in daydreams and delusions.

"After that, we're off to China," Marcy added, swinging an arm around Rex's bony hips and hooking a thumb inside his front pocket.

"Beautiful," I said. You're both gonna die, I thought.

Or maybe not. I tried to imagine them smiling lovingly in thirty-foot swells on their nineteenth straight day without seeing land. It was *possible*. Maybe they'd sail into transcendence. My problem was that Rex and Marcy from Missouri were already blurring with Chet and Laura from Nebraska, Jen and Osler from Texas and a dozen other bug-eyed, manifest-destiny couples I'd watched roll into this yard. If you haven't noticed, people rarely run east in America. They flee west, to reinvent themselves in Vegas and Hollywood or farther north to our deep waters where ice ages conspired to sculpt this boating wonderland.

I can spot these adventure migrants in a blink because strains of this gentle madness course through my family the way diabetes or alcoholism clusters in others. For years, sailing bound us. We were racers, builders and cruisers. It was our family business, our sport, our drug of choice. Yet eventually, sailing blew us apart, too.

"Got an extra beer?" I asked.

Rex and Marcy crashed into each other lunging toward the cooler for a sweaty Pabst I needed for fortitude, seeing as how the black-masted boat gliding past the docks and shirking every NO WAKE sign was likely commandeered by my father. Once it got within a couple hundred yards, I could make out the familiar shape of an old Joho 39 and the large silhouette behind the wheel.

Approaching too fast, he slammed the engine in reverse at the last moment before stepping onto the dock with a midship line and shouting at tattooed Tommy, "Put the slings at the front and back of the cabin top!" He repeated these instructions after Tommy ignored them.

"Heard you the first time," Tommy said from his seat atop the lift.

"Then why didn't you *respond*?" Father asked. "Isn't that why we have a common language? So we can communicate? And tie those slings together so she doesn't slip when you hoist her. Got that, or should I repeat?" Then he found me with his eyes and hollered my name.

Nobody forgets meeting my father. Loud, tall and meaty, he invades your space and claims the right-of-way. There is nothing moderate about him. A leader and a lout, a gentleman and an ass, he never concedes a weakness, admits a sickness or says he loves anybody. Yet the flip side is that when you please him, your body temperature climbs a degree or two. And here he was, in his element once again. Anonymous on the streets, he remains a legend on the docks. Sailors still line up to shake his big hand, and if he sticks around for a drink, they might summon the nerve to ask about all he reputedly made his kids or crew do to help him win, or fact-check the lore and rumors about my brother or, more likely, my sister.

Obviously still agitated, Tommy quickly hoisted this battered sailboat and let it sway in the slings, something he did only when he wanted to remind owners that he could drop their toys if they were anything short of gracious.

"Hey!" Pop shouted, bounding up the ramp to me as Tommy feigned deafness again, lipping a cigarette. "What's with that jackass?"

"Good to see you," I said.

He stared down at me with glossy blue eyes that always seemed to demand forgiveness. "How do you know yet?" he asked.

In an awkward silence, we watched Tommy maneuver the lift while I pieced together the implications of his visit. This old boat was one of the earliest and fastest of the thirty-nine-foot Johos that my family had designed and built. No doubt he'd bought it for next to nothing and now wanted me to overhaul it on the cheap to sell or race.

"C'mon, skinny, I'll buy dinner," he said, then badgered me the entire quarter-mile stroll to the restaurant. "Tell me you finally have a car that runs" was his opener.

"Nope."

"How's a fix-it whiz like you still not have a car?"

"If I need one, I'll borrow it. I've got a bike."

"You're not a twelve-year-old, Josh. You need a car. You could come work for us, you know? We could still use you—more than ever, actually. You know that, right? You could make a whole lot more than whatever you're making down here."

"Think we've been through this a few times. How's Momma?"

He whipped off his ball cap and shook his head like a dog getting out of the water. "Wish I knew."

"She making any headway?"

He pulled out a handkerchief and honked. "Works around the clock. If I didn't put food in front of her, she wouldn't eat. To be honest, I don't even know what she's working on anymore." He looked down at me. "So when does this monk phase of yours end?"

"How many monks do you know who work in boatyards and date online?"

"How do you meet gals on computers anyway?" he asked.

I considered telling him about my latest encounter with a woman whose list of date disqualifiers went like this: *No drinkers or smokers or Leos or Aquarians or unshaven men under 5-10 or guys over 37 who wear weird shoes or are into NASCAR.* After our one and only outing she added another deal breaker: *You can't live on a sailboat.*

"How's Christy doing?" he asked.

"*Kirsten.* Same as I told you last time. Haven't seen her in years."

"I liked her."

"So you tell me."

"Is this the way it's gonna go?"

"I could ask the same thing."

What my father asked me to do over dinner reminded me that he was a cheater. If you didn't watch closely, he'd move the cue ball. Unpoliced, he'd cheat at cards and Monopoly, on diets and taxes. A cheapskate, too, he vastly underestimated the cost of transforming his old boat while trying to make me feel disloyal if I didn't help. "Your grandfather would be so offended if he knew we were monkeying with his original design," he added, meaning: *Keep the circle of conspirators as small as possible.* He didn't actually say all that, most of it coming in grunts and winks. So I looked away to get a break from his lies and expectations and saw a shrieking tern dive headfirst into the bay and resurface with a silver smelt in its beak. I related with the fish.

"A little help here?" Father shouted across the restaurant. "We're celebrating!" When the pouty waitress arrived, he leaned toward her, as if confiding. "So how much would a couple glasses of your finest red run us?"

Blinking and blushing, she handed him a wine list.

"Oh, Christ!" He groaned. "Nine dollars for a glass?"

"The table red's just six," she whispered, flaring pierced nostrils and glancing at the hostess, securing a witness.

"That's supposed to get me excited?" Father said. "And quit looking down your ornamental nose at us. We all know you can't afford to eat here either. So why don't you grab us a couple glasses of your overpriced six-dollar vintage, and then we'll see if we've got enough cash left over to eat."

She stormed off, but I knew he'd win her back before we left and leave a memorably tiny tip. Ahh, to be Bobo Johannssen Jr. By now it looked more like a role he'd mastered than who he actually was. He smirked at me like we'd just pulled off a heist, then blurted, "This is our year, Josh! This is it. *This is our goddamn year!*"

Standard bluster, sure, but it moved me. As it played out, 2012 was quite a year, one that inspired me to try to help my family cheat and dodge shame and fence contraband and maybe even explain something about the universe that everybody else had somehow missed. Add to that my dating misadventures—seven new prospects waiting there in my in-box—and my daily counseling of neurotic boat owners, and you've got a daunting to-do list for a man supposedly thin on ambition in a world seemingly falling apart. The Mayans predicted time would run out before Christmas. A preacher in Oregon asserted much the same, though with Judgment Day arriving six months sooner.

"If you're not thrilled about helping me with this," he suggested after the wine arrived, "do it for your grandfather. Or, goddamn it, do it for Ruby!"

That's what was said in lieu of an ethics debate on what all truly competitive racers secretly do to their boats. "Entirely her idea," he added, raising a palm as if testifying. Then he sneezed so loudly that everybody stared, surprised his skull hadn't popped off his shoulders. It was genetic. His father once sprained his neck sneezing. I waited out the next two bombs. They came in threes.

"She actually called," he said, between sniffles. "Said it was high time for one last family Swiftsure. Ask your grandfather. She finally called!"

He knew all my buttons, how I felt about my grandfather, who'd fainted yet again, and how I knew my sister had a magical feel for steering our family's fastest design in the grandest of Northwest sailboat races, or at least she had at one time. Steamrolled by his optimism, I felt bone weary, like I'd just swum across the bay.

"Your sister's definitely in," he added, sinking the hook deeper. "Completely her idea."

I couldn't hide my smile any longer. It's not just simpletons like me who are suckers for sailing with their sisters. Einstein's idea of an ideal summer was boating daily with his little sister Maja. In a 1929 letter, he wrote that he couldn't wait to get her out sailing on his beloved *Tümmler. You will go into raptures when you (hopefully) visit me next year.*

Raptures indeed.

Einstein dared to imagine a new flexible grid of space and time, but he never learned how to swim or drive and unwittingly dated a Soviet spy. He also moseyed through summers in a rope belt and lady's sandals and loved sailing with his little sister. Without knowing anything about her, though, I can promise you she wasn't anywhere near the sailor mine was. But that's not even slightly fair, because nobody has ever sailed quite like Ruby Johannssen.

# SUNDAY SCHOOL ON WATER

~~~~~~

The second of three Johannssen kids, pinned between a wild older brother and a soon-to-be-famous younger sister, I was the mild child, the hesitant shade of gray in a black-and-white household. Part of it was my comparable lack of gumption in a family that posted goals and inspirations on the walls. Ruby and Bernard had that dazzle of certitude, always seeming to know what they were going to be: Bernard, an astronaut or a boxer; Ruby, an acrobat or a singer. "What was I gonna be?" sounded like a trick question. How could I be anybody but me?

My family rarely went to church, but we had our beliefs and rituals. For years, Sunday meant sailing, regardless of weather; sometimes in the big boat, more often in dinghies with our father shadowing us in a skiff. *Where's the wind?* he'd shout, louder than any preacher. *No! Those waves are old news! Where's the wind now?* His maxims were hammered into us. *Ease, hike, trim!* And his relentless mantra: *Boat speed! Boat speed! Boat speed!*

Once I'd turned ten, Bernard twelve and Ruby eight, there was no getting out of Sunday sailing without a high fever. When there was too much breeze for the dinghies, we'd crew for the two Bobos, Senior and Junior, on our big boat against imaginary rivals. But usually they just anchored two buoys for a starting line and another two for upwind and downwind marks in the shallow bay east of Husky Stadium. Then they'd follow us around in the inflatable with Father shouting instructions and Grumps (the ironic nickname Bernard gave him) relentlessly encouraging us. We'd do thirty tacks, twenty jibes and ten mark roundings before we could even practice starting. Then they'd call off the race the instant it was clear who'd had the best start, and we'd do it again, with countdowns varying from one to three minutes.

We practiced slam jibes and crash tacks, then we'd start, accelerate and stop on command. Like child gymnasts trained to throw flips before they're old enough to fear them, we raced in storms, in fog and in the dark. It didn't strike me how unusual our family was until we crossed the Strait of Juan de Fuca in a gale, and I noticed, while surfing atop twelve-foot swells, that nobody else was out there, much less flying a purple spinnaker. When we slipped behind the tall break-water into Port Townsend that chilly night, it was obvious no boats had even left the dock. I watched grown men eyeball our gregarious father—steam rising off his T-shirt—with the awe and distance reserved for champions and the mentally ill.

Long after we'd learned the basics, he repeated them: how to read water and sails, how to see and anticipate the ever-changing geometry of the fastest zigzags around the racecourse. Most drawers of his life were messy, but he was a sailing perfectionist. If we slacked off on chores or homework, he rarely groused, but miss a ten-degree wind shift and he'd start barking. If the halyards were improperly coiled or—worst of all—if sails needlessly flapped or were improperly raised, adjusted, lowered or folded, there was a reckoning. Mostly, though, he implored us to just sail *faster*. Whether racing or not, he considered it an insult to the boat, the wind and our family name to go any slower than necessary. Something essential was gained—he called it honor—from sailing a boat as fast as possible that made up for most other transgressions. Through this prism of sailing *right,* we had a shot, so his parenting went, to experience inner perfection. Or, as Mother framed it, to understand an invisible force.

Sailing began with a baffling lexicon, and there was no mercy for misidentification. Some things sounded like what they were: *Mast,* okay. *Keel,* sure. And, of course, *boom,* the most lethal and aptly named item on a sailboat, as in *ka-boom* if you didn't duck at the right time. Fine. But left is *port* and right is *starboard*? Why, and says who? Even basic lingo seemed intentionally confounding. Ropes were *lines*? Yes, but they were *halyards* when they raised sails and *sheets* when they adjusted them. And knots were knots except when they were *knots,* as in nautical miles (1.15 normal miles) per hour, which was the confusing term for speed in the marine world, as if simply being afloat altered time and distance.

Yet that was the lingo and nobody veered from it. When we steered the bow through the eye of the wind and the sails swung to the other side, we were *tacking.* Yet it was also called *going about,* which sounded more like a stroll than the right-angle turn it described. *Hard alee!* is what we were instructed to shout before tacking even if it was barely blowing and the only thing *hard* about it was finding enough wind to nudge the sails across.

Over the sailing millennia, apparently nobody ever came up with an apt phrase to describe what it means to sail at angles toward, though not directly into, the wind. The options: *going to weather* (vague), *sailing to windward* (tongue twister), or *beating* (oddly violent or masturbatory). And if you steered too directly into the breeze and your sail fluttered, that was called *pinching,* which conjured a different image altogether. The potential bewilderment was endless. When your sails were on the port side, you were on a starboard tack and had the right-of-way. There were even two winds to keep track of, the *true* and the *apparent.*

Grumps speculated that all the lingo was part of a conspiracy to make the simple act of sailing seem daunting. But I think the nautical glossary was invented by inarticulate men and perpetuated by mumbling successors who clung to it like any tribe clutches a dying language. Our assignment, though, was to master and not ponder the vocabulary. Yet the terms swirled in my head. One phrase that always made sense was *sailing downwind.* Anybody could visualize the oldest and simplest sailing mode, raising an animal hide above the raft and letting the wind push you through the water. This art has since been perfected with blousy spinnakers and surfy hulls, but *sailing downwind* has become *running* or, better yet, *before the wind,* which struck me as a phrase from the Creation Story or the first three words of an ominous fable. Admittedly, I tended to overthink these things. My father called me a *thinker,* which wasn't a compliment. It put me in my mother's camp, at odds with him and the other *doers.* Thinkers, he informed me, don't win sailboat races.

He'd critique us over lunch, playing Captain Second-Guess. Or he'd ask Mother to explain wind or sailing physics yet again. She rarely raced and never fawned over boats, but I never once heard her question the hub of our existence, as if she'd run some equation that proved her resistance was no match for the genetic gravitas of generations of Icelandic sailors distilled into the one and only Bobo Johannssen Jr. Or whatever defiance she'd mustered must've expired by the time Father's medal hung on a nail in the garage. You win a silver in the '76 Olympics, and your quirks, obsessions and chutzpah are all hailed as essential ingredients of your signature genius.

As I said, my family rarely attended church or mentioned God—except Grumps. *Thank God for this breeze,* or *that start,* or *that wind shift.* His casual reverence was a tic he'd inherited from his Lutheran mother, but he'd also praise pagan lords while heading back to the dock, thanking Odin, Thor and Poseidon among others. As Ruby told her Girl Scout troop leader, "Sailing is like praying in our family." This was back when she used to spontaneously perform our family history for visitors with jumbles of fact and fiction.

"Grumps's father, Leif Johannssen, was related to the great Icelandic explorer Leif Eriksson!" she'd begin, before Bernard inevitably pointed out that these two men were utterly unrelated.

I don't think Ruby set out to tell tall tales. She assumed most good stories were bolstered with interesting facts and numbers, not realizing they were also expected to be true. Yet these embellishments suited her. Things never did add up with her, so why should her stories? The only quibbler was Bernard, whose clarifications, footnotes and corrections turned her performances into duets.

"Our great-grandfather," Ruby proclaimed, "braved icebergs and pirates from Iceland to Seattle with his wife, Dora, in a small steel ketch in 1903."

"Actually they emigrated in 1914," Bernard countered, "on a large passenger ship to eastern Canada before traveling overland to here."

"Grumps's father," Ruby continued merrily, "was a boatbuilder, which is why he started Johannssen Boatbuilders in a rotting warehouse he bought for eleven hundred dollars on the Ship Canal. Grumps was named Robert and called Bobby for short, which was finally shortened—nobody knows why—to Bobo.

"When Grumps took over the boathouse in the early fifties," she went on, "his specialty was designing fast and beautiful sailboats called Johos. Whoop-whoop! He and his wife had just one kid, our now world-famous father, Robert Jr., or Little Bobo, as he was originally called, then Bobo Jr., who took to boatbuilding like a dog takes to water [she routinely botched clichés] and, for some inexplicable reason, grew nearly a foot taller than his dad!"

Actually, Bernard argued, it was eight inches and easily explained, considering some of our Icelandic relatives were giants. We'd marveled over an overexposed photo of a bare-chested Great-Uncle Petur with normal men coming up to his nipples.

"By the time Daddy graduated from high school [depending on mood and courage, Bernard might point out that Father dropped out of the eleventh grade] he was building wooden sailboats with Grumps full-time. And in 1967 the business was renamed Johannssen and Sons Boat Company, even though there was only one son who'd soon be heading off to become a war hero. And they went on to design and build the prettiest and fastest fiberglass sailboats in the world!"

"In *Puget Sound,* perhaps," Bernard mumbled traitorously.

"First came the Joho 32 and then the cheetah-fast Joho 39—whoop! whoop!—which wasn't only a popular cruiser but also won its share of races—though usually with a Johannssen at the helm. Hey, what can I say? We're good!

"Grumps sold boats but also an *experience unlike anything you can ever have on land.* His love of boats made other sailors feel like they were getting a steal and weren't going bonkers, though many of them were doing both. And there's a reason we're so good with boats: we have a higher salt content in our blood!"

"That claim," Bernard would patiently explain, "is based on one misleading blood test that showed Grumps had high sodium levels."

"And some people have suggested," Ruby concluded (she loved dramatic endings), "that the reason the Johos have been so popular and Johannssen racers so unbeatable is that sailing runs in our blood all the way back to Leif 'the Greatest Explorer of All Time' Eriksson!"

"Still not true!" Bernard countershouted. "No relation whatsoever!"

While Ruby entertained and Bernard cross-examined, my role was far more subtle. I'd peer over the Bobos' shoulders after they'd unfurl drawings on the dinner table and secure the corners with beer bottles and wineglasses. Then the three of us would silently ponder the lines until my father asked what I thought. A lot of beauty I'd miss, but not this kind.

"I like how this one sits in the water," I'd say, tracing my pinkie along the arc of the toe rail. "I like the sheer and low freeboard. She's got a tall stick and a deep keel. Looks fast and balanced to me."

If I said it just right, his thick bottom lip would stretch into a grin, and he'd swing his eyes at Grumps. In those days, they saw me as their understudy.

There are so many ways to disappoint your family.

Mother was immune to the sport even though she contributed to the obsession, filling us with science as it pertained to sailing and life. A physics teacher at Ballard High, she shared her love of the periodic table when she wasn't reminding us that everything, including seawater, rocks and apples, was mostly empty space. People, too, she'd say, tipping her head toward our father dozing and whimpering in the recliner. Or she'd hit us with such unusual facts as: the earth is an imperfect sphere, 42.6 kilometers fatter than it is tall. Or she'd point out that almost everything in the room—the radio, stereo, refrigerator and TV—had been made possible by math. None of our friends heard so much about Newton's second law of motion or anything about Bernoulli's principle, which explained how sails and keels worked like wings creating two different lifting forces that squirted a boat forward like a watermelon seed squeezed between your fingertips. We understood Bernoulli long before we knew where babies came from. Mother drilled us on Einstein, too. (Ruby's the only toddler I ever heard shout, "E equiz emzee swear!") That Einstein was a lifelong sailing fanatic helped bridge the gap between our parents, between science and sailing. Plus, Mother insisted, just trying to understand him made you smarter. I alone took on that challenge, realizing only years later that I was studying Einstein to better understand my mother.

Early on, I was good enough at math to fool her that I grasped more than I had. She tucked me in one night and whispered, "Sometimes mathematics builds up inside us, and it's like we're climbing some mountain and we get this beautiful view of things that can only be seen by other mathematicians like us."

The most I could muster was a nod, but my scalp tingled.

That same summer she scribbled down two Isaac Newton formulas on the back of a receipt, folded it and handed it to me in private. It was far more than just the mathematical explanations of why planets moved in elliptical orbits. It was as if I now carried in my pocket the two deepest secrets of the universe.

Her information and insights were delivered with a shrill French accent that further confused people trying to sort out our roots. She'd been an innocent Swiss exchange student named Marcelle Gillette when she'd fallen under our father's spell—according to Ruby's rendition of their first date—while sailing in an old wooden Joho 26 with Father snickering at her silent *H*s, how she called us *uman* beings and commented on the *umid* weather or complained about that *Playboy* magazine perv *Ugh Effner*.

As much as Mother taught us, there was no mistaking who our headmaster was. Father shoved sailing down our throats, and early on Bernard and I swallowed every drop. We practiced boat-handling maneuvers till our hands bled while Ruby barely paid attention, not from lack of interest, but as though she'd entered the world already grasping what we'd never know.

# RUBY MOMENTS

～～～

Two early memories of Ruby sailing:

Sunday after Thanksgiving 1995: My father shoved us out into a diagonal rain in our three Lasers. It took 160 pounds to keep these sleek racing dinghies upright in a blow. Bernard might've weighed 150. I was maybe 120, and Ruby had recently cleared 95. So we were all doomed to capsizing, particularly her. Wearing partial wet suits didn't make it more comfortable or less daunting.

After the two Bobos anchored the inflatable buoys and gave us the three-minute horn, we traversed an invisible starting line littered with beer cans, straining to level our boats by either steering directly into the squall and letting the sails flap or pinching so close to the wind that they never completely filled while we dug our shins beneath hiking straps and suspended our bodies horizontally across the decks and out over the water. I capsized at the two-minute horn and was upright by the one-minute blast, already shivering and flustered and irritated that Ruby hadn't flipped yet. We all had the same equipment and differed only in age, weight and skills. As I tacked toward the starting line, Ruby saw my cringing misery, and her mouth flew open with laughter.

While she and I carefully pinched across the line through the froth, Bernard risked filling his sail and surged ahead, tipping wildly before inverting his body backwards over the rail until his boom clipped a wave and he capsized hard. If there was a violent way to do something, my brother usually found it.

More cautious than ever, I continued pinching, but my concentration slipped and I veered off course, a gust straining my sail before I could ease the pressure. By the time my mast hit the water, I was already scrambling over the high side to stand on the centerboard, trying not to panic but feeling numb and helpless, barely aware of my father's shouted commands. Once I got my boat upright, Bernard had tacked and passed Ruby, skimming along at twice her speed and rapidly approaching the upwind mark at an awkward angle, hoping a favorable shift might let him round it without having to tack twice. Stalling, and desperately trying not to capsize again, I slid sideways and noticed Ruby gaining on me, inching along at a better angle toward the mark, her boat tipping less, making steadier progress, as if she'd found a safe passage. Grumps was so proud he began shouting "God loves ya, Ruby!" just as Bernard missed the upwind mark, tacked back and got knocked down like he'd been swatted by some massive unseen hand. Amazingly, I rounded the mark first and began veering toward the downwind buoy bobbing in the waves half a mile away with Ruby still a few boat lengths behind me. As soon as I loosened my sail and swung the boom wide, I started surfing so wildly that I was reluctant to lift the entire centerboard and risk losing more control. I didn't want to get soaked again. Plus, it felt like something might snap, though that—the breaking and the mending—was increasingly thrilling to me.

This was the year I'd started Josh's Small Motor Repairs. I fixed outboards, chain saws, lawn mowers and other two-strokes most people despised and couldn't keep running. About that same time, Grumps gave me his bright orange and quite dead 1974 VW bus as a project. By that Sunday, I'd already pulled the engine and torn it apart and was preparing to rebuild it a year before I'd be old enough to drive. So damage and reconstruction fascinated me, but storms spooked me.

This was Bernard's sort of day. Approaching it like a fight, he dared the wind to throw its best punch. Yet he was distracted by the fact that his baby sister hadn't capsized. So while I froze out of fear, he paused out of disbelief. Regardless, we hesitated, and in those seconds Ruby yanked her centerboard, wobbled atop a wave, leaned forward and spanked the bow twice, as if urging a horse to sprint, then blew past us on a high plane, a foamy wake fanning off her stern like it does behind speedboats. I was close enough to see her relaxed and amused expression as she passed at twice my speed. Following her example, Bernard popped his board and sped up, rocking precariously, though he still couldn't gain on her. My plan was to keep the board halfway down to sacrifice speed for control in hopes they'd both topple and the tortoise could outsmart the hares. But Ruby pulled farther ahead, though increasingly off course and out of control, accelerating toward shore. When Father bullhorned her to drop the board and jibe, she either didn't hear or couldn't alter course and continued speeding toward docks and stone bulkheads. And during this elongated moment, I loathed myself for wishing she'd capsize and blamed the two Bobos for forcing her out here at this age no matter how gifted she was and hated Bernard for making us all so hypercompetitive. I'd braced myself for being sisterless by the time she finally dropped her centerboard and prepared to jibe precariously near the docks in the bay's lone patch of calm water.

How she found this gentle gap amid the frantic boil didn't make sense—so maybe *it* found *her*—but it was still too windy to jibe without capsizing. That's the downside to dinghy sailing. Once the center of mass tips past the center of buoyancy, to use Mother's terms, there is nothing but body weight to counter the heeling torque and keep you upright. So Ruby was doomed to crash into either the water or the docks. Yet she had seemingly somehow calculated all the angles and realized she could turn safely while her sail was briefly shielded from the wind by her nearly capsized hull because her Laser suddenly popped upright, and she sprang to the other side and hiked hard, sailing on a broader, safer approach toward the downwind mark, even throwing us a hoot and a parade wave before rounding the buoy and pinching toward the finish line several light-years ahead of either of us. We raced three more times as the wind slackened. Ruby won them all and, more amazingly, never capsized.

Afterwards, Grumps wouldn't shut up about *my little Ruby* and thanked God, Odin and even Athena. What the goddess of war had to do with any of it remained unclear as he quickly moved on to salute the Nordic god of wind, too. "Thank you, Njord!"

Keep in mind these tales vary, depending on who's telling them, and there are no undisputed accounts of Ruby's early sailing spectacles. Part of the problem is that so much of what she did wasn't plausible. She was also, as I've explained, an unreliable narrator herself. And as fishermen and sailors have proven through the eons—with the help of reflections, mirages and rum—the bar of truth is set lower over the water.

Here's another Sunday: midmorning in mid-August the following summer with heat waves steaming over the lake. The three of us wanted to be anywhere else as the Bobos set up a short course and agreed to let us quit as soon as we rounded it once or within ninety minutes, whichever came first. So began our epic crawl, drifting and baking across the becalmed bay.

Bernard and I tried to manufacture our own wind by roll tacking, which involved rocking our Lasers to temporarily fool and fill the sails with the illusion of wind. So we rocked and flopped, drifting just slightly ahead of our sister, who was pointed in the opposite direction, and gazing up her mast into the sky.

We were almost a third of the way to the upwind mark, thirty yards ahead of her, when I noticed her suddenly gliding, without sculling or roll tacking. Air and water and time stood still, yet our sister was clearly moving, staring up at the top of her mast, as if seeing or willing something. I whistled at Bernard and pointed. "Check her out."

"Oh, shit," he whined.

Unfortunately, we were increasingly accustomed to such Ruby moments. Part of our training involved studying the tiniest wavelets for hints of upcoming wind shifts. Correct reads made up for other blunders by giving you a more direct zigzag around the buoys—a favorable shift lifting you closer to the finish, an unwelcome one sliding you farther away. And this is where Ruby had a sixth sense, saw tiny ripples we'd missed, had more sensitive skin or—Bernard's theory—was just ridiculously lucky. Regardless, she routinely anticipated implications before we ever did. Yet like I said, on this morning there was no wind to shift.

She was still looking up, her weight well forward and leaning toward the side where the sail hung limply. But then things got strange: the only visible ripples on the lake were suddenly right in front of her bow. Bernard and I roll tacked furiously but were too far away to share her private puff, which soon vanished anyway. Still, it had given her enough to sail past us and around the windward mark, where her magic resumed, and her private ripples materialized yet again, *behind* her now. So she swung the boom out wide and sprawled her weight forward to lift the stern and minimize drag, steering with her toes now, seemingly not caring where she was going, just staring up her mast while these mini-zephyrs came and went directly behind her, pushing her toward the finish line. From a distance, her boat looked like an unmanned, motorless craft gliding through a windless calm as Bernard and I finally splashed around the upwind mark. We didn't say a thing. Even Grumps went absolutely mute.

# THE WIND LOVES OUR SISTER

By the time we got home, she'd been off to the roller rink for more than an hour. So we muddled about and tried to make sense of it all, mostly to ourselves. Nobody was shocked to get the call later that afternoon that Ruby had broken her wrist at the rink. She was as clumsy on land as she was supernatural on water. By the age of thirteen she'd already broken two fingers, an ankle, her nose, a rib, a tooth and now a wrist.

Waiting for her and Mother to return from the hospital, we demolished leftover meat loaf and twice-baked potatoes while watching a *Mary Tyler Moore* rerun loud enough for Grumps to hear it. During commercials, he'd pick up a Steinbeck paperback, switch eyeglasses and reread a paragraph or two before the show returned while my father flossed in front of the tube, as he did whenever Mother wasn't around, and Bernard, as usual, bantered sarcastically with the commercials while our black Labs, Isaac and Albert, huddled beneath my chair betting correctly that I'd slip them morsels. Grumps had seen this same episode many times but still outlaughed the canned audience. Then Isaac dropped a slobbery tennis ball into my lap that fell to the floor and rolled southbound toward the windows.

Over time, the Johannssen manor, with its cracked foundation, increasingly leaned toward the blackberry hill and the lumberyard and, across the water, the Space Needle and the rest of the urban mirage out our windows. We lived near the Ship Canal, a man-made boulevard of fresh water curling west from Lake Washington to the Ballard Locks and Puget Sound. Everything felt stuck in time until the houses around us started selling and getting demolished and replaced with lot-stuffing mansions, leaving nowhere for dogs to crap but in our overgrown yard. Waves of peppy Realtors kept knocking like Jehovahs to let us know how much our "teardown" was worth.

Visitors were often openly surprised to see how and where we lived, assuming such famous sailors and boatbuilders would be living so much larger. Yet the Bobos were more like struggling artists selling sculptures to the wealthy, a sticking point for Grumps, who prided himself on making boats that normal people could afford. Even when business roared, there were few home improvements and never any cash sitting around. The less we're worth, the Bobos liked to say, the less appealing we are to sue. They packed sack lunches and never paid to park. We were the only kids in our class who didn't get braces; orthodontists, we'd been taught, were shysters. If we ate out as a family, it was fish 'n' chips at Ivar's snack bar. We never made it to Disneyland, Hawaii or Paris. Our vacations were all boating. And when Granny died of Benson & Hedges, as Ruby summarized, Grumps moved into the Teardown, which meant me and Bernard doubling up on Goodwill bunk beds.

After *Mary Tyler Moore*, we watched dueling TV ads attacking Dole and Clinton while Bernard piled on, mocking them both. When I asked about the difference between Republicans and Democrats, Grumps blew his nose, one nostril at a time, then carefully folded the handkerchief like it was valuable. "Democrats are sailors," he said. "Republicans are powerboaters."

"Clinton sails?" I asked doubtfully.

Grumps hesitated, deferring to my father, who was clipping his toenails now. "No," he said, "but he'd take it up long before Dole would."

That made sense, but Clinton didn't look like he'd be of any use on a sailboat either.

"Republicans drink all day and just motor their stinkpots from one marina to another," Grumps elaborated. "Democrats have the decency to wait till they drop sails and anchors before getting plastered."

The ironies would come in time, of course, with Grumps puttering around in a comfortable stinkpot and my father turning conservative. But now my grandfather was bolstering his case, rattling off famous Democrat sailors—"JFK and FDR, by God!"—when Ruby slipped through the front door and was immediately confronted by Bernard.

"How'd you do it?" he demanded.

"I just fell," she said, looking down at her bright plaster forearm. "Stephanie shot ahead, and I was just like trying to catch up when—"

"No," he interrupted. "On the course this morning. How'd you do *that*?"

At this age, Bernard's features were an arresting mix of Mother's puffy lips and long eyelashes and Father's large nostrils and massive forehead. But watching anger rise in my brother or father was the exact same thing, their eyes bulging, their jugulars swelling to make room as the blood barreled to their brains. Yet both of them often smiled while furious, flaunting their incongruities. Later that fall, Bernard would get kicked off the Ballard football team for tackling too hard in practice during the same month I saw him liberate house spiders the size of small turtles and read butterfly guidebooks so many times their spines fell apart.

"How'd I do what?" Ruby asked, though her smirk said she knew.

After Mother set a bowl of canned minestrone in front of her, she started slurping and disrobing, her rust-colored bangs sticking to her sweaty forehead, breathing audibly through her nose. Everything she did seemed to generate heat. With Mother still an enigma to me, too, at this point, I assumed all females were mysterious.

Breaking her wrist didn't make Ruby cry, but the sight of a purple starfish or the exuberant flight of a swallow might. Mother called it hormones, though Grumps had the same problem with getting choked up at the beauty or humor of things. He watched *M\*A\*S\*H* reruns with a hankie.

"Where's your jacket?" Mother asked, still standing there watching her.

Ruby blushed. "Gave it to Stephanie. Doesn't fit anymore."

"Sure it does. Get your coat back, sweetie."

It was a recurring problem, Ruby giving things away—her lunch money, tennis shoes, Halloween candy, my box kite.

"How'd you do it?" Bernard pressed.

She shrugged unconvincingly. "What?"

Bernard looked to us for help. "How. Did. You. Find. Wind. When. There. Was. No. Wind?"

Grumps quit shelling pistachios and hunched forward to make sure he didn't miss a syllable of her response. My father finished his wine, swallowing noisily, missing Mother's scowl as she swept his toenail clippings onto a sailing magazine and then into the trash before grabbing herself a beer. (They were always a booze-gender switcheroo, with people mistakenly handing her the glass and him the bottle.)

"I go where I think the wind's gonna be," Ruby finally said.

"That," Bernard snapped, his eyes flashing, "is complete bullshit."

"Ber*nard*," Mother scolded halfheartedly, having given up on policing his language long ago.

"There was no wind to *think* about." His voice had recently deepened, and all of a sudden he sounded like yet another demanding grown-up in our shrinking house. "None at all. Zero."

"It was light," Ruby conceded, her slightly elevated eyebrow telling me how much she enjoyed torturing our brother.

"No," he corrected her, "there wasn't *any*—except whatever was filling your sail."

"Maybe she just pays better attention out there," Father suggested. "Have you considered that?"

"No, because it's bogus."

"We've all seen enough," Mother interrupted, "to know there can be pockets and gusts anytime and anywhere." Tucking her bangs behind her ears, she was in her final year of waist-length hippie hair before it abruptly went wiry, gray and short. And with her accent fading, she would, amazingly, begin to blend with the other moms.

"All it really takes," she reminded us, "is a little expanding air. And maybe Ruby was just creating more *apparent* wind than you were and it snowballed. The more you generate, the more lift you get and the faster you go, right? And that creates more apparent wind, which makes you go even faster and so on. That's why iceboats can sail four times faster than the true speed of the wind, remember?"

"Gee, wow, that's terrific stuff," Bernard retorted. "Except for the fact that four times zero's still zero."

"Sometimes I see wind," Ruby volunteered, "like colors on the water."

"Nice try," he said, sounding bored. "Makes you sound cool, but it doesn't explain why you're always looking up."

"I just have this hunch," she said, "this feeling about where it's going to blow next. Now *here* . . . then *there*."

"So you hear voices," Bernard sneered.

"Just Daddy's." Ruby couldn't hide her delight any longer. "But even you can probably hear that."

Our brother waited out the laughs. "Why *are* you always looking up? There's no telltales up there. What're you watching?"

After a long pause, she said, "Just the sail and the air, I guess. Doesn't Momma say that in light winds you gotta keep the air molecules in contact with the sail?"

"You can't watch goddamn molecules," Bernard growled.

"If you say so, Captain Slowpoke."

After the laughter fizzled all of us stared at little Ruby, slouching beneath an impish smile and a sunburned nose. At this juncture, she was baby soft and boy chested in a Madonna T-shirt she'd later be aghast to see herself wearing in photos. Her hands, though, hinted at the unusual, her fingers strangely longer than mine or Bernard's. You noticed them when she got excited or messed around on a piano or told stories. And she had that showstopping left eyebrow, which she could lower, lift or curl independently of the other. Her pupils also were peculiar, oddly tiny, leaving us all lost in her big green irises.

We killed time, waiting for whatever she'd say next. Mother jotting numbers on the back of a grocery receipt. Father quietly grabbing himself another glass of red. Grumps popping another tiny white pill and stroking his mustache. Bernard methodically cracking his knuckles and then his spine, *click-click click*. Me opening the freezer and prying loose a grape Popsicle.

What I wanted to ask was precisely where her wrist broke and what the X-ray looked like and whether her arm ached and how long it would take to heal and was it susceptible to breaking again in the same spot or would it be stronger than ever like a welded joint.

"I look," Ruby said slowly, milking the attention, "for which way the wind wants to go."

Bernard snorted. "Very funny, but wind doesn't think. It just blows or doesn't."

Tearing the plastic with my teeth, I pulled out the Popsicle, split it in half and handed a purple stick to Ruby.

"Tell that to the wind," she said before sliding it into her smile.

"Why does this keep happening to her?" our brother whined.

The two Bobos rumbled with laughter, then Ruby pretended her Popsicle was a microphone and started into that love-shack song while Mother looked on pensively. She was the last of us to admit there was anything bizarre about Ruby's sailing.

There are so many variables, she kept reminding us. At her suggestion, we switched boats and sails. We strapped thirty pounds of weights to Ruby's cockpit. We started at different ends of the line and veered to opposite sides of the course. Still, she almost always won, and eventually Mother became as moved by her daughter's sailing prowess as she was drawn to mysteries and unsolved problems.

Yet she rarely had satisfying answers when it came to Ruby. On this August evening, she sighed, leaned back and said, "Einstein loved to sail when there was little or no wind so he could scribble down ideas."

Bernard laughed bitterly. "I doubt there's much deep thinking going on in Ruby's boat."

"Then perhaps it will just have to remain a mystery," our mother said. "As Albert liked to say, 'Mystery is the source of all true art and science.'"

Bernard shrugged. "Wow, that's so insightful it makes me weepy. But sailing isn't art or science."

"You're right," Ruby said. "It's both. And have you ever considered that maybe the wind just loves me more than you?"

Her left eyebrow soared, then her giggle turned into snorting laughter after she dropped her Popsicle into the lime-green-and-white carpet Mother had vowed to replace years before.

"Just our luck," Bernard grumbled before marching out of the house. "The wind loves our little sister."

# SATANIC GEOMETRY

Nine of us were working the boatyard most days in the momentous spring of 2012, not counting two desk jockeys, a parts guy and a few seasonal bottom painters. There was the occasional sober scholar studying manuals, but we were mostly wing-it boys with fix-it skills. What we tended to share beyond the usual handyman swagger was a tolerance for discomfort and a knack for improv with drills, wrenches, adhesives and blowtorches. Most of us—including Lorraine—squinted beneath ball caps all day and swallowed cheap beer till midnight, then rinsed and repeated, our bodies Christmas trees of cuts and bruises. If we had girlfriends—no telling with Lorraine—they didn't last. But don't pity us, especially if you own a boat and care deeply about it. We are the medics and surgeons of your inanimate world.

The morning after my father's ambush, I bounded into the yard with my brother so big in my mind that I almost felt him striding beside me. He'd *written*! Just a brief and cryptic postcard sent inside an envelope wedged innocently against the side wall of my post-office box but definitely his handwriting. I hadn't realized how much I'd worried he was dead until I saw proof that he wasn't. It'd been years since he'd sent me manifestos about American hypocrisies and ocean polluters. All his feisty irreverence had subsequently been reduced to terse postcards—then nothing for the past twenty-eight months. And now, it appeared, he was coming home!

*Gonna need new boat and new buyer. Tell Yoshito, yoshito999@gmail*
*.com, that Minke will only deal with him.*

Just seventeen words, but I read them several times in hopes of squeezing out a little more meaning. *Gonna need* implied urgency, didn't it? For Bernard, it probably felt dangerously specific. When he'd last risked visiting—for one night—I asked him how it felt to be back home. He'd paused, like it was a philosophical question, then licked his split lip and said, "I see any land as an *intrusion*." That comment stuck with me, as did his eyes, which had turned a milkier blue as if he'd stared at the sun for so long that they'd faded like hull paint. Yet the unstated clues were clear. The April 3 Manila postmark—stamped just seven days ago—suggested that he was planning a spring slog across the Pacific. A *new* boat meant a *different* boat, no doubt larger, roomier and faster, though still small enough to solo; so thirty-seven- to forty-five-footers capable of quicker crossings. That he wanted me to find a boat for him meant he either had money or intended to *liberate* one. As for *new buyer,* he clearly expected me to help him smuggle again, and Minke must be his new alias. He also apparently needed both the boat and buyer badly enough to risk coming home. At least that's what I squeezed from those familiar backwards-leaning letters on the back of a creased postcard with a bony off-balance Filipino woman in a flowery bikini.

The only customers in the yard this early were Rex and Marcy, clumsily applying a second coat of cheap bottom paint. "How's it look?" she asked, lowering a filthy dust mask to bare her teeth.

"Sweet," I said, as if this were the smoothest, raciest shellacking I'd ever seen.

"Two coats will last us four years," Rex announced.

"Maybe three," I said. "But you'll still need to dive-clean her every six months or the barnacles will kill your speed."

They nodded fervently, then showed me the boat-maintenance and storm-sailing books they'd gathered, as if preparing to explore the world's largest ocean in a small tattered sloop was just like cramming for any other exam.

Eyes wandering, I scanned the backlit yard and the hull silhouettes looming like fiberglass whales on blocks, my gaze bouncing between a rudderless Ingrid 38 and a blistered Valiant 40. Rigged for soloing, either might be perfect for Bernard. Circling the Valiant, I was picturing my brother safely surfing the swells inside this bulbous vessel when Noah strode up in his oil-splattered overalls, sucking a Camel down to his fingertips, his other hand wrapped around a Red Bull.

"Could get to Pluto and back in this bitch," he said, pinkie-pointing at the Valiant. "The great Robert Perry designed her for durability right down to her loins." I looked away as he grabbed his. "Now don't go phobic on me, Josh. We're all somewhere on the homo-hetero spectrum, a matter of degrees is all, predetermined shortly after conception in those intrepid first cells clinging to our mothers' uteral walls. Am I right?"

"Noah," I said, stepping back. "Think I might enjoy my coffee here in a little peace?"

"Not a chance." He closed in again. "Pretty much all you can hope for in this crazy world, my friend, is a fingerhold on one thing you can know for certain. And you know what that is?" He chain-lit another cigarette, then exhaled through his nose like a dragon. "If you don't replace the zincs, the propellers will corrode."

None of us ever knew what Noah would say next, whether profound or nonsensical, insulting or hilarious. Sometimes he'd yak himself right off a cliff or zag midsentence into politics or religion or some date I'd had months ago. "She was fine but pretentious, right?" We tried to keep him away from customers, which wasn't easy; as our diesel savant, he had a bizarrely precise memory for substitute part numbers and a hand in most projects. A preacher's son, he spoke in melodious rants and without warning would shift into impressions.

His Obama was decent, but his Morgan Freeman was pitch-perfect: *And they will march just as they have done for centuries, ever since the emperor penguin decided to stay, to live and love in the harshest place on earth.*

Another reason we tried to keep him out of sight was his out-loud testimony about growing up in a house where the Nativity scene graced the front yard year-round. Just to mention the name of his hometown alone—Boring, Oregon—could spark a harangue, as would any reference to his father ever since his Christian talk-radio program went national. In February, he'd used his swelling audience to predict the end of the world. Our world. This one. *Yet again.* He'd foretold it once before, in 1998, conceding afterwards that he'd simply made an easily corrected mathematical gaffe. This time he was certain. The rapture was coming on June 24—two months and fourteen days from now. Noah claimed he rarely thought about it, though the side effects kept mounting. His latest tic? Two or three involuntary head jerks, like a boxer dodging jabs.

Then Big Alex came bounding toward us, so I set my coffee on the garbage barrel and braced for impact as he compressed my rib cage and scraped his whiskers across my cheek until he turned to Noah, who rolled his eyes in surrender. A recovering boozer, Alex had added a thirteenth step of his own, hugging friends and strangers, that made him yet another employee to shield from customers.

"What a blessed day!" he gushed.

Topping everything off, bowlegged Mick strolled up for his own morning hug. Short, young and bloodshot, he pointed at my father's bedraggled Joho 39 in the corner of the yard. "What's the story there?"

Among thirty-one boats of varying values, sizes, shapes and conditions, Mick had somehow smelled a rogue.

"You painting her?" he asked.

"Eventually," I said.

"What else?"

"He's Frankensteining her ass," Noah told him. "It's an old Joho 39, as they're affectionately called, a plastic classic built by his diddy and granddiddy back in the Pleistocene era of fiberglass construction. And our boy Josh is gonna Frankenstein her ass for Swiftsure or some other ridiculous race."

How could he possibly know what I hadn't yet fully admitted even to myself?

"And you want us to get freaky on her, too," Noah said. "Just say it, my friend. You'll feel better." He stared at me. "Testify."

"You're a wack job," I said.

"True enough, but can't you at least admit you're gonna ask for my help? 'Oh Noah, good buddy, would you lighten the rigging and strap on a mini-bowsprit and recommend a rudder with less drag?' All of which I'll happily do if you'll just answer the one bloody question no sailor has ever adequately addressed: How can you get so amped up about going slightly faster than somebody else when you're both going so fucking slow?"

"It's hard to explain."

"Try."

"Well, it takes training and intuition. And it helps if you understand hydrodynamics and aerodynamics. Think about it," I said. "To most boaters, wind's an obstacle, but it's our fuel. We're harnessing an invisible force. So it's got some magic to it."

Noah laughed. "You're *speed walking.* If you're going slightly faster than the moron next to you, who cares?"

I finished my cold coffee. "Do you consider the fastest rock climbers annoyingly slow? Why go to all that trouble when you could hop on a motorcycle and ride up the backside of the same cliff in five minutes?"

"My point exactly," he said. "Now explain Swiftsure. You guys act like you're heading off to Lollapalooza or Burning Man, as if you can't call yourself a real sailor until you've busted your Swiftsure hymen."

I shrugged. "It's the biggest race around, an overnighter with hundreds of Canadian and American boats. I mean you head out into the ocean a bit, and then you surf the swells back to Victoria in the dark. It can be a wild ride."

"Wow." Noah gave me his zombie face. "How courageous."

I quietly backed away as customers finally rolled in and began shuffling in tight orbits around their boats, waiting semi-urgently to yak with Jack, the rotund, self-described *crippled midget* who ran our yard.

He used to work alongside us before a falling mast crushed three disks. Now Jack spent his days behind the question counter, and it couldn't have happened to a more adaptable man. Part diagnostician, part psychiatrist, he was always on everybody's side. With us, he lampooned delusional and fastidious boat owners. With them, he commiserated about soaring costs and scandalous fees and taxes.

He was out front now in the thick mist—rising or falling, who could tell?—beneath the same faded red ball cap he never removed, not even to scratch his scalp. "Gotta understand," he was telling a hefty man in a linen suit, "they build these things with the tops off and cram all the wiring and plumbing inside and then glue and screw the tops down so you can't get at anything that matters ever again. So when things go wrong we cut into housings and crawl beneath the damn floorboards. Then, of course, there's the satanic geometry of sailboat engine compartments. All my mechanics bring cells down with them so they can call us when they get stuck. Had to pry Big Alex out with a crane just last week." Then he looked up and shouted "Josh!" as if he hadn't seen me in months. "Got someone here you gotta meet."

I duly shook the large, silky hand of Randall P. Dodd, who turned out to be the owner of the shatter-cracked fifty-three-foot Carver near the fence line. Dodd's midlife crisis, I was to learn, involved taking up *yachting* and splurging on this behemoth he'd humbly named *Goliath*. A tech exec, he'd ordered every last automated gizmo available until his computerized skipper could practically run his yacht from marina to marina. But on his third outing—during a surge of postcoital, single-malt hubris—Dodd overrode the autopilot and was actually steering, relishing his imperial wake and the virile roar of his twin 450s snorting $180 of diesel an hour, plowing ahead at three-quarter throttle and standing like Zeus on his flying bridge, when the depth alarms started honking. Fuck 'em, he thought. He could see damn well where he was headed as his twenty-three-ton novelty crashed into the well-marked although submerged Wyckoff Shoal at seventeen knots, gutting his transmission and launching his mistress, Candi, across the galley below and snapping her left clavicle.

"Fix my boat, ASAP," he told us, even after Jack warned him there was likely seventy grand in repairs. "Was just starting to get the hang of it," he confided. "It's part of who I am now, understand? I'm a boat captain."

After reassuring him we could rebuild his toy, I shuffled outside to join the smoke breakers listening to Noah mimic the Dos Equis pitchman—"'Stay thirsty, my friends'"—until he noticed me and demanded an update on my dating misadventures.

The boys gobbled up these stories. For some, they conjured time-enhanced memories of their dating primes. For others, they were joke reels. Even if I played it straight or dull, they smirked like jackals. And *then?* they'd ask.

"Number Thirteen was the youngest," I said. "She kept staring into her cell like it was a makeup mirror. Finally, she admitted she'd hoped I'd seem younger the way Brad Pitt seems younger. 'But you really don't,' she said. 'You seem pretty old.'"

The boys hooted.

I didn't tell them I had Mother's math on my side. She'd penciled out my dating master plan on Thanksgiving after Father had wondered aloud during dinner how I'd turned thirty-one without finding a potential wife yet. The last census, she estimated, showed seven thousand single women within five years of my age and thirty miles of my location. At least 10 percent were dating online, she estimated, with about half of those on Match.com. So if I dated thirty-five women on that site, or 5 percent of the available pool (more than the standard polling margin of error), the math suggested I'd find true love. At least so went her calculations. The unspoken assumption being that when Ms. Right showed up, I'd know. By this juncture, I was twenty-three dates in, well over halfway through the experiment with no romance in sight.

"The closest I got to feeling like I had a girlfriend," I informed the boys, "was with Number Twenty-One. I thought we were into each other. Bought her four dinners before she informs me she keeps dreaming that I'm making out with her sister. So I remind her I've never met her sister. 'I'm sorry,' she says, 'but I'm having a hard time forgiving you.'"

The boys roared.

"Number Twenty-Two dumped me," I explained, "because I drank out of a Styrofoam cup."

"What?"

"She picked me up in the yard, and I asked her to stop at the port office so I could grab some joe to go. They had paper and Styrofoam cups, but I made the wrong choice, and that was the final straw."

"How is that even a straw?" asked Leo, a pudgy fiberglasser famous for getting so stoned that he spray-painted BRING IT? on a freeway overpass, his sloppy exclamation point looking more like a question mark and leaving thousands of drivers to ponder what, in fact, they'd forgotten.

"Styrofoam apparently oozes chemicals like styrene," I told them, "which she says can kill you. I looked it up. It's outlawed in California. Same stuff they used in Legos."

"I used to suck on my Legos," Noah said. "And I survived."

"Till now," I pointed out. "She says she's okay with my lack of a degree and the fact that I smell like Jiffy Lube, but she cannot *abide*—

she actually used that word—my drinking from Styrofoam cups. It's a sign, she tells me, that we'll never be compatible."

"Or a sign that she's completely insane," Mick suggested.

"They have wings but cannot fly," Noah began. "They are birds but think they're fish. And every year they embark on a nearly impossible journey to find a mate."

"What the?" asked one of the new bottom painters.

*"March of the goddamn Penguins,"* Mick muttered as we dispersed.

The rest of my day sputtered through a succession of half-finished projects, none of which involved my father's boat, though he'd called three times without leaving messages.

By closing, Jack summoned me for a conference call with Blaine Stanton, the hospitalized owner of the nearly demolished thirty-six-foot sailboat we'd begun senselessly repairing.

Blaine's stents hadn't helped. His aorta had ruptured, and he now was calling in before his next surgery, whispering that he was about to receive his last rites.

"When I wake up I think about her," he rasped through the speaker. "The thought of leaving her like that is too much for me to ponder." We waited through a painful throat clearing. "I'm serious, Jack."

"I know you are," Jack offered.

"I want *Sophia* saved regardless of what happens to me," Blaine whispered. "Hear me? I just wired you guys another twenty K."

"Don't you worry about her, Blaine." Jack stared at the ceiling so his tears wouldn't overflow. "She's in capable hands, my friend. We'll do right by your *Sophia* no matter what happens."

# A SWEET VINCIBILITY

Of the boys, I was the only boater. Everybody used to be, of course, but by now they were like bartenders who no longer drank. *Me, own a boat? Do I look fucking crazy?*

Meanwhile, I owned two, an old wooden Star and an older Joho 32—my floating home. Both were squeezed into my discount double slip on the A Dock at Sunrise Marina, a ramshackle of piers, sheds and boats hitched to the western rim of the bay, a ten-minute bike ride from the boatyard.

These docks were a magnet for every bad idea and flawed design on water, every wood, steel and ferro-cement blunder; a Chinese junk made of teak so heavy it took typhoons to move it, rotting Chris-Crafts and other relics from the '60s and '70s, as well as the occasional pampered sloop like *Princess,* a twenty-three-footer so beloved by its owner that jealous neighboring boats wouldn't speak to it. Mostly, though, these were unloved seagull-shit palaces mossed over and nosed into the dock like drunks leaning against walls, with inverted masts, decomposing canvas and stiff mooring lines strewn about moldy cockpits like dead snakes. Yet somebody somewhere, amazingly, kept paying moorage out of guilt, ignorance or senility.

Neglected boats tell stories. People get distracted, fired, sick or divorced, and their boats hint at sad messy lives, the blue tarps temporarily concealing the decline until the wind shifts and the harbor manager gets a whiff.

There was a barracuda-thin, sixty-three-foot schooner that hadn't left the dock in twenty-two years. Its psychologist owner tried to sell it once, asking twice what it was worth, predicting people would assume it must be exotic. They didn't. Now it was full of rats the size of raccoons. That cute purple mini-tug on the C Dock was available for 14K, down from 17K last month. Prices fell by the week, and some boats sold twice or three times a year to the onslaught of delusional buyers overconfident about their renovation skills right up until they ran out of cash or visualized, in one alarming flash, all the work ahead. That was when they tracked down that liveaboard handyman they'd heard about who'd coach them through it for free—maybe even do it for them. Which was why I snuck aboard my Joho some nights without flipping on the lights and lay there in the dark, because otherwise: *Tap tap. Josh? Got a minute?*

Few places turn more motley than a hobo marina that welcomes liveaboards. There were some professionals, a few state workers, an occasional world traveler and plenty of dreamers, eccentrics, addicts and ex-cons like Trent. Nobody knew if that was his first, last or real name, and the fine print on his business card boasted that he offered paid instruction on tree climbing, marathon swimming, windsurfing and Frisbee golf. Toss in two lesbians, several stoners, an elderly nudist couple, a narcoleptic we called Rem and a former nun named Georgia who lived in a large black catamaran and call it my neighborhood.

There was a sweet vincibility to Sunrise, the grass and ferns sprouting from rotting piers reminding us that our time here was limited. Yet people kept coming and going, their abandoned boats auctioned and demolished. My problem was that I wanted to rescue them all. Sloops, ketches, schooners, powerboats, I couldn't resist. Similarly indiscriminate with women, I liked them short and tall, skinny and

stubby, quiet and brash, brainy and simple, sane and nutso. I wasn't
an ass man, a boob or an elbow man. If anything I was a laugh man, or
maybe a voice man because I knew that might become the soundtrack
to my life. The smart ones sensed my lack of discernment and focus
almost immediately.

See, Sunrise had wireless, so my dating two-step usually began
with dinner at the marina tavern with its brassy waitresses and addic-
tive clam chowder. Plus they all wanted to see my home. Yet no matter
how truthfully I described it, they'd envision a swanky yacht instead
of a dank hovel of tools and books with a drop-down table, a triangular bed and a closet toilet. What it definitely didn't look like was the
home of their future husband. And that's what many of them were
hunting for—whether they realized it or not.

Getting dates wasn't the hard part. As Ruby once put it, my angu-
lar face, messy hair and spaniel eyes made me appealing to all those
girls who fell for stray dogs. If there were second dates, I'd take them
sailing and study their reactions as the boat tipped and the plates,
pots and life preservers fell to the floor, as if the inanimates below
were enjoying raucous sex while we got acquainted above. They didn't
have to instantly love sailing, but they couldn't act like they'd rather
be at some mall.

As new prospects popped into my in-box every day, I'd lean back
and study their pictures for beauty only I could see, then scroll down
to the books they'd most recently read. Number 23 mentioned *Sophie's
Choice*. So I couldn't resist meeting her, though her pictures were poorly
lit and she'd described herself as "Hillbilly cute."

Tacking out of the marina now, I smelled Grady Rollins's eighty-
two-foot yacht. If you squinted you could see its former grandeur, the
knife bow, fantail stern and curved pilot-house windows. But now?
You could kick a hole in her side without straining a hamstring. And
if you stepped inside, the mildew reek snapped your head back.

"Got some nasty deck leaks," Grady had admitted after coaxing me aboard the first time. "Especially above the bedrooms, but I just push the mattresses aside."

I reluctantly toured his dilapidated yacht with one eye calculating the enormous restoration costs, the other filling out my insane-boater checklist.

Minimal boating experience. Check.

Blindly in love with a hopeless boat. Check.

Vastly underestimates maintenance expenses. Check.

The gleaming eyes of a zealot. Double check.

Yet it was hard to dislike Grady. His cheerful twang matched his crisp Wranglers and Western shirts with their yokes and snaps. He was a salesman, though nobody knew what he peddled beyond optimism. While his fence-post posture and courtly manners suggested he'd served, nobody knew where or when. Perhaps it was just his Oklahoman sensibilities. See, Grady was yet another adventure migrant who'd washed up here.

From inside the wheelhouse, his boat didn't even appear to be compromised. And after we dropped into the refurbished dining room, I sensed some of the effortless elegance she'd obviously once generated and began to sympathize with him.

On the coffee table next to a brown couch was a hardbound version of *Yachting* from 1975. "Go ahead," he urged, "take a look." Without my leafing, the magazine fell open to a two-page spread on his boat, temporarily restored to its 1915 splendor. He shared the yacht's history, its foreclosures, title fights and lawsuits escalating until he'd snatched it at what *sounded* like a steal if you didn't think very hard. All of which meant, of course, that I was getting played. Like the others, Grady was fishing for free help, having heard, no doubt, about my unusual philanthropy.

"People say all the time I should just put this old girl out of her misery," he said. "They tell me I should sink or demolish her and move on. 'Get over it!' Know what I'm sayin'?"

"Most people don't understand love," I heard myself respond.

"Thank you! That's exactly right! It's like they're all sayin', 'Why're you still bangin' this old hag when you could be boppin' some young thing?'"

"Love," I said again.

Down below, he showed me the huge twin diesels, which looked strangely clean, almost new. He offered to turn them over, and, believe me, I wanted to hear them knock, but again I felt that tug of free labor and passed. Then I trailed him to the stern cabin—twelve hundred square feet in all, he told me, like a Realtor pitching a condo—and down a comically narrow spiral to three disheveled bedrooms, where the mold stench tripled. Still, the sporty tiled and teak-laid head was a jewel of a tiny bathroom that would've looked regal anywhere.

"My girlfriend loves this boat," he assured me. "If she didn't, I'd have to cut her loose because I'm gonna die on this thing." He told me that a second time. I nodded so he wouldn't say it again.

Stepping back onto the dock, we walked around gazing quietly at his rot-softened hull. "I'm renamin' her *Shangri-la*," he said, beaming like an expectant father. "Gonna get a real artist to paint the name freehand on her stern. *Shangri-la!*"

He's a loon, I reminded myself, once he told me his master plan called for not only removing the rot but also raising the bow. Yet his optimism seemed so genuine it felt contagious. I'd seen this trait before, of course, but Grady had taken it to another level of batshit craziness. I nodded along, not wanting to offer any buzzkilling estimates of what his fantasy might cost. By now I was rooting for him, but then I innocently asked why he wanted to raise the bow, and he doubled down on the madness.

"Oh, Josh," he said, as if it were obvious, "I'm gonna put a piano in her. Gotta lift the bow so it'll fit!"

This felt like the moment when he'd enlist me in his quixotic absurdity, but he didn't. At least not yet. He was just sharing his dreams with a stranger on a dock. "A baby grand," he said, smiling and shaking his head like even he couldn't believe how fantastic this was all gonna be. "Not a grand. A baby'll work just fine."

"You play?" I asked.

"Hell no!" He dragged his hand back through his hair, leaving the impression that his retreating hairline wasn't the result of natural balding so much as the consequence of being continually astounded.

I tried to look at him like he wasn't deranged. "Your girlfriend?"

"What about her?"

"She play?"

"Not a lick." He laughed. "I just love pianos, Josh."

In the bright daylight he actually didn't look nuts at all, even after explaining with an Okïe mumble that he was running dreadfully low on cash. His expression was serene, not cuckoo.

"You won't need to raise the bow," I told him as pigeons swooped and banked in formation over our heads toward the B Dock. "The piano should fit as is."

It'd been weeks since that exchange, but I recalled Grady's delight at my observation as I tacked my Star twenty feet from his rotting bow and glided out of the marina toward the crowded racecourse.

# EVERY CELL IN YOUR BODY

My racing sidekick this evening was eager Johnny, a 120-pound Japanese student at the college. His real name was Hideaki, but to make it easy for Americans he told everybody to call him Johnny. My response was to insist that he call me by my Japanese name of choice, Kazuhiro. So when we sailed he called me Kaz, or Captain Kazuhiro if he was feeling particularly respectful.

His legs were too short for him to get his butt out over the rail, but his enthusiasm nearly made up for his size. What was endearing, though, was how much he loved everything about racing: the rigging, the waiting, the jockeying, the near collisions, the shouting matches, the absence or excess of wind, seemingly even the losing. Whatever he knew I'd taught him, but since language often fouled us up I kept his assignments simple, along the lines of "Where's Mario?"

If you'd just met our fleet of Star sailors, thirty-three men and nine women, you'd never guess Mario was our Buddha. No, you'd fall for the enchanting accents and assume the eloquent Brit or the loud Lithuanian or perhaps the handsome Aussie was the chosen one. You might even pick any of several blustery Americans before you'd point to sheepish Mario. The first hint, though, was that at six three and twice Johnny's weight he possessed the ideal length and mass to keep these boats level and fast when it blew. But at the southern end of Puget Sound we'd often get a whole lot of nothing, which is why some skippers preferred light crews, though Mario usually won those drifters, too. On water, he oozed command, rarely speaking or protesting. You never heard him shout *Starboard!* because everybody knew where he was and that he either had the right-of-way or wouldn't hit you. You also noticed his swiveling head, his fast strong hands and his unruly shrub of hair that looked like he'd never been indoors. To top off his dominance, he beat everybody with a geriatric crew.

Technically over seventy, Yvonne moved like fifty, with silky white hair and a Mona Lisa grin beneath her wide-brimmed hat that made you want to paint her. Still, what it all said, without Mario having to, was: *I can beat you hacks with a dated hull, shit sails and a spinster on the bow.* It was her boat, you see. Mario was a racing bum who'd never owned a single floating object. Beyond his size and unknowable age, he didn't offer many clues about himself other than that he worked in transportation logistics. What else we'd clawed out of him was that he was single and kidless, living alone in some random apartment equidistant to three sailing clubs where dozens of race-boat owners begged him to steer theirs and make their pricey obsessions, at least for a day, seem sane. But what Mario apparently liked the most was racing cheap old Stars down here with the rest of us.

Crouched low in the water beneath an enormous mainsail, these boats resemble birds with wings too large for their bodies. Conceived in 1911, a Star is twenty-two feet, nine inches long and just five foot eight wide. Its tall, flexible mast is easy to bend, shape and, unfortunately, snap. Attached to it and swinging perilously low over the cockpit is an endless boom, making the Star perhaps the most uncomfortable, head-banging two-man boat out there. You don't just duck when you tack, you go facedown like you're in a foxhole under fire. Throw it all together and you have a sleek boat that's fended off a century of design revolutions, even if racing it feels like playing tennis with an old wooden racket.

That Yvonne's boat was the only red one in the fleet made it easy to spot, though all you really needed to do was look toward the front. Comforting ourselves, we collected excuses and theories. Maybe her boat was slightly lighter, her mast better tuned, her sails cut in New Zealand. After a few beers, we'd indulge the notion that Yvonne herself was the secret weapon, a mermaid or sea witch masquerading as an elderly hippie.

By the third and final race, Johnny and I were parched and discouraged after finishing in the middle yet again, the wind too frisky for us to keep stable and fast. But it now had lightened enough that we had a chance. I followed Mario, timed it right and flew out beside him. For the first time in weeks, we were close enough to watch him in action.

Unlike me, he wasn't squeezing the tiller, holding his breath and studying telltales, nor desperately trying to go in a straight, fast line. He was in perpetual motion, tightening and easing lines, reshaping the mast and the mainsail like a man playing a stand-up harp, bowing the sails and accelerating, then steering more directly into the wind without losing speed. When he and Yvonne tacked, their footwork and body movements looked choreographed. Trying to copy them, I whacked my skull on the boom, and Johnny missed the hiking strap with his foot and nearly backflipped overboard. Then we pinched, stalled and fell farther behind.

One of Mario's advantages might have been that he didn't have a mother who'd pointed out to him that sailing was more complicated than flying. Mine wrote an article for *Sail* magazine that confused thousands by mixing laws of motion and fluid dynamics with forces of gravity, torque, kinetic energy, wind, lift and drag to explain the science behind the sport. Even as technical as she got—"water is 800 times denser than air"—she warned that her tangled equations were oversimplifications because once a boat tips or the wind gusts the calculations change again. In other words, as soon as you think you've grasped sailing physics, there's something else to factor in and you're back to bafflement.

At some point, almost everyone had ribbed me about being a mediocre racer. A Johannssen who can't sail? That's like being Aretha's tone-deaf daughter or Einstein's dimwitted son. But Mario never brought it up. The only thing he'd ever said about my family was how much he hoped my sister would race with us down here someday.

"I still don't see the upwind mark," Johnny admitted after a long silence.

"Don't worry," I said. "Mario will show us." He rounded the buoy a moment later and surfed toward us, his main fully eased, his jib poled out wide, with Yvonne lounging belly-down on the bow in her straw hat, as if poolside in Monte Carlo. Like I said, *she* got into our heads, too.

After the last race, we all glided home in the buttery twilight. Just an hour's drive or a day's sail from noisy Seattle, Olympia used to be the end of the wagon road heading north from Oregon. From the water, the southern end of this inland sea still has that dead-end feel. The tides get more extreme, but just about everything else mellows, with enough greenery crowding the modest city to imagine nature reclaiming downtown, its shabby buildings floating out on the next big ebb.

With just enough wind to return, nobody spoke, not wanting to spoil the moment, all of us happy mutes with bright faces and no chance of explaining this sensation, even to ourselves. Perhaps that's part of why I keep taking people sailing, hoping somebody will eventually put the feeling into words. My mother's the only one I've ever heard try.

"So why do we feel so good out here?" Ruby had asked one night after a week of cruising that ended with us all lying on the deck, spinning around the anchor.

Mother loved these sorts of questions. Why do we laugh when something is funny? Why do we dream of flying?

"Well, it's the same feeling we get when we walk along the ocean, isn't it?" she began indirectly, as usual. "It's that ionic lift from salty water, sure. But it's more than that, isn't it?"

We were all yeahing and nodding and listening hard in case she put her finger on something revelatory.

"And it's even more powerful when you're out on the water all day because the rise and fall of the ocean connects you to the sun and moon, right?"

With her eyes squeezed shut, we knew not to rush her.

"That alone might make us feel good, but let's not forget we live on a planet that's mostly water—and so are we, right?"

We were too tired to respond. Sure, whatever, yes!

"And we know *all* of life began in salty water. So maybe the reason we feel like we're glowing or buzzing at times like these is that when we're out here every cell in our body is saying, *Momma!*"

After a thoughtful lull, Ruby broke the silence by shouting, "Momma!"

Our night of Star racing ended with Johnny and me rolling the sails and offering each other farewell bows.

"Thank you, Kazuhiro," he said, "for another night of sailing."

"No, thank *you*, Hideaki," I replied. "Good job out there."

He bowed. I bowed back. He dropped his head again, wanting the last word, but I was not about to be outgratituded tonight.

Afterwards, I shuffled up the A Dock through the early evening cacophony of metal, hip-hop and classical—the mix, as always, reflecting the drugs du jour on the docks. You could tell the age and sobriety of the new liveaboards by their music. Whenever a meth head moved in, we heard from howling bands with names like Bone Cancer followed by fights and evictions. Then the tunes would improve for a spell until the next addict turned up.

Glancing up at the noisy tavern above the marina, I noticed a bag lady waiting outside the gate for the A Dock.

"Hey," Mario said, surprising me as I strode past his boat. "How'd you do out there?"

"Another beautiful night of discouraging sailing," I said.

He gave me a wincing smile. Mario had usually finished his cheeseburger by now and was slipping out the back door. Uncomfortable with placing second in one race, though, he'd been tweaking something probably only he'd notice, tightening an upper shroud a half turn or reinspecting the battens.

"Hey," he said, "I was wondering . . ."

"Yeah?"

"Is there any chance your sister . . ."

"Yeah?" I wasn't about to help him.

"If, you know, she might come out with us some night this season."

I knew he'd sailed against her in Lasers back when she was a teen phenom and had seen her beat everybody, himself included, years before all the hullabaloo.

"Like I've told you, Mario, she hasn't sailed or lived around here since high school. Okay?"

"But maybe she'll visit this summer and go out for a night?"

People like Mario were the most unsettled by Ruby's saga, as if her mythology mocked their passions.

I looked past him to make it appear I wasn't reading his mind and saw the posse of liveaboards waiting to ask me about their balky bilge pumps or their weeping hull-deck joints or their jammed halyards or haywire autopilots . . .

The rumpled woman still waiting behind the gate suddenly looked familiar. But who the hell was she?

"Maybe," I told Mario. "I'll tell her, the next time I talk to her, that we'd both love to see her out here if she could pull it off."

He nodded doubtfully, and that's when I placed the bag lady. She looked better in her dimly lit headshots.

*Hillbilly cute.*

I bought her chowder and a beer, and we discussed that devastating moment in *Sophie's Choice* when we discovered the meaning of the title.

She was missing an eyetooth, but I liked her attitude and didn't want to appear entirely uninterested. So when she thanked me for dinner, I gave her that neutral line about how we should stay in touch.

She sighed. "I'm sorry," she said. "You're so nice, but, to be honest, not my type. Too skinny."

Back aboard my boat, I stared gloomily at my new batch of potential dates before obsessing yet again over Bernard's latest postcard. Creating an anonymous e-mail address took no time at all, but I lost an hour of my life choosing the words for this simple message: *Minke coming to Seattle soon with product. Will deal only with you.*

Pressing SEND, I felt a fever wash over me, soaking even my socks.

# LIVE YOUR OWN LIFE

~~~~~~

"The great Leif Eriksson sailed to North America in the year 1001, centuries before the overrated Christopher Columbus ran aground and told the world he'd *discovered* this place, which is why we should be celebrating Leif Eriksson Day instead of toasting some second-place wannabe who finished almost *five hundred years* behind the winner!"

Not even Bernard challenged this portion of Ruby's childhood rendition of our Icelandic lore, but his interjections and clarifications were coming.

"Leif Eriksson was a strong and handsome [embellishment] young man when he discovered America [Canada, actually, Newfoundland to be more specific]. But he just called it Vinland—the land of wine, wink-wink—and threw wild parties [embellishment]. Soon enough, though, the Indians got jealous of all the fun [speculation] and killed a few drunken sailors. So Leif and his crew packed up and sailed home. Not being a braggart, he didn't make a big deal out of finding a continent. And the rest of the world apparently was clueless about the Vikings and didn't know Jack Squat. [Ruby assumed Mr. Squat was a noble Icelander because Grumps kept griping about people not knowing him.] So that's how the overrated Christopher Columbus was able to gobsmack [another word she routinely misused] the world into believing he discovered America, which is silly, since oodles of Indians had *already* found it.

"But the people of Ballard knew better!" Ruby shouted. "That's why there's a ginormous statue of Leif at Shilshole Marina. Still, when they put up all those fancy words beneath him, they almost made the silly mistake of calling him the *son of Norway*. Bah! They stopped that foolishness after Grumps said he'd bust some heads unless it said Leif was the great son of *Iceland*! [Iceland's consul general, not Grumps, had threatened to sue.]

"What people don't realize," Ruby maintained, "is there are only four thousand [actually, forty thousand] Icelanders in the States, and that makes Icelanders rarer than two-headed sharks [no such thing] and people like Grumps really exotic, considering he's even a blood relative of the Great Leif Eriksson! [Not even close to true.]"

Fortunately, our Sunday instruction went beyond lectures on sailing, physics and Icelandic reverie. We had texts, the heaviest of which was *Chapman's Piloting: Seamanship and Small Boat Handling*. You could spend several lifetimes mulling his advice in those 624 mercilessly dense pages and still miss thousands of tips on knots, navigation, boat handling, anchoring, line splicing and so much more. Bernard was outraged to learn that the long-dead Charles F. Chapman—*Chap*, to his pals—was a powerboater. No wonder his section on sailing ran only twenty-six pages! Chap owned a stinkpot!

But there've been fifty-seven editions of that book for a reason, the Bobos told us. And Chapman, while hardly Mr. Excitement, nor even alive, was one of our professors. Otherwise we wouldn't have been repeatedly asked, *What would Chap do?*

Yet our required reading wasn't all tedious. We also were assigned our namesakes' books: Bernard Moitessier's *The Long Way* and Joshua Slocum's *Sailing Alone Around the World*.

Slocum set out to sea from Massachusetts in a stubby oyster sloop just shy of thirty-seven feet on April 24, 1895, back when it wasn't considered possible, much less advisable, to circumnavigate the planet by yourself in a small sailboat. Many people—probably not the Mensas of their time—insisted it was impossible to go *around* the world seeing how it was so clearly flat. *Mr. Slocum, don't you mean you intend to sail* across *the world?* But Slocum didn't care what anybody thought. He just did it and told his story in the breezy fashion of a fearless captain who'd already witnessed everything the oceans could hurl at him. When he waxed about his boat, as sailors must, he lauded and defended it like a loyal spouse and occasionally veered into anthropomorphic zeal, but never once went batshit.

"I heard water rushing by, with only a thin plank between me and the depths . . . But it was all right; it was my ship on her course, sailing as no other ship had ever sailed before in the world."

People write memoirs about drug binges, suburban angst or raising llamas and try to make them sound unique and harrowing. Slocum did the opposite. He understated exotic adventure, at one point offhandedly describing how he fended off cannibals by changing clothes and hats whenever he emerged from the cabin to make it appear that several men were on board. I recall some of his sentences like they were my own, but the line our father made us memorize was: "To know the laws that govern the winds, and to know that you know them, will give you an easy mind on your voyage round the world; otherwise you may tremble at the appearance of every cloud."

I read Slocum with an awe dwarfed only by the mounting burden of being as horrifically misnamed as all the clumsy Graces, gloomy Hopes, stingy Charitys, and disingenuous Franks. Even photos of big waves made me queasy despite a birth certificate swearing that I was, indeed, Joshua Slocum Johannssen.

However, Bernard's namesake would become his North Star. A so-called mystic, Moitessier was in position to win the very first solo, nonstop, round-the-world race in 1969 when the Frenchman said, Fuck it (*Le baiser*, actually), and instead of heading north to the finish line, he'd continued sailing his ketch eastward through the Indian Ocean. "My intention is to continue the voyage, still nonstop, toward the Pacific Islands," he wrote in a note to the London *Sunday Times,* which he'd *slingshotted* onto a passing ship. (How cool is that?) "I am continuing nonstop because I am happy at sea, and perhaps because I want to save my soul."

Yet the Moitessier quote that Bernard stapled to the wall above his bunk was: I FEEL HAPPY, LIGHT, AT ONCE DETACHED FROM EVERY-THING AND IN CONTROL OF EVERYTHING, AS WHEN ALL DEBTS ARE WIPED AWAY AND YOU CAN LIVE YOUR OWN LIFE.

There it was: *Live your own life!*

Moitessier's decision to swap victory for peace of mind played a role in the evolution of every Johannssen kid, but who could have predicted all that would unfold? And determining whether the Frenchman deserves credit or blame is like assigning intent to a meteorite. Regardless, our readings coincided with Bernard's burgeoning disdain for rules and authority. He shunned seat belts and helmets and drove without a license. If he saw signs warning SHOPLIFTERS WILL BE PROSECUTED, he looked for something to steal.

I doubt Father ever slowed down enough to read *The Long Way* or grasp how much Moitessier's philosophies contradicted his own. Peace, he'd assured us, came with *winning.* The unspoken goal of all his schooling, of course, was to create a dynasty of Olympic-caliber racers, though it was increasingly obvious that only one of his children inherited that chromosome. Even on big boats. Ruby never glanced at instruments to see if we'd sped up or the wind had mellowed. She knew.

Most people don't give wind much thought. Ask where it comes from and why it goes where, and they'll shrug. Except Mother. Wind, she told us, usually begins with the heat of the sun changing the density and moisture of our atmosphere. I had this memorized by age nine: *Wind is the consequence of variation.*

And without wind, how would the planet express itself? If dead calm was the norm, trees would never sway or dance. Lakes would be as flat and dull as a Thorazine buzz. The windiest city on earth is Wellington, New Zealand, where it blows an annual average of sixteen knots. Half the days of the year it averages over thirty. So people stay the hell away, right? Nope. Wellington's among the world's most-beloved destinations. The least-windy place on earth? Oak Ridge, Tennessee, averages a three-knot draft, barely a mouse fart. So it must be a getaway for honeymooners and yoga retreats? Nope, they built atomic bombs there in part because *nobody* wanted to live there.

We want and need wind. Sure, it's a complicated psychological relationship, starting with the first lullaby we hear. *When the wind blows, the cradle will rock. When the bough breaks, the cradle will fall.* How comforting. Yet for some reason we treat even the most villainous windstorms like endearing alcoholic relatives. Why else would we christen violent hurricanes with names like Andrew and Katrina? Earthquakes and tornadoes generate similar mayhem, yet we don't name those brutes.

Ruby's understanding of wind was wildly out of proportion with her grasp of everything else. She always took everybody literally and never saw the point of apostrophes or nonphonetic spelling. Nobody bit her tongue more often or broke more nails or swallowed more gum. By her teens she began attracting a succession of dubious boyfriends—as Bernard put it, the Who's Who of Ballard Fuckups. She'd fall for lame pranks onshore. Yet at the helm she was steady eyed, unfoolable. Something about reading the wind focused her. I should know. Nobody watched her sail more than me.

Once I got my license, I'd drop her off at the lake after school and return early enough to see the final race. She competed mostly against older high school boys. The general rule: the less wind, the bigger her lead. In little or no breeze she'd be so far ahead it looked like she was in a different race. Nobody maximized their time in gusts better or read the conditions as well, not just the shifts but the lulls disguised as shifts, as if she'd downloaded a bird's-eye view of the course with its invisible overlay of ever-changing tacking lanes.

But like a musician who plays by ear, she couldn't teach it. And she wasn't always right, occasionally finishing near the back when she'd gamble on shifts that never came. Usually, though, she won easily.

Most of us learn the basics, how to pull the strings that shape the sails to make the boats move reasonably well at different angles to the wind. The more skilled puppeteers, like my father or Mario, could make sailboats fly like birds. And then there was Ruby. She *was* the bird.

Between races, I'd watch her do the mortal things, stretching her arms and neck with no more tension than if she were moseying around the yard. At fifteen, she was growing into herself and sliding from cutie to beauty. Mario Seville and the rest of these older boys getting trounced by her every Tuesday afternoon were no doubt already helplessly in love.

# BOAT PORN

Sailboats and women. The wiring of men gets messed up here. There is something so irresistibly feminine about sailboats that men forget they are things. Why else would even the surliest of mariners name their boats *Roxanne* or *Juliette*? It's not just love but lust. Trust me, there's something oddly carnal going on. Sailboats arouse.

Why else would a marketing juggernaut like Pfizer shoot a Viagra commercial that shows a middle-aged man sailing a J/29 *by himself* and suddenly having to replace a failed boom shackle. Why it fails at all is a mystery. There are maybe three knots of wind and barely any pressure on the sails. But that's missing the point because: "You've reached the age where you've learned a thing or two," says Voice-Over Man, who sounds like he gets laid twice a day. "This is the age of knowing what needs to be done. So why would you let something like erectile dysfunction get in your way?"

Of a little boat maintenance?

Apparently. Because this MacGyver wannabe pulls a strap off a life preserver and ties a makeshift tether to secure the boom and sail long enough to find a substitute shackle in the cabin below. After he screws that on, he removes the tether in a swift sensuous tug, as if discarding his own belt.

"Isn't it time you talked to your doctor about Viagra? Twenty million men already have."

So what's the takeaway here?

Fixing small problems on your boat with an erection equals good times? That's more than a little confusing. Cialis ads are all about being ready when *the moment is right*. There's always a fetching middle-aged woman somewhere in the commercial. But Viagra strands you solo on a sailboat in no wind, with your jib oddly back winded because your boat's getting towed and you're an actor who doesn't know how to sail. Why Viagra advocates woodies in solitude is another mystery. Yet near the end of the ad, as the fake sailor glides toward the dock amid the disclaimer that these pills might leave you blind, deaf and permanently hard, he looks so sated you half expect him to light a Marlboro. Confusing? Yes, but the point is these marketing geniuses in the boner business understand how to exploit the peculiar wiring of men when it comes to sailboats.

Or consider *Boat Porn*. That's the subject line of thousands of e-mails sent daily when men share photos of their fantasy boats, with juicy high-resolution gigapixel images of curvaceous hulls, swanky interiors and mouthwatering sterns. Listen closely to men talk about their dream boats, and you can hear the infidelity in their voices.

It was Grumps who first suggested the libido link. He'd driven us to Shilshole Marina to stroll the docks, as usual, but there was one particular beauty he wanted to show us—an old panther-sleek schooner named *Rainbird*. It didn't take a trained eye to see she had all the salty charm that forty feet of wood, glass and bronze can conjure. Still, he clearly saw something more.

"Just looking at her almost brings me to orgasm," he volunteered, not realizing how weird that sounded to his three teenaged grandchildren. From his vantage, though, he was earnestly sharing an unvarnished truth.

As a part-time surveyor, I see infatuation in the eyes of potential buyers like the man I met last April at a Bremerton yard to examine a forty-year-old Alberg 30.

Upright on stands, dripping like a bikini model, her cruising curves and varnished teak glistened in the early sun. She looked young for her age, with a spoon bow and a heart-shaped stern slightly narrower than the one belonging to the buyer's wife, who stood at a disgruntled distance to size up her latest rival.

Assessing a boat this old is a bit like giving your middle-aged date a physical. You tap her decking to check for rot (bone loss) and listen for structural weaknesses (bum hip or shoulder). You hunt for deep blisters in the hull (skin cancer) and see how worn-out her sails (lungs) are and make sure her engine (heart) sounds reliable and that she hasn't been sailed so hard (lived so recklessly) that her rigging or mast step (adrenals) are fried.

Sliding a bare hand along the base of her keel, I could feel where she'd grounded but found no voids or delamination. I wiped bottom slime on my jeans and looked up, knowing the couple's eyes would be all over me.

When he started firing questions, I offered discouraging grunts and climbed a ladder to the deck without glancing at either one of them, then went to work with what Noah called my little hammer of doom, hunched over and tapping the deck, listening for ominous thuds.

Afterwards, I spent a couple hours exploring the cabin, with a flashlight and mirror, checking and touching, testing and even tasting everything like a kid left alone for too long in a doctor's office.

Fire extinguisher loaded with current tag? Check.

Operable shutoff valve to galley stove? Check.

All thru-hulls double clamped? No. Corroded clamp on the raw-water-intake seacock.

Operable running lights, cabin lights and VHF? Check, check, check.

Crawling beneath the cockpit, I pulled out the noise insulation and wedged myself beside the twenty-horse Yanmar to look for abrasion, corrosion or oil leaks. Then my hip started vibrating so I gingerly fished my cell phone from my pocket without checking the incoming number.

"This is Josh."

"Tell me you've got that damn keel off already," my father began, his voice breathy and halting as if he'd been lunging up stairs.

Exhaling through my nose, I wiggled my thumb over the OFF button. He'd gone from calling but never leaving messages to bludgeoning me with daily demands and updates.

"They're casting the new one right now," he declared. "Should've already been done, but you gotta be ready to roll when it arrives. New rudder will be trucked to your yard on Thursday. Friday at the latest. Well?"

"What?"

"Sounds like you're in a tin can. You've had that boat for nine days now, but I bet you haven't even taken a look at the keel bolts yet. Surprise me! What've you got to report?"

"I've been busy." Dizzy from diesel fumes and sweating profusely now from the waist up, I wiggled my torso to give my chest more space to expand between the engine block and the curved hull. "Getting to your project in my spare time hasn't been my top priority."

He pushed a few breaths into the phone. "Feeling sorry for yourself? You still never pounce on anything, do you? You walk around in circles like a dog figuring out where to piss. Always have. Sometimes you have to pounce!" He filibustered for several more minutes before closing with "And I sure hope you realize we need to keep this *family* project as quiet and affordable as possible."

Translation: *Don't let anybody know what we're doing to this boat, and forget about getting paid.*

"Seeing how you're so worried about time," I said, hyperventilating slightly and closing my eyes to brace for impact, "shouldn't you let the Swiftsure handicappers know about your little design changes? Shouldn't you *pounce* on that?"

There was a pause, like the delay and click before a detonation, yet he came back calmer. "You worry about your end. When we have something to tell them, I'll handle it. Get that keel off. No more lollygagging."

Back in the brilliant daylight, I climbed down the ladder, still cooling from my father's words, my resentment spreading to include my brother for adding another stressor to my days—incessantly wondering if and how some bogeyman named Yoshito would ever respond to my e-mail.

After lighting a cigarette, another theatrical touch I'd stolen from Grumps, I circumnavigated the vessel again, triple checking that the rudder lined up with the keel, that the hull was true. The buyer was a desperate dog by now, silently begging me to throw him a ball of information, and his wife heaved herself out of the backseat of their old sedan to hear what I had to say, praying, no doubt, I'd deem the Alberg an overpriced lemon.

Exhaling slowly, I penciled a shopping list in the margin—*cereal, bananas, beer.* Surveys bring out the sadist in me. When a boat's overpriced junk, I rush to crush the dream with lines like *Run away and don't look back.* But when she's a peach, I often stall and withhold oxygen before sharing the verdict with the nearly ecstatic buyer.

"So," he finally asked, "is she solid?"

"She's got voids," I said solemnly. "Four-to-six-inch gaps in the cockpit decking." His face fell; hers lifted. "But so do most boats," I added, "even new ones." They swapped expressions. Then I exhaled another thin cloud and said, "But you've also got rot here."

"Rot!" The man looked like I'd informed him he had leukemia. "How bad?"

I shook my head. "You might drill some holes and dry it out some. Beyond that it gets pricey."

The wife made a fist and gently pumped it.

"But that's true for most old boats in this climate," I continued. "If they've got wooden cores, rot comes with rain. This isn't so bad. For this vintage, her decks are decent. The sails and running rigging are toast, though that's no big deal. Her mast is bent to port, but you should be able to straighten that out. And while the auxiliary looks clean—and isn't leaking oil or coolant—she looks like she's been run hot at least once."

He nodded like a bobblehead. "So, what would you say overall?"

I blew a smoke ring and shot a smaller one through it, something I'm fairly skilled at unless you compare me with Grumps. When there's no breeze, he can pop out five perfect rings so fast he can skywrite the Olympic insignia.

"Her body—the hull—is flawless," I said, staring at the wife who was pacing now like a caged rhino. "I'll need to run market comparables, but I'm guessing she's worth the asking price. Wouldn't take her on the outside without an overhaul, but she can handle inland waters right now. You're not gonna win races, but Albergs are still popular, which helps with resale when it comes time to move on."

Within a few days they'd receive a report filled with enough minutiae about things to fix and ponder—*missing split-ring on clevis pin holding starboard lower lifeline to bow pulpit*—to fill many weekends. I wished them luck and stepped back before I got slapped by the wife or hugged by the husband, who I predicted would immediately buy new heaters and refrigeration and solar panels that he didn't need, hastening their inevitable divorce when the wife would insist on keeping the boat just to twist the knife.

Glancing beyond the doomed couple, I took in the rest of the yard. Hunters and Catalinas getting their bottoms painted. A Nordic Tug with a new bow thruster. A weathered black schooner near the corner of the yard that, if I hadn't been dodging their eyes, I never would have noticed. Even though it was sixty yards away, and sixteen years had passed since I'd seen it, I knew exactly what it was and could make out a handwritten FOR SALE sign on the lifelines as well as its name. *Rainbird.*

The same forty-footer that had made Grumps groan with lust!

Starting to pant, I simultaneously wondered what they were asking and if it might be the ideal *new* boat for my brother. Or fix it up and give it to Grumps on his eighty-eighth birthday! Or buy it for me! Yes! Check out those lines! The sultry *Rainbird* down on her luck and falling into my price range! That's called fate, right? Then it hit me, how much time and money she'd guzzle, how fast she'd decay, how she was probably slow through the water and gloomy down below, how she'd bust my heart.

I flicked my smoke into a puddle, spun on a boot heel and ordered my legs to carry me safely away as an unusual black-and-yellow butterfly flitted into view and dive-bombed my face before flapping away, as if Bernard had been enjoying my internal melodrama and couldn't resist swooping low for a taunt.

# OUR LEVITATING SISTER

~~~~~

As startling as our sister's sailing mastery rapidly became, it still alarmed us the first time Father showed more faith in her than her brothers in the biggest race of the year.

Beginning and ending near Victoria Harbour, the annual Swiftsure International Yacht Race called for sailing out into the Pacific and back on the last weekend in May, with most boats finishing the following morning or later, depending on size, wind speed, patience, bravado, skills and luck.

We were running *Freya II* as a family that year, along with two of Father's pals who'd been racing since woolly mammoths roamed, as Ruby liked to say. But Bernard and I still outranked her on the big boat. So why let our fifteen-year-old sis call out sail adjustments right after we crossed the starting line?

Swiftsure is notoriously volatile, capable of dramatic shifts in wind and waves that send so many sailors, me and Grumps included, scrambling for Dramamine. Nothing pleased the Bobos more than placing well here in one of their own designs. They'd last won it in 1986 and had finished in the top five three times afterwards, but even that was increasingly unlikely, since new ultralights were turning the final downwind leg into a drag race that left the Johos behind.

Like most races involving vessels of various designs, Swiftsure uses a handicapping system that enables any boat to compete against another regardless of size, speed or age. Unlike golf, the handicaps apply to the boats, not the sailors. The higher the handicap, the slower the boat.

If boat A is a 0 (a dead giveaway it's large and fast), and B is a 60 (still pretty fast and likely large), A would need to beat B by sixty seconds per nautical mile. In a ten-mile race, regardless of wind speed, A needs to finish at least ten minutes ahead of B to place higher.

So it's not about who hits the finish line first because you won't know who really won for sure until everybody crosses and this calculation is run: $c = e - (r \times d)$. Or, corrected time (in seconds) equals elapsed time (in seconds) minus the rating (handicap) times the distance (nautical miles). Waiting for the math often makes for belated celebrations when—after the fifth postrace beer, or the next morning— the results are finally released.

This is the norm for sailboat races yet remains as awkward as trying to handicap a road race between an old El Camino, a Hummer and a new Ferrari to ensure that the best driver wins. A derelict sloop sailed by drunken rookies gets the same handicap as the same design in mint condition commandeered by America's Cup winners. So rich owners, who can keep blowing cash on new sails, get rewarded. As do rogue cheaters who lighten or refashion their boats without informing race officials of speed-increasing, handicap-altering changes.

By the spring of 1998, the Bobos were desperately hoping to goose sales by winning Swiftsure with their already dated Joho 39, which meant they were betting the family business that Ruby was already better than the rest of us at calling sail trims from the bow. Lying on her back, she eyed the curvature of the sails and the slot between them, shouting out subtle adjustments in her kid soprano.

*Too much twist in the main . . . Lower the traveler . . . Another inch! . . . Too much! . . . That's better. A little more. There . . . Now slide the jib car forward an inch . . . Good. A bit more jib halyard . . . That's it. Yes!*

The larger revelation, however, came during the moonlit downwind run back to Victoria. Fearing we were falling farther behind, Father kept glancing from Ruby to our stalling spinnaker and back at her. "What?"

"Nothing," she said.

I noticed Mother studying the clashing and overlapping waves behind us again. "There's probably a secret proof behind all this movement," she told me when I got closer. "We use equations, you know, to predict currents and blood flow or to know how long it'll take for a stirred cup of coffee to become still." Her smiling face turned into the light. "There's only chaos until we come up with the right math to explain it."

Meanwhile, Father kept peeking at Ruby. "What?" he demanded again.

She exhaled. "Why don't we just head up forty-five degrees for a hundred yards, and then jibe and ride the next gust. The puffs seem to be coming every three or four minutes, and more directly from the south, so we'll be able to head off at a faster pace on a more productive course, right? And then we'll do it again and again until the pattern shifts or we gobsmack these posers with boat speed. Maybe it won't work, but it beats sticking with this course and watching boats continue to pass us, doesn't it?"

We looked around for the gusts she was talking about. Yet outside the moonbeam, the water was a black mystery. Perhaps she'd been tracking boat lights, but how could we be sure the gusts would be there, much less at the same angle, when we arrived? To our astonishment, though, Father stepped back and relinquished the wheel. "You do it," he said.

Maybe he deferred out of exhaustion. He routinely drove longer than anybody could concentrate. Or perhaps it was resignation because we'd lost too much ground to have a shot at winning even our class of similarly rated boats. Still, it was surreal to see him break the rotation and surrender the helm to little Ruby, and not out of love or preferential treatment but a raw desire to finish higher.

Traveling farther, but faster, we passed half a dozen boats. Even Mother tuned in, telling Ruby when the wind waves and swells were synched to encourage surfing, and she'd steer more perpendicularly to the swells, speeding up again by veering more upwind until the next surfing opportunity arose.

Our newfound speed cheered us all, with Ruby now calling trims and jibes from behind the wheel and Bernard handling the challenging spinnaker-pole maneuvers in the rising blow as Grumps hurled out gratitude to the deities. "Thank you, Aeolus! Much obliged, Njord!" And just as we were weaving and surfing at our fastest, Ruby began humming, a flagrant violation of the Bobos' racing superstitions. Yet nobody flinched even when she started singing, softly at first, *"I'm bein' followed by a moonshadow, moonshadow, moonshadow,"* and everybody except Grumps, who didn't know the lyrics, joined in.

Then our sixteen-foot spinnaker pole inexplicably buckled, and as the pole fell to starboard, the massive flimsy sail collapsed to port. Bernard lunged for the pole and unlatched its jaws from the sail and then the mast before holding up the bent aluminum tube for everyone to see while Ruby steered more downwind to refill the unbraced, free-flying spinnaker, and the boat pounded onward.

I didn't hear what anybody said next because I was already scrambling below. Without the pole, I knew we'd either have to keep sailing more carefully and directly downwind or, more likely, drop the spinnaker, either of which doomed our performance. Scanning the cabin for a solution, all I saw was the tapered teak leg on the collapsible table latched to the bulkhead, and I snapped it off at the hinge, then grabbed a roll of duct tape and popped up on deck, where everybody was shouting. Scrambling forward, I told Bernard and Clive to hold the damaged pole straight while I taped my makeshift splint, turn after turn after turn to the buckled section. Then they reattached the pole to the spinnaker and then to the mast and gave Ruby the thumbs-up to change course and fill the sail. After it survived two gusts in a row there was applause.

If my father was ever more proud of me, I've forgotten the moment.

The pole would fail again within the hour, but we amazingly finished first in our class that year, fifth overall. We probably wouldn't have cracked the top ten without Ruby steering.

Word of her prowess, both accurate and apocryphal, continued to spread, and Bernard fueled the rumors. "She *smells* wind shifts," he'd tell other racers. "Watch her nostrils flare." Her success on water obscured the fact she was flunking classes and, as Mother put it, picking the wrong friends and still giving away everything she owned. Yet her failings and travails went unnoticed by Father. Like I said, sailing well was the hall pass in our house.

But looking back, I see her uncertainty in some of those old photos. She didn't know what was going on either. There were several shots in which we three Johannssen kids stood side by side, yet inexplicably only her hair was blowing. Others showed her sailing with tiny rainbows encircling her boat and, in one picture, her head. Another one Bernard and I obsessed over was taken from behind with her hiked out on her Laser, her torso suspended horizontally over the water. Sheer physics required her butt or thighs to be pressed hard against the gunwale, but there was light beneath her rear, too, as if she were floating. Bernard studied another *Hovering Ruby* photo for days, trying to figure out what trick explained the illusion that she was standing an inch above *Freya II*'s deck.

Mother toyed with us, speculating on the scientific possibility that a powerful magnetic field could levitate a human ever so slightly and that perhaps some people were more susceptible to such forces.

But Bernard cried bullshit and found a magician's handbook that described how he took advantage of an audience's inability to see his grounded foot to give the impression that he was floating.

"*See!*" Bernard exclaimed, balancing on one foot.

I said yes, but it didn't look anything like what Ruby had done.

By then, Ruby also had turned into Grumps's personal masseuse. She'd have him lie belly-down on the couch and tell him to breathe loudly enough for her to hear. Then, during his exhales, she'd press small circles into muscles along his back and behind his knees. After several of these moves he'd giggle and pass out, and his bulging disk would usually stop aching by morning. Asked what she'd done, she'd shrug and say she was just encouraging his body to heal itself. Which it seemingly would for a couple weeks until she'd do it again. Soon she was performing similar exorcisms for half the old-timers on our block, easing kinks and aches, tendinitis or arthritis.

Bernard dismissed them as Ruby's placebos. But what gave her the notion and confidence in the first place that she could ease somebody's pain? And what about the bigger question? Were these *phenomena* the product of luck and coincidence, or was she occasionally bending reality? Bernard wouldn't indulge such conundrums. He was out to debunk her. My brother wasn't investigating our sister's inexplicable or supernatural moments but rather looking into her unfair advantages. In other words, whether or not she was cheating.

During the heat of his inquisition, I found her lying in the backyard, her eyes fixed on the azure sky.

"What're you doing?" I asked, plopping down next to her.

"Making a cloud with my mind," she whispered.

Snickering, I said, "If you're a cloud maker, you're fired."

"Quiet," she hissed. "Sometimes it takes a while."

Her eyes began watering, and mine wandered plenty over the next several minutes, so I might've missed something, but when I next looked up there was a tiny oval cloud the size of a minivan a few hundred feet directly above us.

She wasn't impressed. "I've made better ones," she told me, rising to her feet and then flicking grass off her jeans. "You could make them, too," she said, "if you'd concentrate."

I won't admit, even to myself, how many times I tried.

# FOUR PLANETS IN SCORPIO

Upside down in the engine compartment of a Peterson 42, my head throbbing, my hands bloody, my boots in the air, I struggled to loosen four stubborn bolts. Finally dislodging one, I came up for air in the cockpit and heard the fidgeting owner tell me, as if I were his mildly retarded servant, that this wasn't supposed to take so long.

"Electrical problems are unpredictable," I told him, a line I'd offered a hundred times. Usually it worked, and most people would give me the I-get-it grimace, the do-your-best shrug.

"At ninety-three bucks an hour," this one grunted, "I expect more than vague excuses."

I inhaled the toxic boatyard aroma of solvents, bottom paint and epoxy. "Wanna take over?" I asked. "I could coach you on what you need to do and what you're up against."

He vibrated his lips. "You're just removing the solenoid, right?"

"That's right."

"How hard could that be?"

"Well, seeing as how it won't detach from the starter, you'll have to pull that, too." I took a deeper breath. "There's three more bolts down there to loosen, and good luck with them. It's too cramped for a socket, so you gotta hang upside down and bust 'em loose with this customized Allen I sawed off for you this morning. And you might have to attach a pipe to the end of it to get enough leverage. Hopefully you won't break the heads off or smash your hands, but the odds are good you'll hurt yourself."

"I don't care for your tone," he said.

Looking past him, I continued, "And to get the starter out, you'll have to pull the alternator, of course. But you might want to snap some quick photos beforehand so you remember how it's all supposed to look. Then you just pop the alternator off and yank the starter and remove the solenoid, right? Wrong. First, you gotta loosen the freshwater reservoir or the starter won't come out. And in pulling the starter you'll probably jostle some coolant hoses—metal tubes, actually. Volvo prefers metal over rubber, I'm guessing, because they're more expensive. But you won't fully appreciate this complication till you try to put the starter back in with its new solenoid, which you might find at Al's Alternators. He'll know without looking whether he has one or not. If he doesn't, he'll order it and charge you sixty-nine bucks. Then you'll have to jostle the coolant tubes again to get the starter and new solenoid back in there. The antifreeze might start leaking now, but you can't really tell until—"

"Look," he snapped, his mouth twitching. "Like I said, I don't care for your tone in the slightest."

"I don't either," I admitted, sighing and scanning the yard, where Big Alex was hugging limp customers.

"Sometimes these things never get solved," I told the guy as gently as I could. "The truth is the solenoid might not even be the problem. When it comes to electrical systems and salt water, there's corrosion you can't see. There are gremlins and ghosts. Sometimes you have to start over and replace everything. But I'm betting and hoping it's the solenoid. Anytime you want me to stop, just say the word, and I'll move on to less-exasperating projects." I opened my bloody hand and offered him the sawed-off wrench.

I knew he'd complain to Jack and I'd get the mini-lecture, but when he started grumbling about *gremlins and ghosts,* I dropped back into the engine compartment and bonked my temple. Fortunately, by the time I resurfaced with the other three bolts, he was gone, and I sat on deck with my head throbbing and watched Lorraine working on *Audacious* yet again. The dermatologist who owned it tried to compensate for his mediocre racing skills with the most extravagant bottom-painting ritual in the fleet. He pulled *Audacious* twice a year to have Lorraine sand, paint, burnish and repaint the bottom and then burnish and paint again. She'd indulge his every head game, applying sheets of copper paint that ran four hundred a gallon and scared off sea life a mile away. Whenever the doc won anything, he'd swing by and hand her two Ben Franklins out of gratitude or perhaps backhanded lust.

To be fair, Lorraine had odd powers over all of us. It might have been her eyes, so brown they looked black, or her ability to outwork and outswear everybody with her spectacularly foul bilingual mouth. *Hijo de puta machista,* we learned, means "sexist motherfucker." Besides that, though, we knew little about her beyond the tattooed bird that peeked over her worn jeans whenever she bent over, though most of the time we couldn't see the bird, her jeans or her face beneath the sexless zippered suit and the industrial respirator she wore while making sailboat bottoms obscenely smooth. She'd had a weekend fling with Noah, a year ago when he was sixty pounds lighter. Afterwards, he pretended to be okay with being just friends, but all she had to do was give him the slow eye and he got so light-headed he'd almost pass out. As overhyped as her work might have been, I knew I'd probably be asking for her help before long.

With that thought, my eyes swung across the yard. Just glancing at my father's tattered Joho hurried my blood. Since his *lollygagging* lecture two days ago, I'd been sending his calls straight into voice mail and then deleting them as soon as he started to get pushy. This morning, though, he'd made Grumps leave the message.

"I hope you're getting a chance to work on that Swiftsure boat we've got down there," he said woodenly, followed by muffled background murmuring. "Well, what do you want me to tell him? Oh, hell." Then directly into the phone: "I'm sure you'll do the best you can, Josh. You always do."

I peeled my eyes off the needy Joho—Grumps obviously had no clue what all Father wanted me to do to it—and focused on Rex and Marcy shuttling boxes of canned food up the ladder into their freshly painted boat. Days earlier, they'd shown me the full library they'd assembled, mostly dated dramas of similarly unprepared couples heading out to nowhere.

Climbing down now, I strolled over and asked them if they'd found the charts they'd need, and Rex unfurled a small-scale map with a yellow highlighter marking their route to Alaska.

"Nice," I said. You might as well navigate with a globe, I thought.

"You guys taking any sailing lessons?" I asked.

"Nope," Rex said.

"Navigation classes?"

He shook his head.

"Registered or documented the boat yet?"

"Nah."

"What about survival gear?"

"You can overthink these things," Rex explained. "We're experiential. We learn by *doing*."

So there I was once again, trespassing through delusions while Marcy devoured a banana. "You meet Josie and Paul yet?" she asked. "They're from Boulder. We're giving them pointers—well, Rex is— since they're heading out, too." She pointed at a young tattooed couple slumped beside another neglected sloop that probably couldn't make it to Seattle.

Not wanting to meet any more adventure migrants in my dream-trampling mood, I checked on the progress Mick and Leo were making on grinding and reglassing *Sophia*.

When Jack waddled up, I tried to preempt his lecture. "I gave that guy the business after he accused me of running up the bill."

Jack waved me off. "I told him you're the best and said I'd talk to you. Now we've talked." He twisted his mustache and pointed at *Sophia*'s bow. "Blaine rang me the minute he got out of surgery again. Said he felt fantastic. Told me again not to worry what this costs. Said he'd just mix the receipts with the kitchen remodel and score points with the wife for investing so much in *her* project."

When customers began lurking for Jack's attention, I shuffled outside to join the smokers and, without even a prompt or a request, began recounting my latest dating fiasco.

"So Number Twenty-Four invites me to her parents' place on the west side. Her mom's frantic in the kitchen and has so little to say I'm already sensing her disappointment in me. And her old man's all gold watch and pricey scotch. Only drinks Glenlivet, he informs me. 'Everything else is piss.' Says that twice, maybe three times. Still, I was almost liking him till he started razzing me about sailing. 'Never understood the attraction,' he says, like I'd asked."

The boys hooted.

" 'Takes all day to go absolutely nowhere,' he tells me. 'And all those tangled ropes? No thank you. Don't understand why anyone would consider it worth the hassle unless they couldn't afford a powerboat.' "

More hooting.

"This guy's killing me, but the catch is I wanted to sleep with his daughter again. She had this zest for sex that made me feel nineteen again."

Their eyes widened and the hooting resumed, but then I described the family-style dinner we'd had with her triple-chinned father, a self-made man, as he constantly pointed out, who suddenly disclosed that he owns a forty-seven-foot Bayliner, something his daughter had failed to mention.

"So your flying bridge is about eighteen feet off the water," I tell him.

"That's right," he says.

"And I'm guessing you've got twin three-thirty Cummins diesels? Freshwater cooled."

He bunches his lips. "Impressive," he says, glancing approvingly at his daughter.

"You go fast and put out a huge wake, don't you?"

He nods proudly, though one bushy eyebrow starts to lift.

"Know what my father calls boats like yours?" I ask.

His smile is cold. "Stinkpots?"

"Something like that," I say. "But guess what my brother calls boaters like you."

He tilts his head to get a better bead on me.

"Cocksuckers," I say.

The boys snort and howl. "That is so dogmatic," said Mick, boatyard leader in vocabulary gaffes.

"*Pedantic,*" Noah corrected, then spasmodically jerked his head back twice.

A billboard had gone up that morning just a block away from the boatyard with a simple message: THE END IS NEAR. Everybody figured it had something to do with Noah's doomsday father, but nobody dared ask him about it.

"So how'd all that go over with the zesty daughter?" he asked.

"Amazingly," I said, "she never called me again."

As usual, I didn't want to tell them about dates who'd dumped me because I was too dull or too desperate, too withdrawn or too candid. In less than an hour, Number 25 and I went from bonding over similar childhoods to knowing too much to ever want to see each other again.

I looked past the boys to the limp marina flags. Johnny and I had put in a practice day that week, so we were theoretically as ready as ever to do well if the wind remained light tonight.

I backtracked and told the boys about Number 9. "She seemed crazy about me till she did my chart and found out I had four planets in Scorpio. 'It was never gonna work,' she told me. 'I can't be with a man who's secretive and misogynistic.'"

"Massage a what?" Mick asked.

"She dumped our boy Josh," Noah said, "because he had four planets in Scorpio. That's the takeaway."

"Which planets?" Leo asked.

"For twenty days and twenty nights," Noah began, "the emperor penguin will march to a place so extreme it supports no other life. In the harshest place on earth, love finds a way."

# THE GRAVITY OF ONE SAILBOAT

We began our prerace rituals as the rising wind turned the bay from placid green Jell-O to corrugated iron. The entire Star fleet was out tonight, so when the countdown began twenty-one boats were traversing the invisible starting line like manic hamsters.

"At the two-minute horn," I told Johnny, "we're gonna head directly away from the line for almost a minute, then jibe around and come screaming back and hit the middle at full speed right at the gun. Got it?"

"Yes, Captain Kaz!"

Once we'd nearly executed that plan, we were turning heads because, for once, we were moving faster than everybody else, especially Mario, who as usual was stalling near the less-crowded left end of the line, which suddenly was where we were heading now that the wind had shifted. But before we got alongside him, we lost our uninterrupted breeze to two other boats, both of which Mario left behind with his mysterious acceleration until he squirted free into clear air, his lead growing as we drifted toward the rear.

Once we could finally tack, we were yet again too light or too clumsy to keep the boat level. After finishing second to last in the next two races, I snapped at Johnny to quit apologizing for things that weren't his fault, which triggered another apology before he caught himself. We jibed back toward the marina in quiet awe of our inadequacies.

Why did I race at all? To remind everybody I was no Bobo or Ruby Johannssen?

The dock offered no relief. A flock of liveaboards loitered near my pier, distracting me enough that I didn't notice we were arriving too fast, and Johnny didn't have enough time to stop us from thumping the dock and crunching the brittle bow. Waving off his further apologies, I glared at my needy neighbors who were hoping, no doubt, for just a little advice.

"Not tonight," I nearly shouted.

Most of them immediately retreated, but Rem, the B Dock narcoleptic who'd recently bought a rotting yawl for next to nothing, stepped forward. "I just got one quick question," he said, an empty Pabst dangling from his pinkie.

"Sure, Rem, but it'll run you a buck-fifty a minute starting"—I glanced at my watch—"right now."

"Okay, okay," he said, holding up filthy palms and backpedaling. "Ex*cuuuse* me."

Johnny helped roll the sails in abashed silence and knew better than to bow to me tonight.

Then I seized the corner booth of the tavern, but Number 26 never showed. Or maybe she looked inside, saw a brooding tramp clutching a foamy pint and moonwalked right back out. She'd later blame it on an emergency involving her half brother's girlfriend, though she never rescheduled. Her insistence that dates share her *recycling ethic* had already struck me as an unromantic deal breaker anyhow.

The first beer went down like it was trying to put something out. The second agitated me to the brink of calling Pop to tell him to get his pipe dream out of my yard. What had he called it? *A family project.* No, this was a selfish scheme for one reckless Bobo Johannssen Jr.

While other Star skippers brayed away at their table, Mario strolled over with his beer to interrupt my bitter blues.

"So your family's sailing Swiftsure this year?" he said.

I chuckled, then stared till he started fumbling with zippers. "Where'd you hear that?"

"I hear your sister's gonna be there, too."

"No kidding. You might want to get your hearing checked."

"We never actually dated," Mario abruptly disclosed. "I mean, I always liked Ruby and didn't date anybody else till I was older."

I shook my head. "What beer are you on already?"

"I wrote letters when she was in Africa, least one a month for that first year. She never replied, but that didn't stop me. That's kinda why I started coming down here three years ago, because I kept thinking she'd eventually come out sailing with you."

I whistled. "That's some seriously flawed thinking."

"All I'm saying," he said now, his chest rising, "is I'd love to sail with that girl again."

"I get it, Mario. We all would."

He stared, waiting for more. "Just holding hands felt like a holy experience." His voice actually quavered. Then he turned and hustled out the back door.

My third beer replaced martyrdom with wonder at all Mario Seville had just disclosed, which in turn somehow made me feel guilty about snapping at the liveaboards.

Grabbing a tool bag, I began my rounds in the gentle rain by climbing inside Georgia's port lazarette and tightening hose clamps on both sides of her bilge pump to regain the suction. Then I showed the former nun how to do it herself and fended off her offer of cheap wine and Doritos. Next stop was Trent's mildewed powerboat. Listening to his struggling diesel, I speculated aloud about a clogged fuel line or a weak injector pump. Then scrambling around the stern, on a hunch, I banged and reamed the fuel vent with a screwdriver until crud spilled out. The engine started easily, and I waved off Trent's eight bucks—"all I got handy." Next came the nudist couple who eagerly wanted to know the pros and cons of propane and diesel heaters. When I finally got to Rem, he was sitting hatless in his cockpit in the steady rain, listening to a piano concerto—conducting it, actually.

"Hey, Remy."

His hands froze in midair, then his eyes opened. "Oh, shit. I'm sorry, man. I didn't know . . . I mean, like I—"

"What ya got?"

He pointed at the port-side deck, where water pooled an inch deep between the cabin and the toerail. "Leaks like a mother right down into the cabinets. Bucket a day sometimes. Wanna peek below? Maybe the railing needs rebedding, I don't know. But there's a million fucking screws poking through, and I don't know how to . . ."

I tuned out the rest while I pulled out my drill, inserted a three-quarter-inch bit and bored through the bottom of the toerail at the boat's beamiest point. "Hey!" Rem sputtered. "You can't do that, can you?"

After I recoiled the drill, the new hole gushed like a hose. "Doesn't solve your problem, but at least slows it down. You need more scuppers so the water doesn't gather here. Once the hole dries I'll come by and coat it with epoxy so the rail won't rot."

"Wow, man. That's totally awesome, but like I mean I don't have—"

"See ya, Rem. Get back to your Bach."

The rain fell harder, its familiar encore rattling tin roofs, thumping tarps and swamping decks and drains. Live on a boat in western Washington, and rain becomes your roommate. We get those monsoonlike dumps, but our specialty is intimate and unrelenting rain. You hear its percussion on your cabin top and feel its dampness in your nose and clothes even when they're both dry. No heater or dehumidifier or thermostat or detergent is a match for this moisture. The first R-rated movie I ever saw was *Fatal Attraction*, with Glenn Close playing that psycho mistress who tells Michael Douglas, "I'm not gonna be ignored!" That's the sort of rain we get.

Finally retreating to my own boat, I stopped on the dock to answer my trembling phone.

"Hey, Josh," said a friendly woman's voice. "How the hell are you?"

"Ruby?"

"Who else?" she asked, as if we talked every third day instead of every third year. "Hello? Can you hear me? Josh?"

"Great to hear your voice!" I yelled.

She laughed. "You think I've got just one?" Then she unleashed a lungful of elegant French before channeling some choppy African dialect. "I've gotta run soon here, so tell me how that boat makeover's coming. Dad says"—she mimicked his sulky baritone—"'He's not doing a damn thing yet.' I told him, 'Don't play me, old man! That doesn't sound like my brother.' What's wrong with Momma anyway? She sounded like a dial tone. She okay? Hello, hello?"

"I'm here! So Dad put you up to this?"

"What? The other way around. I'm putting *you all* up to this. Swift-sure, Josh! It's time! Hold on a sec." Her phone sounded like it had fallen. "Put that anywhere!" she shouted into the background, then said, softly, to me, "So tell me you can make that boat fast."

"Hardly." I snorted. "It's a stupid old piece of shit."

She sighed. "Listen to you! Who pissed in your Cheerios? Somebody's gotta win. Why not us? I told Grumps to double up on the blood thinners because he doesn't want to miss this humdinger. Hello?"

"I'm here."

"Hello? Josh?"

"I'm here!"

"You heard anything from Bernard?"

"Yes!"

"Josh? Can you hear me?"

"Yes, Ruby! Yes!"

"You there?"

"Yes!"

"Well, if you can still hear me," she said quietly, as if talking to herself, "plan on dinner at the Teardown the Saturday before the race to plot our brilliant strategy." Then she giggled and hung up.

After the line died, I frantically redialed and a robotic voice informed me that the message box was full.

Only then did I look up and notice Trent and the nudists staring at me as if I'd just lunged so far out of character they no longer recognized me.

Instead of retreating to my bunk, I found myself pedaling blindly into the soggy night, my sister's voice reverberating inside me as I glided past mumbling street guitarists and the buzz and rustle of downtown back out to the soaked boatyard.

The Joho 39 had been sitting there for eleven days, but I hadn't given it more than nervous glances or, for that matter, looked closely at any of these models since my father sold *Freya II*—against everybody's wishes—during another slump at Johannssen & Sons. Spotting one crouched at a dock, much less under sail, unhinged me. But this boat came with so much baggage, had such an offensive name—*Hell Bitch*—and looked so neglected, as if she'd been banging against a dock for the past decade, I hadn't felt any affection until now. With her to myself finally, her graceful bulky silhouette felt like family.

The design had lost its prestige long ago. Too spare to be a posh cruiser, too heavy to race competitively, she'd still managed to hang around for twenty-eight years and circumnavigate the planet at least three times and had, no doubt, been in and out of almost every celebrated harbor on every continent, not to mention every cove and cranny of our inland sea.

I was a toddler when the Bobos invented her, but long after we're all dust, there'll likely be a few restored Joho 39s hurtling downwind, buckling the knees of boaters who can't resist old curvy low-slung sloops that meshed Father's desire for speed with Grumps's insistence on beauty and comfort. The compromises were obvious. An overhanging bow for elegance and anchoring ease combined with flat hull sections aft and forward to boost downwind surfing, velocity and control.

This design was the yardstick by which I assessed all others. Length 39 feet 1 inch, waterline 33 feet 3 inches, beam 11 feet 4 inches, displacement 13,700 pounds, sail area/displacement ratio 18.8. Sailboat stats relax me. Show me the numbers, and I'll tell you how she sails in different conditions. Given the age and general condition, I can tell you what she's worth, how pretty she is, then dial up her racing handicap within ten seconds a mile.

Walking around her several times, I wondered how the eight of us—counting Grumps and the two Labs—got along at all inside this plastic shell less than half the size of a mobile home. Yet stuffed with ropes, chains, fenders, sails, cereal, books, beer, wine and sleeping bags, this had been room enough. We did so much more together when we were aboard it—more reading, laughing, conversing and singing, with Grumps leading us in ridiculous sea chanteys before invariably leading us aground.

We hit bottom twice on the same day in Active Pass, first on the east side, then on the west. Three days later, we were marooned on a sandbar in the Georgia Strait. So we raised sails and gathered on the lower rail, except for little Ruby, whom we left at the wheel in case we broke free of the mercifully soft Fraser River delta. This went on for almost two chilly hours until Grumps and Bernard winched Father halfway up the mast, the harness squeezing his crotch enough to make his voice climb as he ranted about everything that was annoying him, including the snickering below.

Finally a puff of wind in tandem with the rising tide sprung us free, under sail and accelerating at an extreme tilt with all of us bracing to hit bottom yet again while Father dangled more precariously by the minute and shouted to get him the hell down, sending Ruby into hysterics. Yet nobody risked lowering him or relieving her for fear of jinxing our escape into deeper water.

The last time I saw Grumps, I asked why we ran aground so often. "Were charts that poorly marked back then?"

He stared into his beer, contemplating the bubbles. "I have no idea," he said. "Your mother claims Einstein ran aground all the damn time."

It's true that a peculiarly high percentage of Einstein's sailing stories ended with him hitting bottom or getting rescued or towed home in the dark. And when the famous scientist messed up in a boat, the world heard about it. In the summer of 1944, the *New York Times* considered it newsworthy when the sixty-five-year-old sailed into a rock and capsized in a lake high in the Adirondacks, where the genius was temporarily trapped beneath his sail, his leg entangled in rope before he clawed to the surface.

During our longest family odyssey, we lived together on the 39 for twenty-four straight days. We ate s'mores every night. Grumps taught us Nordic myths and how to yodel. We played countless games of Yahtzee. In one quiet Canadian marina, Bernard put on his Zorro mask, fake sword and cape and had me winch him off the deck so he could swing over the crowded boat of strangers next to us and shout, in a bad Spanish accent, "How much for your leetle girls?"

*Freya II* was so much more than a boat. She was our portal to the rest of the world. Aboard her, we saw orcas and humpbacks, porpoises, dolphins and menageries of seabirds and tidal crawlers. Near the end of one trip, we lay on the deck and stared at the blazing constellations while Mother informed us that we were all an inch longer lying down than standing up because gravity wasn't compressing the tissues in our spine. She also told us how the moon would've spun off into space long ago without the earth's suction holding it close, and that all objects asserted pulls. Neptune, she explained, wasn't discovered until an alert astronomer detected a wobble in Uranus's orbit around the sun that hinted at some unseen sphere tugging it slightly off course.

Staring tonight at the pleasing shape of this downtrodden Joho 39, I hoped that if properly mended she might possess enough gravity to tug the family back together again, at least for a weekend.

Next thing I knew, I was removing the warped teak floorboards to examine the keel bolts and the integrity of the reinforced keel trunk with its familiar final layer of twenty-four-ounce roving and its trade-mark I-beams supporting the thick mast step. I spent the remaining hours before sunrise sanding and silently vowing to make the hull as smooth and true and flawless as it was when this 1984 Joho 39, Hull Number 13, emerged from the mold at Johannssen & Sons.

# HEARTLESS HUNKS OF PLASTIC

Families split over money, betrayal and abuse, over resentments, infidelities and misunderstandings, over people being jackasses. Most anything can rattle the fault lines. Yet I know of only one family torn asunder by a sailboat race. Actually, by a single moment and a spontaneous push of a tiller. Other smaller quakes preceded the big one, but during most of those, my father, not my sister, was the skipper.

When racing, he dictated not only boat maneuvers but mood and emotion, too. If he joked, we all loosened, but you wouldn't intentionally distract him any more than you'd heckle a man listening to the tumblers of a bank vault. Shoot the breeze at the wrong time, and he'd turn his bulging blues on you. He expected everybody to talk, think and daydream about how to make us go faster, as if a tad more teeth-grinding, spoon-bending concentration might will our boat ahead of the fleet. You didn't pack beer or an ounce of unessential weight. You ate lunch discreetly, if at all.

David Binstein violated all these tenets.

Built like a three-hundred-pound boar, Binny was popular with shorthanded skippers struggling to keep their overpriced, underballasted boats level and fast. And he'd raced enough to understand his role as prime railmeat, nimbly switching sides with each upwind tack, cantilevering his heft out over the lifelines at just the right spot and moment. His weight, though, was simply hurting us on the final downwind leg of this disappointing day of summer racing in 1999 when he launched his third frat story of the afternoon while mauling an egg-salad sub and chasing it with a Busch Light.

This one began with some pledge attending his first football game and Binny waving him toward the middle of the student section, shouting that he'd saved him a seat.

"So this pimpled dweeb heads out to me, excusing himself past maybe forty or fifty students with his huge smile and a foot-long hot dog." As usual, Binny's giggling slowed his own storytelling. Veins pulsed in my father's forehead as two more boats gained on us.

"This kid had no idea we were such great friends," Binny continued. "I mean, I saved him a seat, right? He's flattered! So when he finally gets to me, I lift him up and yell, 'Body pass!'"

Pop's jaw muscles twitched as a Synergy 1000 passed us. I knew he saw this final run as the last chance to salvage the day. We were on *Freya II,* which felt sluggish downwind compared with pricey new lighter designs like that goddamn Synergy. The economic inequalities of the sport infuriated Father, especially this recent wave of dot-com newbies who'd drop a couple hundred on a boat and sails. *Buying trophies,* he called it. Stubbornly, we continued racing our aging boat against these young peacocks like the one skippering yet another featherlight blowing past us with its sexy see-through sails.

"So this kid gets passed all the way down to the front row. And everybody's been leaning in and taking bites of his hot dog." Binny's neck jiggled with suppressed laughter. "So by the time he reaches the cheerleaders, there's about this much left." He held his thumb and forefinger a half inch apart and loudly inhaled, dizzy with mirth. "And that's the part that gets me," he squeaked, wiping his eyes, "the expression on this kid's face at what's left of his—"

"Off!" Father thundered. "You're a waste of space, Binstein! Get the hell off! Now!"

Binny dropped his can, and what beer was left sloshed along the toerail.

"Off!" Father yelled again.

Binny looked around in disbelief.

"Dad," I said gently, being the closest to him, "take it easy now." See, I'd watched his rutted forehead do the math, estimating our total crew weight at fourteen hundred pounds and realizing the difference three hundred might make in the final mile. He'd probably also factored in that it was late July and the water was warmish, that we were out of sight on the edge of the course.

"Now!" he demanded. "We'll pick you up after we finish!"

Then we finally all started objecting at once, but to our amazement Binny lifted one of his meaty legs over the lifelines. I don't know what Bobo Jr. thought would happen. Regardless, he didn't object when Bernard followed Binny's *kerplunk* by shouting, "Man overboard! Douse the chute and prepare to jibe and rescue!" And he did start the engine and execute the U-turn while we tackled the spinnaker, dropped the main and powered back to our bobbing frat boy, his undersized life preserver barely keeping his chin above the small waves.

"C'mon!" Father said, trying to laugh it off. "Who seriously thought he'd jump?"

"Dad," Bernard said, loud enough for everybody to hear, "you're an asshole."

Our father forced a smile and glanced around, counting on his cartoonish ability to reinflate himself. "Sometimes," he said slowly, "we all are."

"Nice try," Bernard said, "but you can't spread this blame. Too many witnesses to warp reality this time."

He was right. Our crew that day included three youngsters who sailed and drank with just about everybody, which meant this story would be passed from bar to bar, race to race, year to year, along with more exaggerated lore about our father illegally pumping or sculling or hitting marks or ramming boats on purpose or shattering a Coke bottle on the mast when he was upset with how the spinnaker was handled.

By the time Ruby began her senior year later that fall, the wheels of normalcy were coming off. She'd glance at the phone *before* it rang. Or she'd turn to me and say "It's about to rain" seconds before it did. Or she'd suddenly whisper "Visitors" right before the dogs yelped. Maybe her hearing was bizarrely acute, but that didn't explain the early September evening when she blurted, with obvious alarm, "Where's Momma?"

"Safeway?" Grumps said, looking up from a letter he was writing to the latest critic who'd denounced Steinbeck as too political or too sentimental. "She shops on Thursdays, right?"

My father folded and creased the sports section and glanced at the clock. "What's the problem? It's not even seven yet."

"Something happened," Ruby mumbled. Her new haircut made her distress even more palpable. She'd started cutting it extra short to avoid the double takes it generated when long and curly. Still, mothers asked ours which dye Ruby used to get that burnt-orange hue. They'd always look disappointed, then suspicious, to hear it was *natural*.

It was another hour before we got the call that our mother had been rear-ended on 45th at what had to be nearly the exact instant Ruby had inquired about her whereabouts.

Before skidding to the hospital in the flatbed, we all stared at her until she shouted that she had no idea how she felt the jostling of our mother's remarkable brain.

Just the week before, Mother had sat me down to tell me the saga of Fermat's famous last theorem.

Pierre de Fermat was a French mathematician whose final brainstorm came in 1637, when he declared that no three positive integers can satisfy the equation $a^n + b^n = c^n$ for any integer value of $n$ greater than two. Not a holy-shit revelation to most of us, this theorem became a pillar of nineteenth- and twentieth-century mathematics despite the fact that Fermat never provided the proof to back it up. Not surprisingly, re-creating this missing evidence became the holy grail of mathematicians for well over three hundred years, until a skinny Brit named Andrew Wiles pulled that rabbit out of his cap in 1995. Mother showed me a video in which Wiles described his quest and how he spent years working secretly in his attic before presenting his findings at Cambridge in 1993—only to discover a critical error. Devastated, he quietly returned to the task until he realized that an idea he'd abandoned long ago provided the missing link. "It was the most thrilling moment of my life," he said, choking up and turning away from the lens.

That's when I noticed my mother was weeping, too. "His name," she whispered, "will always be attached to this grand achievement. There is nothing anybody can do to improve his proof. It stands on its own like Mozart's Requiem. Hundreds of years from now, people will still know his name."

It was the first time I'd sensed her ego, her need to leave her mark. Call it my mother's version of the midlife crisis. But that was just part of it. She also was at war with the Bobos about the ongoing educa-tion of her children, the most recent flash point coming when they persuaded me to continue working in the boathouse—*for just one more year*—instead of heading off to college. Though she'd objected when Bernard went straight from high school to the boathouse, she'd thrown a mini-tantrum when I did the same. "I refuse to be the only educated member of my own family," she'd declared. "I did not bear and raise children to work in your damn boat factory!"

As the Olympic trials neared, Father implored Ruby to train harder, pointing out that other racers wouldn't have an extra pound on them. Ruby persisted in ignoring him and sticking to her own habits, gorging on Cheetos and giving her possessions away to friends and acquaintances, her bicycle, snow skis and sailing gloves, her watch and necklaces, my skateboard. "They're busting their butts five hours a day, every day, even Sundays," he'd chide her over dinner.

"It's just sailing!" she finally erupted, then doubled the blasphemy. "And sailboats are just heartless hunks of plastic!"

The Bobos stared at their plates. Grumps cracked his toes. Father ground his teeth, outrage misting off his skin and hair. Mother and Bernard twitched in and out of grins.

Ruby's stack of unread racing books continued to grow, and I couldn't blame her. Why study something that came as naturally as breathing?

Though it wasn't like she *always* won. She'd lost races steering big boats. Yet on her lonesome, in a Laser, when it mattered, she'd won every major local and regional competition she'd entered since she was twelve. At fifteen, she won the Youth Nationals, easily. Now she was about to face the best women sailors in the country for a spot on the 2000 U.S. Olympic team bound for Sydney next summer.

Even to me, this sounded like more than *just sailing.* More like legacy, as if generations of genetics and ambition and lore had been bubbling toward this climax.

# THE FAMILY PIG PILE

No girl Ruby's age had ever won the trials. Still five five and a teen-soft
one hundred twenty pounds, she was up against thirty-two adults,
gym-sculpted women in their twenties with sponsors, husbands and
abs like boxers. Once again, the math and physics and odds were
against her. But she'd qualified, and our father had immediately
entered her in the regatta, serendipitously held this year half an hour
from the Teardown, which made her the local darling underdog complete with an Olympic bloodline.

I was more nervous than she was. Her rivals were grown-up wizards
who'd traveled from the lakes, bays and rivers they'd dominated all
across America. Sailing was their life, and Ruby was barely seventeen
and seemed even younger.

A humbling opening day that left her with two thirds, a fifth and
a seventh was softened by the fact nobody had really dominated yet,
except for a former collegiate champion from Lake Superior who was
twenty-five, six one and a mother of twin boys. Mother Superior—as
we called her—had a first, two seconds and one disqualification.

Ruby was in the top three for the next seven—including four
firsts!—and in second place overall with three races remaining on the
final day. So there we all were, stacked along log-strewn Golden Gardens Park to witness the potential coronation of our family obsession
on a record hot day.

The two Bobos wore matching floppy sailor hats—as if they might be called to duty at any moment—and yakked nonstop. *Oh boy* this. *Christ almighty* that. Bernard rocked in place a few paces apart from us with half his head shaved, the other half flaunting Nordic locks. He'd recently become a vegetarian and a mountaineering zealot, scaling Rainier three times over the summer while reading everything Edward Abbey ever wrote. His T-shirt insisted that we TAX THE RICH!

Also in attendance was Ruby's latest boyfriend, a sallow, indoorsy Ballard teen with a gold hoop earring that made Father twitch his jaw muscles. His name might've been Zach or Jack, but all I remember for sure is Father called him the Latest Mistake. Mother was also there in the flesh, but so distracted she might as well have been in her office.

Ruby popped out front in the first race and tacked away from Mother Superior toward the right side of the course, even though both Bobos simultaneously pointed out the left side looked windier and that she should be *covering* Superior, blocking her wind. She made good time toward the windward mark before the breeze shifted ten degrees, at which point she tacked again and rode her new course straight for the buoy while most of the fleet had to tack twice to get on the same path. Rounding the mark, she was twenty yards ahead of the second-place boat.

"Still backseat driving?" Bernard asked the Bobos.

Through binoculars, I watched Ruby build speed downwind despite the fluky breeze. Near the finish, she jibed once more than necessary, second-guessing which end of the line was closest, and got nosed out by a former Olympian from Florida. Mother Superior finished fourth.

"Let it go," Grumps told my father, who kept demanding that somebody please explain why she picked the wrong end of the goddamn line, though second place kept her in contention.

Between races it got hotter yet, as if some orbital wobble had tugged us closer to the sun. Bernard used this break to stride up the beach shouting, "Will the person who left an Australian shepherd inside a gold Lexus SUV with the windows up please free her now!"

The two Bobos stopped arguing long enough for Father to ask what the hell Bernard was yelling about. "The kid's out of control," he said to Mother who gave no sign she heard either of them.

The next race started well, but Ruby picked the right side of the course again while most of the fleet went left, apparently gambling on another favorable shift that never happened. She finished third.

"What in God's name!" Father roared. "Why can't she play the odds? Is that too much to ask of her?"

Bernard checked to see if I was catching this, seeing as he'd told me earlier that Father wanted her to win for *him*.

Ruby's Latest Mistake picked this moment to go confessional as we stood silently overlooking the Sound. "My parents want me to get a job," he told me and my brother. "Like at Red Robin or Walgreens or some boring shit like that. I won't take just any day job, though. Know what I mean? Get that on your résumé and you start to look like a lifer."

"Know what I think?" Bernard casually asked. "You should lower your standards and realize it's highly unlikely that anybody would want to hire you to do anything."

It took the kid a moment to digest this. "Well, fuck you, too," he finally said.

"Fuck me?" Bernard grabbed the boy under the arms and threw him, upwards as much as backwards. To his credit, he stuck the landing and immediately held up his palms in surrender.

Bernard stormed off toward the parking lot again, then down to the most crowded stretch of the beach. "Will the douchebag with the pretentious Lexus please free your overheating dog right now!"

After the Bobos reworked the scores, Mother calculated that Ruby should be able to still win the trials if she finished in the top five and ahead of Mother Superior in the final race. By then the northerly was generating foot-high rollers that favored longer, stronger sailors. Yet Rube nailed the start so perfectly that we feared she was over early, surging a boat length ahead of Mother Superior and using her rights to force her to tack. Then she covered her, back and forth across the course, blocking her wind and expanding her lead to the windward mark, which Ruby rounded in third and her nemesis in fifth.

Father continued questioning her decisions, saying she should just sail to win. Yet on the downwind leg, she was the fastest boat, and by midpoint, she'd climbed into second. For the last loop, she played the shifts and overtook the leader by cutting inside her around the windward mark. From there Ruby was just one smooth downwind run to the Olympics. Cheers rose up as word spread. Locals and Ballard High friends and fellow racers like Mario Seville all started shouting out over the water. The two Bobos spouted nonsensical cheers. Even Mother, who'd been almost morose till now, yelled, "Go, Ruby! Go!"

Leading by thirty yards approaching the finish line, she was guaranteed to win unless she capsized. People began crowding around us to experience the family's reaction. Mother hugged the two Bobos while I hid tears behind the binoculars. Her speed, once again, didn't make sense. How does *anybody* separate from sailors *this* good?

Then things suddenly turned strange.

She was headed for the left end of the finish line, which made sense given her location and wind direction. If she stuck to it, she wouldn't need to jibe. Yet at the last instant she did exactly that, pivoting ninety degrees and sailing parallel to the line like she'd done on that earlier race, but at a sharper, more inexplicable angle.

"What's she . . . ," my father murmured. "Did the wind shift that much?"

"She's just . . . ," Grumps muttered, hugging himself.

"Did her rudder snap?" Mother asked.

"Is she doing a penalty turn?" Bernard wondered aloud.

"She must've already finished!" Father insisted.

"Give her the horn," Grumps pleaded.

Then we watched her veer past the buoy marking the far end of the finish line as the boat behind her crossed and received the horn followed by another congested threesome, including Mother Superior. *Honk-honk-honk.* Then another three, *honk-honk-hooonk.*

As this spectacle unfolded, I could already tell it would be one of the indelible moments—amid billions of faded and meaningless ones—that would make up my life.

Earlier that week, Ruby had asked what my dreams were like. I hadn't said much other than that they kept waking me up. In hers, she told me, she was rarely herself. "When I wake up it startles me to remember that to everybody else I'm always just this Ruby you see right here. It's so much more personal."

"What is?"

"Being awake."

Wrong-way Ruby sailed off toward the center of the Sound as the rest of the fleet crossed the line in clumps and bleats. Onshore, Father seized up like an engine that'd run out of oil. Years later, he'd call it the single most hostile thing anybody had ever done to him. I admit tasting some of that acid, because if given Ruby's gifts I'd have served them like a slave. Bernard, however, found her decision nothing short of exhilarating.

"Moitessier!" he shouted, jamming his wolf smile up near our father's purple mug. "Serves you fucking right! *Moitessier!*"

I'm not sure Father could've connected those dots at that instant, how Ruby passing up victory could be seen as a nod to the mystic Frenchman he'd forced us to study. At that instant, I doubt he could have told you who Moitessier was. Perhaps Ruby wasn't channeling the guy anyway. Afterwards, she told a reporter and the rest of the sailing universe that she wanted to sail less, not more, and to work at things she wasn't already good at, like the piano and French and religion and boyfriends. She also said she wanted to go to Africa for the Peace Corps more than she wanted to go to Australia for the Olympics, a comment mulled by millions, toasted by many. By then, though, her explanations barely mattered. Her meltdown was a two-sentence national news brief. As it turned out, had she finished that race she would've been the favorite in Sydney.

Two months later, Ruby and our father were mentioned in *Sports Illustrated* in an article about kid stars snapping under parental pressure. That mortification was followed by an unrelated business-journal story about the Puget Sound boatbuilding landscape, with one anonymous competitor saying Johannssen & Sons had been an obsolete family enterprise for more than a decade. It took me years to realize that in Bobo Jr.'s mind, Ruby's Olympic run was his financial ace in the hole. Her success, he'd envisioned, could resuscitate the Johannssen brand.

What actually transpired inside her head at the end of the race remained unclear. She thought of Moitessier, yes, but only *after* she'd abandoned course. Asked point-blank what she'd been thinking when she decided to jibe, she said, "I wasn't."

How different would our lives have been if she'd simply finished?

To get Bernard out of his face, my stricken father backhanded the air, as if fending off yellow jackets, his knuckles grazing my brother's cheek. Seemingly innocent, accidental contact, though as Mother would later point out: For every action there is an equal and opposite reaction. Regardless, Bernard responded by planting both hands in Bobo Jr.'s chest and sending him reeling, his fleshy neck whipping loosely backwards but then forward as his skull bounced off a log, which sent me airborne into my brother's ribs, tackling him into the sand.

What happened next turns fuzzy and fractured for me, but I believe my father crawled toward us like an incensed bear until Grumps, galloping in our direction, tripped on the same log and yelped like something had snapped.

I have no idea what Ruby's Latest Mistake did during this or how my nose bled on everybody. But I know plenty of people saw the family pig pile and tried not to make eye contact with any member of our barbarous clan. And I recall Mother's strangely detached inventory of injuries and how my ubiquitous blood made everything seem worse than it was.

In hindsight, I think of this whole episode as our family's big bang, jettisoning Bernard to the South Pacific, Ruby to Africa, Mother to Arizona, and me and Grumps right down the road. Within a year, Father would be living alone in the Teardown, and more than a dozen would pass before the whole family gathered in the same room again.

While the rest of us regrouped on the beach, Bernard stormed into the parking lot with a rock the size of a softball. He set it on the roof of the Lexus, grabbed a gallon jug of water out of a nearby pickup and cut the top off with the knife he carried on his belt, then used the rock to shatter the driver's window of the SUV. With the alarm blaring, he opened the door, freed the unsteady dog and guided her toward the water.

What lingers next is Mother saying, during our shameful hobble to the cars, "It's finally over." Leaving me to wonder if she meant our childhood or our family unit. Or, seeing how Ruby's sailing magic had stitched us together for so long, the central drama of our existence.

She found a tissue to dam my nose and told me to tilt my head back. The sky, I saw, was milky blue, but the moon was surprisingly clear and full yet so oddly ringed, and I told her so.

"So what do you think is going on with the moon?" she asked.

"Some kind of reflection?" I guessed.

"Yes, but of what?"

"Just tell me."

"It's sunlight," she said, "bouncing off the moon and reflecting off crystals in the upper atmosphere. Nice, huh?"

She looked up at me, her smile gone. "It's over," she said again.

When we'd get home, she'd retreat to her office to unpack the Dob-sonian telescope I'd helped her pick out, including a foot-wide mirror that cost $850 and a smaller one for $150, expenditures we'd hid-den from the Bobos. She'd sucked me into her astronomy mania, at one point insisting that I slow down and imagine what it must have been like for Edwin Hubble to discover in 1925 that the universe was expanding, the galaxies moving apart from one another faster and farther all the time.

"Guess what they call that moon?" she asked now, handing me another tissue. "C'mon, you can get this." Her eyes were still on the sky. "What's it look like?"

"An eyeball?" My nose felt cold and numb and large beneath my hand. "I don't know, Mom. A poached egg?"

I waited, knowing she'd eventually tell me.

"A moon halo," she whispered, her hand clutching mine. "Isn't that beautiful. It's called a moon halo."

# DANCING ON A COP CAR

~~~~~~

The next time we saw Bernard he was on television.

He'd packed all his climbing gear and left home before we'd returned from the beach fracas and read his simple note: *I'M OUTTA HERE—B.*

Six days later, he left a message on the house phone when he knew nobody would be there, telling Mother he'd landed a job and wasn't coming home anytime soon. *So don't leave the light on.*

After I called around, a friend of his finally shared a number for one of his new mountaineering pals, who told me he'd been hired as a climbing ranger at Mount Rainier.

Irritated that I'd found his bunkhouse number, Bernard reluctantly disclosed that he was making *first ascents* and *decent coin*—he had lots of new words—and had found a sassy waitress to play with at night.

"Everybody wishes you'd just come home," I said, though I was mostly speaking for myself. "The Bobos need you at the boathouse."

He snickered. "I've got a job outside on a magnificent mountain. Why would I want to go back to laying fiberglass indoors?"

"Loyalty" was the word that popped out of me.

His laughter hurt my ears. "Then just come visit," I said weakly.

That busted him up again, though by then I wasn't sure if he was laughing at me, at the notion of a *visit* or at the antics of his sassy girlfriend on his end of the line. What astonished me was that he didn't apologize for leaving me to patch the family back together.

Another five weeks of unreturned calls whirled past before Ruby and I drove to Rainier. We poked around the bunkhouses but couldn't find anybody who knew him. So we wheeled up to the lodge at Paradise, asked where we'd find the climbing rangers and received the same useless phone number. His waitress, though, was easy to spot.

"He left the mountain eleven days ago," she told us.

"Quit?" I asked, trying to place her accent.

"Fired, technically, but the case could be made that he quit."

"So what'd he do?"

She looked at me long enough to rotate a wad of blue gum around her mouth three times. "We were having our monthly staff meeting," she said, glancing into the kitchen. "The supe was giving us the same old customer-service crap. He was more worked up than usual, though, like maybe his wife was holding out, you know? And Bernie just told him off in front of everybody."

*Bernie,* I thought. "Brilliant," I said.

"Listen, y'all want anything to eat?"

"What'd he say?" Ruby asked.

She leaned closer and rearranged our water glasses. "The supe was reminding the climbing rangers they weren't getting paid to have fun. He'd heard how often they were skiing off the summit and whooping down the mountain. 'Sends the *wrong message,*' he told them. Then he bitched about our lack of cheeriness and even went after Travis, the bug guy, saying his *insect tours* were running too long and screwing up other schedules. That's when Bernie stuck his hand up and told the supe it'd be a whole lot easier working here if he wasn't such an *imperious fuckstick.* We had to look up *imperious* afterwards. *Fuckstick* we knew."

"Fired on the spot?" I asked, marveling at Bernard's penchant for mouthy beauties.

She nodded. "Like I said, he seemed ready to go."

"Where to?"

She shrugged. "I'm just a junior-college girl from Louisiana, but I'm guessing he would've told his family if he'd wanted y'all to know."

An obese customer waved for her. She rolled her eyes and her gum again before taking a long last look at the huge black x on Ruby's white T-shirt and hustled off, her hips rocking out figure eights.

The shirt hinted at one of Ruby's many postsailing phases. When the yearbook came out the following spring, she'd look like the most outgoing senior imaginable. Group photos would show her in the Cultural Awareness Club (for two weeks), the Environmental Club (quit by the third meeting), the Thespian Club (auditioned but never acted), Knowledge Bowl (never competed), the Mountaineers Club (went twice), the Japanese Club (just for the picture). The only out-fit she stuck with was the Red Cross Club. Her classmates probably assumed she craved popularity, but I think Ruby was just trying on new identities. At this stage, four weeks into her senior year, she'd recently finished reading *The Autobiography of Malcolm X* and couldn't quit yapping about how he'd reinvented himself in prison. If he could do it in jail, her thought bubble seemed to say, why can't we do it out here in freedom? So when I saw that shirt, I bought it even though it fell to her knees.

As Bernard's girl sashayed back past us, Ruby stepped in front of her. "Please tell him his sister and brother *need* to hear from him." Then she tilted her head to the side and cracked the smile that had always kicked open every door in her path. "Please," she said again.

And maybe she did, but we still didn't *see* or hear from Bernard till Ruby spotted him two months later on television. It was day two of the soon-to-be-famous WTO riots, which she'd attended that after-noon with her latest dubious boyfriend, a chubby kid with big ears, a lopsided grin and a vocabulary consisting of *man, like* and *awesome*.

The Bobos and I were reeling from nine straight days of work, with

Grumps's neck locking up again and Father denying, as always, any soreness or fatigue, though he moaned and dozed in the recliner. The house already felt awkwardly muted with Bernard's absence, Mother's self-seclusion and Father ignoring Ruby.

After he pretended not to hear her account of getting mildly tear-gassed hours earlier, I finally snapped. "Quit your pouting already. You wouldn't stand for it in any of us. She's your daughter. Grow up."

I hadn't raised my voice, but coming from me I might as well have swung a sword.

To his credit, he didn't erupt. He dropped his fork, stared into the middle distance above the TV, rubbed his nose a few times and resumed eating. Twenty minutes later, not even he could ignore Ruby's announcement that Bernard was on the tube.

I was so nonpolitical back in late 1999 that the WTO fiasco baffled me. What sort of protest could inspire people to throw rocks at Niketown *and* block intersections with inflatable whales? On this broadcast, downtown looked like footage from some foreign uprising. And the story line swung swiftly from dismay over the protesters' vandalism to anger over police striking back at citizens. The outrage tripled once a television crew got gassed. Now every channel was questioning the cops' behavior. And that's when a camera shifted to a strapping young masked man shouting and gesticulating on the roof of a city patrol car.

"Bernard," Ruby whispered. Then louder, "That's Bernard!"

Mother popped out of her office, and we all crowded the twenty-four-inch Zenith for a closer look.

"No, no," Father mumbled. "Can't be."

But then, as if to prove him wrong, this Zorro-like protester, cape and all, started clogging on top of that Crown Vic, hands on hips, kicking his feet in a rowdy rendition of the Icelandic folk dance Grumps had taught us.

"Sweet Jesus," Father said.

"C'mon, Bernard," Grumps pleaded. "Get down."

"He's too skinny," Mother said in such a remote monotone it was hard to tell whether she meant too thin to be her son or that she wished he'd eat more.

"What's he thinking?" Father asked, then louder, "What's he thinking?"

After a brief silence, Ruby answered: "People who make a peaceful revolution impossible will make a violent revolution inevitable."

The Bobos gaped as my sister raised a Black Power fist before clearing unfinished plates of meat loaf.

Since Ruby's sailing rebellion, Mother had rarely cooked, as if her daughter veering off course had freed her from her ordained roles, too. Not that it was the end of parenting, but that she had *her* time now, too, to make her own observations, to be Darwin in the Galapagos or Hubble peering at the cosmos. Let the Bobos learn how to cook.

They tried for a few weeks before letting me take over. My repertoire was limited to burgers, tacos, fish sticks and meat loaf. Predictably, my father buried everything in ketchup, and Grumps, still trying not to overstay his welcome, loved it all exactly as it was served. Midway through my apprenticeship, Ruby announced she was a vegan.

"At Sixth and Union today," a big-haired TV lady said, "the First Amendment was suspended."

As they cut to commercials, we all asked questions at once, except for Mother, who grabbed a warm hat and stepped outside.

Others also must've recognized Bernard and his televised jig, because within an hour two police officers came knocking.

"Mr. Johannssen?"

"That's right."

"Mind if we come in?"

"Of course I mind," Father said. "Why wouldn't I?"

"We'd like to speak to Bernard Johannssen."

"Well, congratulations. So would we, but we don't know where he's at. Hasn't lived here for months."

"We'd sure like to talk to him, sir. Where exactly might we find him?"

"I just answered that question. You got any others?"

"Sir, your son is suspected of potential criminal activities in connection to the protests going—"

"We have a television."

"Well, sir—"

"Last we heard, he was working on Rainier, rescuing those climbers who get stuck and expect taxpayers to save their fannies."

They kept peeking past the Bobos at me.

"That's Josh, Bernard's little brother." My father snickered at the notion of his middle child clogging on a cop car.

"Somebody upstairs?" the cop asked after hearing footsteps above while his sidekick looked wildly for a staircase.

"This is the upstairs," Father said. "My wife's on the roof."

Sidekick unsnapped his gun holster at the sound of more movement above.

"I see," the cop said. "And what exactly is *she* doing up there?"

"Telescope," I interjected, before Dad could insult them again. "She's an astronomer."

The two cops exchanged glances. "I'm sorry, but we're gonna have to take a look. You understand, Mr. Johannssen?"

"Of course! Having the police investigate my wife's stargazing while there's rioting going on downtown makes perfect sense."

One cop held the ladder while the other ascended with a flashlight. What he found was a middle-aged woman in a Russian fur hat and a faded yellow bathrobe, sitting on a folding chair and staring through a large telescope.

I'd built her a level platform on the flat tarred section. In exchange, she'd taught me about constellations, planets and supernovas—or exploding stars, as I preferred to call them. She'd learned how to measure the brightness and location of stars so we'd notice if anything changed. I went along with her but couldn't fathom how we could spot anything that telescopes ten times as powerful somehow missed. Still, I jotted the numbers she called out, as if sharing in her quest to monitor our galaxy.

"Venus," she said to the cop, pointing at what looked like easily the brightest star in the sky. "It's as close as it gets. Wanna see?"

Subsequent articles would paint Bernard as one of the masterminds of the riots and a member of something called the Ruckus Society. We had no idea what was true, though there was no stopping his police-car clogging from playing over and over in our minds.

# THE GETAWAY SAILBOAT

~~~~~~~~

A month later, on a Wednesday afternoon three days before the new millennium, I was watching my grandfather light a cigar and crack his first Rainier of the day, his 3:45 p.m. ritual, up fifteen minutes from the prior year and a full hour from the year before that. If I could have just one short video of Grumps, I might choose this moment for the focus and appreciation that came over him when he puffed a new cigar to life, rocking it between thumb and forefinger, as if gauging its symmetricality, then dipping his nose closer to the smoke before straightening, rubbing his hip in a circular motion, dragging his thumb under his shirt to scratch his spine and finally exhaling very slowly before handing out stale bread to the geese.

No one had a bigger soft spot for Canada geese. He preferred these boisterous turkey-sized, black-and-white beasts to swans or eagles, pelicans or flamingos, and their nasal honk and jumbo turds didn't annoy him at all. Not surprisingly, his expanding goose family returned to our boathouse every spring, then eventually quit traveling altogether and stayed year-round—his affection and generosity single-handedly transforming them from migrants to residents. He'd named at least eight and recognized them all on sight, or so he claimed; the loquacious matriarch he called Dora, after his mother. But Parks and Rec had recently declared their poop a health menace and began gassing the geese en masse in mobile vans, inciting Grumps to speak publicly for the first time in his life.

"I've lived all my years in this fine city, and most people who know me would consider me a reasonable man," he told the Parks board. "And I certainly didn't come here with the intent to liken you to Nazis. But after hearing your rationale for systematically killing thousands of innocent and glorious birds, I can't think of a more accurate way to describe you people."

After he smoked and drank and shoveled shit off the dock, Grumps sat and scrawled in his big red journal. I'd always assumed it was design ideas or contract logistics until I found his pages open to what looked like the beginning of a screenplay he'd entitled *Against the Wind*. His cast of characters? Otto Helm, Max Ebb, Slack Tide and Swirling Eddy. While Grumps scribbled ideas, I continued glassing the hull of an experimental race boat, a Falcon 35, that Father had designed for some fast-talking orthodontist.

Traditional Joho construction involved eight layers of mat and roving through most of the hull. On this one, though, we were using just four layers. And instead of three-quarter-inch plywood for bulkheads and coring, we went with half-inch. Father swore builders—at least those who wanted to stay in business!—were going even lighter to build competitive boats. Grumps cursed the drawings and refused to let Father call the design a Joho, first quietly, later forcefully, before apologizing to everybody for losing his temper, though holding his line.

The other boat we were building, an original thirty-one-footer, was the latest testament to Grumps's ongoing insistence on grace and durability. Step aboard and you immediately sensed integrity and elegance even if you didn't notice all the bronze, the Burmese teak, the curved cockpit trim and the laminated beams below.

We were behind on deliveries, but even after Bernard's exit the Bobos wouldn't hire more than part-time help, though we routinely needed at least two more glassers and another woodworker. My father responded by exhorting us to work harder, especially himself. Today he was really grinding, and I'd seen him only during his mini-breaks, when his sweat-blistered forehead would briefly rise above the bulk-head. I was listening to Grumps shovel poop and discuss world events with Dora when Bernard slipped inside the back door.

"Hey, Josh," he said, like it was just the two of us. "Got a minute?"

I followed him outside without telling anybody, not wanting him to think I let the Bobos know my whereabouts at all times.

Smirking beneath a wool ski hat, he stuck out his fist and offered me a stick of Trident.

"I need you to survey a boat for me," he said. "Just docked near Gasworks Park. I've only got an hour. Think you could swing that?"

This all felt normal somehow. Checking out a boat on a one-hour deadline? Fantastic! I was flattered, giddy and blushing.

We talked nonstop to the dock, him trying to catch up on the Ruby saga, me trying to find out where he'd been and whether he was still a fugitive or had *plea-bargained* the two malicious-mischief charges for damaging a police car and a Starbucks window.

"They've dropped hundreds of charges," I said. "Everybody's getting off." I told him how the cops had come to the house and climbed up on the roof, though I was too jacked to register his responses. When he boasted of living on the streets in Eugene for a week, I finally realized the odor following us down the street was his.

Walking up to the boat, I didn't need to see the shadows of the recently removed vinyl letters to know her name. *Bravado* was an old Cal 36 owned by an officious local racer whom Grumps used to point to as an exception to his rule that all Republicans were powerboaters.

"So you stole it."

He laughed. "It's just a thing, Josh. You heard Ruby. Sailboats are bloodless *things*."

"But this thing isn't yours."

"I don't believe in personal property."

"That's convenient. So you stole it."

"I received it," he said. "Somebody else liberated it. Or, if you prefer: it was *donated* to me," he said, chortling at his word choice.

"Who makes a getaway on a sailboat?" I asked him. "Ever see Bruce Willis or Schwarzenegger or Stallone leap on a sailboat and escape danger at two-point-three knots?"

He rocked at his hips and grinned at me. "I forgot how funny you get when you're pissed."

"Why're you running? Those stupid charges aren't that big a deal."

"Up to ten years in jail and twenty grand in fines sounds pretty big to me. And there might be more. I've participated in a few other actions, Josh."

"Actions?"

"I'm leaving on this boat. You helping or not?"

"So now I have to go to jail, too?"

"Can we skip the melodrama? All I'm asking is for you to look this over and tell me how well it's equipped for the outside."

"Outside what?"

"The ocean, Josh! What're you missing here?"

"It's a race boat!"

"Used to be. Now it's basically a pretty fast cruiser. And that's what I want to do—cruise fast. So what's she need? You know this stuff so much better than me. The boat's open. Look around. Tell me what's missing."

"Autopilot?" I asked, stepping aboard.

"Affirmative."

"Backup autopilot?"

"Negative."

"Radar?"

He grinned. "I've got an air horn."

"How 'bout anchors?"

"One thirty-pounder."

"You need at least two, and one should be forty or bigger. How about a bunk to strap yourself into?"

"Got climbing harnesses and ropes."

Scrambling through the boat, I tried to focus, but my vision pulsed while Bernard kept glancing out the window, watching the dock behind us, cracking his knuckles, one by one.

"You'll need three reefs in the main," I said, "instead of two—if you've even got that. And you need a jackline along the cabin top to tie into when you go forward. If you clip into the lifelines, you'll just beat against the hull before you drown. Pick up a solar panel or two, when you can, and rig the reeflines so you can handle them from the cockpit. Might need a backing plate and a block right here to do that."

"Man, you worry."

"What're you really doing?" I asked, suddenly so frustrated I was afraid I'd cry. "I mean, is there a *plan*?"

"I'm gonna be a citizen of the sea." His smile was almost sad. "I'm headed out, Josh."

"Have you noticed that it's late December?" My voice squeaked. "You checked the storm patterns?"

He reached for my shoulder, but I wouldn't let him touch me. "Like I said," he whispered, "you worry too much."

"What about food? Or are you just planning on catching seabirds with your bare hands?"

"Got enough cans of bad chili to last a few weeks. You've always known I'd be going, Josh. Don't act so fucking astonished."

Then I just said it: "What makes you think you can leave us?" I couldn't have sounded any whinier.

"What makes you think you have to stay?" he asked, so calmly that this sounded like the easiest question ever.

The ensuing Johannssen brothers standoff dragged on for a few seconds before I finally understood. "You don't really want me to check this boat out," I said, wincing at my gullibility. "You want money."

He glanced up the dock again, then directly at me. "Actually, I want both."

After jogging to the bank, I emptied most of my account, loped back to the boat and handed him a fat roll of fifties totaling $1,350. Then I helped him power through the locks so I could hear his diesel, like a doc listening to an old heart, but mostly to spend another hour with my brother.

The lake water gushed out the front gate as we gradually lowered to salty Puget Sound with just two other boats along for the descent and a few thrilled tourists pointing at us, as if we were exotic chimpanzees trained to operate boats.

I made a list of all the spare engine parts he needed. He smiled, glanced at the scrap of paper and tossed it below.

When I told him Father was still ignoring Ruby, his eyes flashed, but he didn't say anything.

"Why were you on top of the police car in the first place?" I demanded, feeling like I'd paid for some semblance of an answer by now.

"That's a longer conversation, Brother. And you can tell Dad he's an ass."

"Tell him yourself," I said as it began to rain.

"And look out for Ruby," he added. "She needs you. Mom and Grumps do, too."

"Thanks for telling me to do what I'm already doing."

"I'll write as soon as I get somewhere that feels safe," he continued. "For now, though, this has gotta be our secret."

I laughed. Another damn secret, this one coming a day after Ruby confided she'd be leaving once she graduated and never coming back. Two days before that, Mother had told me she'd applied for professorships in Arizona and Texas as well as the UDub. But don't tell anybody.

He dropped me off at the Shilshole gas dock without tying off. "Josh," he shouted, peeling away beneath the now-deafening rain, "you're my hero!"

"Yeah right," I mumbled to myself, the rain seeping down my forehead as he puttered away without a visible flicker of regret or fear in the slowest getaway vehicle imaginable.

Foolish as this appeared, I would've left with him if he'd invited me.

I wouldn't see Bernard for five years. Far more would happen than he'd ever share, but that's to be expected. As a psychologist friend once told me, a sailboat's just a mechanism for a journey.

Perhaps. But from my mother's vantage, a sailboat is a mechanism for transferring the motion of wind into the motion of water. The wind pushes the boat, the boat pushes the water.

# THE INTERNATIONAL SIGN OF FORNICATION

Most people have never sailed. So when you take them out, they wear clumsy shoes and start calling you Ahab or Bligh. Or if they're particularly nervous, they'll quote Whitman—*O Captain! my Captain!*—and shout *Bon voyage!* or talk like pirates, as if this were the freshest improv: *Arrrggh! Keelhaul the wench!* They'll offer to help, but what they really want to know is where to sit and what to hold on to and when you'll get them a drink.

If timing and elements cooperate, it all begins gently with hoisting the sails and killing the engine. If they're not too spooked they might even start to notice how different the world sounds and looks out here at this strolling pace, as if we'd popped out of the atmosphere and were gazing down at our blue planet. This is when they just might suspend the everyday humdrum. You see it in their glances at shore, where time has stopped and this breeze is having no impact whatsoever. For some, bells start ringing. Why don't we get out on the water more often? Or they start vowing, openly or secretly, to take lessons, the pledge softening with the return to land. But they have right now. And as twilight approaches, the rising warmth of the sunbaked ground creates thermals that need somewhere to go. Voilà! A side rail eases toward the drink and our speed doubles. So I ask them to steer and watch them feel the wind transfer from the sails to the rudder to the throbbing tiller in their grip. Their eyes widen as if I'd handed them a snake, and we rush toward shore as the depth sounder drops—twenty feet, sixteen, thirteen, then eleven. We better tack soon, I say, but you're the skipper, so it's your call. They look wildly about, then shout, *Hard alee!*

There's a shrink in town with a business called sailingtherapy.com. He takes out bickering couples, mother-daughter squabblers and the chronically depressed. He readily admits he offers little beyond the natural high of sailing. It doesn't hurt that they're mostly women and he has dreamy eyes and an FM voice, but the ride alone usually solves or at least eases their problems.

Yet as therapeutic as sailing is, it's awkward for romance. Cramped, mildewed boats don't conjure foreplay. My initial online pitch—*Sailor looking for love*—attracted women seeking novelties. Many were freshly divorced and disrobing before I knew them at all. Afterwards, some dates looked so remorseful, like they'd just cheated on somebody far worthier, which in turn left me bluesy, wandering the docks. Even Kirsten, who'd been with me long enough for everything to bloom and wither and bloom and wither yet again, felt so wholesome compared with these escapades. But they continued, though few truly enjoyed the sailing. Many were nervous, some uninterested, their faces sagging with boredom.

Number 27, however, was thrilled. On our third sail, she suddenly insisted we do it on board, seeing as how there was no wind. She was older, never married, seemingly stable, often funny. I hoped she'd last. We admired many of the same books. This wasn't common, and in fact it had evolved into my lone date disqualifier. *Your favorite authors can't be romance novelists.* This woman was a Tom Robbins fanatic, and she admitted after a third mojito that she occasionally thought of him while getting off.

I laughed. "He's gotta be pushing eighty."

She puckered a grin. "Have you read *Jitterbug Perfume*?"

During my family's early cruising days, we'd passed a seemingly unmanned vessel flying a tiny jib and a JUST MARRIED banner. "God bless them," Grumps said. The next time we saw the same setup, I overheard my father call it "the international sign of fornication." I didn't have a banner, though I did fly my smallest jib on this eerily calm Sunday afternoon.

We were below, in the bow, fully engaged, when I heard water suddenly gurgling beneath the hull. I'd strapped the tiller to the middle but sensed a puff pushing us to port. Eyes clenched, she seemed so close I didn't want to interrupt things and ask her to look out the hatch to see if we were headed toward shore. Who knew what writers she was fantasizing about now? A young Vonnegut talking filthy? Melville in waders? Faulkner in nothing but a cowboy hat?

I was pondering all that while also trying to calculate speed and location, tidal height and likely depths, without getting too distracted, when my cell started blaring behind us—my father, I knew without looking, demanding a progress report or exhorting me to *pounce* or informing me the new goddamn rudder should've already arrived.

As anybody who's ever tried to please a woman or get a small sailboat up on a plane knows, it can take a whole lot of tweaking and tightening and gentle adjustments. Then either *yeowwww!* or you slam, precrescendo, into a sandbar like we did, thudding to a halt as gently as I could've hoped, though firmly enough to eject Number 27.

She couldn't have been more alarmed or embarrassed if we'd been abruptly boarded by the Coast Guard. Even after I'd backed us off the bar into deeper water, she couldn't look at me, much less laugh.

I called Grumps during his happy hour the following day to recount the fiasco. His opening chuckles deepened into full-throated cackling as I described the mounting complications, then turned asthmatic once I told him about Father's untimely call. His ensuing coughing spasms had me contemplating hanging up and dialing

911. None of his health threats sounded too dire, but add them all together—ministrokes and tiny blood clots, rising prostate numbers and elevated liver enzymes—and the little man seemed to be under siege. "She wouldn't have lasted anyway," he finally rasped. "No sense of humor. Although maybe you're no Captain Casanova."

From what I've gathered, Einstein wasn't either. If photos tell us anything, his sailing dates were overdressed and constipated. Mostly, he went out by himself.

Perhaps sailing is a vehicle for thought, not seduction. Maybe Einstein's boldest notions and thought experiments came to him while riding or awaiting wind with no risk of phone calls or visits from students, friends or family. Where better to ponder light and gravity, time and relativity?

During our homeschooling Sundays, Grumps once made the case—after a few Rainiers—that the history of the world was written by whoever sailed best. Early on, the Egyptians topped the heap because they figured out how to sail goods *up* the Nile, he told us. Then business boomed for the Arabs once their new triangular sails enabled them to travel upwind. And China's early dominance, he assured us, coincided with the advent of its sturdy sails that folded up like venetian blinds.

In my early days in the boatyard, Jack used to tell us we were performing a community service. Without us, he said, the motorized boating world would fade away and all waves would come from wind, with no sounds other than the occasional flap of oars or sails. That scenario always appealed to me. Maybe we'd all think more clearly. Sailing and big ideas go together. That's why boats attract some people the way churches lure others. Knowingly or not, we sail in hopes of answering larger questions.

In the summer of 1939, in between solo afternoon sails on Cutchogue Harbor along Long Island Sound, Einstein sent FDR a letter urging him to build an atomic bomb before Germany did. Other than that fateful letter, it was a serene summer of sailing and playing music with a fellow violinist who owned the local department store.

In the end, all Einstein wanted to know was how God created this world. "I want to know His thoughts," he used to say. "The rest are details." He spent his final years working on unifying theories that could explain and connect everything. Light and gravity. Atoms and solar systems. Violins and sailboats.

# A CRUSH ON EINSTEIN'S BRAIN

My mother encouraged us to revel in historical flash points when conventional wisdom got kicked in the nads. Like when Copernicus suggested the sun didn't revolve around the earth. Even better, the moment Galileo used his homemade telescope to prove that Copernicus was right and our humble planet wasn't the center of anything other than the orbit of one puny moon. Her favorite Einstein moment came fourteen years after he first jolted the scientific community with daring theories he'd generated during his midtwenties in his spare time. Those ideas made him famous among his peers, but his fanfare was about to flash to the masses.

In Newton's universe, time and space were constants, but Einstein came along and said, Hold on, Isaac! I don't think so. The speed of light—671 million miles per hour—is the only constant we can truly count on. And I'm also pretty sure energy and mass are connected by the square root of the speed of light.

While scientists debated his brain-twisting abstractions, a solar eclipse finally offered a world stage to prove or disprove his bewitching premises, that gravity bends light and distorts the night sky far more than anybody realized and that Newton's long-accepted grid of the cosmos was an oversimplification.

On May 29, 1919, the moon obscured the sun for slightly more than seven minutes, providing a dark-enough sky to measure the difference between the real and apparent location of a star positioned slightly behind the sun. The star should not have been visible from earth. Yet because the sun's gravitational suction bent the starlight around it by the precise amount Einstein's general theory of relativity had predicted, the star appeared beside, not behind, the obscured sun. His far more precise understanding of gravity suddenly changed the way Man looked at the cosmos.

"Think about it," Mother marveled. "The world had to go dark in order to be illuminated." And for one grand moment—this was her favorite part—a *scientist* was the world's biggest celebrity. As Charlie Chaplin told Einstein, "They're cheering us both: you because nobody understands you, and me because everybody understands me."

Mother might have understood Einstein better than she did us and never passed up an opportunity to explain and extol him.

When the first pocket GPS came out, she took one aboard with us so we could use the latitude and longitude readings to plot our location on the chart. "How can it be so accurate?" she asked, then explained how the device calculates its whereabouts by triangulating signals from satellites. To be precise, though, it needs to know exactly how long it takes to receive those signals to within a billionth of a second, which is tricky because satellites are moving and their signals are passing through the earth's gravity. Getting an accurate reading wouldn't have been possible, she told us, had Einstein not accurately predicted that the earth's gravity sped up time ever so slightly, leaving time on a satellite thirty-eight-billionths of a second behind time on earth. Without his math, she explained, errors would grow by the hour and a GPS would be useless. "We know where we are thanks to Einstein."

What I knew was that our mother had a crush on Albert's mind.

By mid-2000 her astronomical research made diminishing sense to me, though I suspected she was ransacking the sky in search of anything that might help her get hired as a professor. Along with her résumé, she sent the UDub a summary of her findings, including a short paper on supernovas she'd published in *Astronomy Now*. A faculty friend assured her she was the front-runner. Yet the form letter response thanked her for applying, *but unfortunately, due to such stiff competition for this position, we are unable to grant an interview.*

It was the first setback I saw her unable to process. Ruby snubbing the Olympics or Bernard clogging on a police car were mere shudders compared with this derailment. She had the experience, the volunteer hours, the awards. She phoned the dean to make sure it wasn't a mistake. They hired a young man from Amherst who would quit three years later for a post at Berkeley. They could've had our mother forever.

Suddenly her high cheekbones made her look gaunt. Her lips flattened, and her eyes narrowed. Her default expression became a thin frown. She forgot to wear bras. Chin whiskers went untweezed. She took to wearing thicker glasses and speaking in incomplete sentences. On clear nights, she'd stay on the roof till four o'clock, regardless of the temperature, then take a nap and rise for school only a few hours later.

I wanted to believe she was responding like a champion, by working harder, like Einstein after he got turned down for a high school teaching job.

Ruby's response was to turn her senior project into an oral essay on sexism in science. "Given that less than five percent of research physicists are women," she began, rehearsing her performance for me, "isn't it remarkable there are three women on the top-ten list of scientists *robbed* of Nobel Prizes?"

She went on to cite, very convincingly, and at great length, the brilliance and brainstorms of Lise Meitner, who'd discovered that some of the missing mass involved with nuclear fission is converted into energy; Chien-Shiung Wu, who proved the daring theory that the widely accepted parity law didn't apply to all nuclei; and Jocelyn

Bell Burnell, who detected a radio pulse that led to the recognition of pulsars as a previously unknown phenomenon coming from stars. In each case, of course, male colleagues or bosses or rivals got all the Nobel credit and love.

"My mother, as great a scientist as any of us will likely meet, could write you an equation to illustrate how women have to be twenty-five percent better and work thirty-five percent harder to get seventy-seven percent as much money for the exact same job," Ruby told the panel of teachers and parents. "All of which might explain why the overrated physics department at our local university—an institution I will never attend or root for—has turned down my mother's efforts to teach there. Twice!"

Wrapping up, Ruby offered a couple quotes: "As Gloria Steinem said a long time ago: 'The truth will set you free, but first it might piss you off.' For our purposes today, please keep that in mind."

By this point, Ruby was blossoming into a persuasive public speaker, especially when it came to charming strangers into writing checks, first for the Red Cross and later for Mercy Ships, a floating hospital offering free medical care to impoverished Africans.

On this drizzly Wednesday morning in late May, she concluded with: "I will give the last word to my brilliant and patient mother, who says: 'The pursuit of truth and beauty is a sphere of activity in which we are permitted to remain children all our lives.'"

She waited a couple beats, then bowed.

One of the panelists broke into tears. None of them, including Ruby, realized this stirring closing line belonged to Einstein, not our mother.

The week after Ruby graduated, Mother pulled me into her office, her eyes blinking excessively. I thought Bernard must've phoned or that he'd been arrested or found dead in the Pacific.

Instead, she showed me a web page about some institute offering million-dollar rewards to anybody who could solve any of seven unsolved mathematical problems.

She tried explaining further, but her words started jumbling so she just scrolled and pointed.

*For the past 150 years, the Navier-Stokes equations have been used on a daily basis throughout the world for all sorts of applications of fluid dynamics. Yet the equations remain mysterious. They aren't as well understood as mathematicians would like, which is why we are offering a $1 million prize to whoever makes substantial headway into understanding these important equations.*

"This one's mine!" she hissed, clenching both fists. "You remember me talking about them, right? Waves and fluids and making sense of chaos?"

I nodded too vaguely.

"Navier and Stokes! C'mon, Josh! The French bridge builder and the Irish mathematician. Remember?"

"Yeah, sure, right."

She was hard to listen to because I couldn't get past her pained expression.

"It's all about turbulence," she said, "about what happens to these equations when complications mount. Throw in a little chaos, and everybody runs for the hills. But just because it gets complicated doesn't mean the equations don't continue to work! It's still just an extrapolation of Newton's laws of motion with an additional term for energy lost, okay? And I'm good with differential equations. I'm gonna take a run at this, Josh, but your father can't hear about it or all he'll see is money. No, this is for me." She tapped her temples with her fingertips as her voice dropped to a whisper. "For *me!*"

# FRANKENSTEINING HER

After a neurotic early spring of rain, sunshine and hail, summer seemingly arrived prematurely in late April with vegetable gardens exploding—FREE LETTUCE!—and massive mudflats exposing themselves to the warmth during one of the largest tidal swings of 2012.

The heat wave sent frantic boat owners scrambling to get their forgotten and neglected vessels into the water. Now! Before the rains returned or they ran out of cash. Now! Because their well-being, their biological clocks and the narratives of their lives suddenly hinged on getting their boats fixed and ready to launch. Whatever the cost! Erase months of inattention in a weekend. Preferably an hour. Now!

The yard bustled with boat brokers and surveyors and another wave of seasonal bottom painters like Austin, a tattooed dropout who got around on a skateboard towed by a pit bull named Fiona. As soon as Tommy launched one boat, he lifted another to take its place. Dozens more anchored in the deep end of the shallow harbor, waiting for an opening.

On our first break of the day, the boys huddled along the launch railing, seagulls wheeling overhead in search of leftover fries. Launch day had finally arrived for Rex and Marcy, the manifest-destiny couple from St. Louis. Everybody liked Marcy so much we'd all helped them for free. Even the port gave them a discount on lay time. Just two days earlier, I'd found them a storm jib and some used charts. I almost started liking Rex after he begrudgingly took my advice on tethers and strobes. But we were all about Marcy.

Tommy carefully lowered their Catalina toward the floating dock below, offering Marcy his first smile in weeks. We crowded the railing to watch the big-eyed couple. Rex kept scowling and readjusting his hat while she pointed at us and rocked with laughter.

"Why do the biggest blowholes always get the best girls?" Mick asked. "Makes me think I need to become more of a prick."

"Don't sell yourself short," Noah said. "You're getting there."

"Marcy's just so real," Mick continued. "I mean, all that food on her face and paint on her hands? Any of your computer dates that adorable, Josh?"

"Not even close."

"Most of 'em are one-offs, right?" Leo asked. "Not many repeats, no?"

"True, but lately it's been my call. Weird things start bugging me. I bailed on Number Twenty-Eight because she couldn't spell. Hey, my sister can't spell and I adore that about her. But this woman's e-mails had at least one misspelled word in every sentence. When she spelled ass*hole w-h-o-l-e*, I asked if she was referring to the entire butt and never heard from her again. Number Twenty-Nine was a divorced Realtor who put all her incoming calls on speakerphone no matter where we were or what we were up to or who was calling. How appealing is that? The next one must've read all those *Cosmo* articles you see in the checkout line about the fifty sizzling moves guaranteed to seduce a man. She had so many moves I didn't know what to do."

"Fifty moves?" Mick said. "I think I've got one."

"You've got a move?" Noah said. "That must be a doozy."

"Thirty-One was smart but freaked me out when we got ready for sleep," I admitted. "She inserted these thick mouth guards, top and bottom, then locked them together, almost like a muzzle."

"This is a story about love," Noah began in his Morgan Freeman voice-over. "Like most love stories, it begins with an act of utter foolishness."

Lorraine laughed, and we all turned, surprised to see her slightly downwind, smoking in her nuke suit. She'd been in the yard since sunup, as usual, and hadn't taken a break in days, at least not with us. Our theory? She was making too much loot to stop. Painting two to three bottoms a day now, she collected far more than the yard charged—nobody knew how much—because after three boats in the spring series sailed to glory on her obscenely smooth bottoms, she could set her own rates.

"Went out the other night," she said, "and I was laughing so hard with my friend that this dude asked if we were lesbians. I mean not, Are you dykes? But, Hey, you two *together*? The same question, basically."

The small hairs in our ears vibrated. So she isn't? She gave us a slow smile and then walked off.

"Anybody ever have the balls to ask her out?" Austin asked.

"Just Noah," Big Alex said. "Our hero."

"She asked *me* out," Noah corrected. "And just once. It must've been on a dare, or maybe she lost a bet with somebody."

The others nodded.

"But no Marcys, Josh?" Mick asked, our eyes returning to the launch below. "Nobody like her online, huh?"

"The Marcys of the world don't need to go looking for somebody," I explained. "Soon as a Rex dumps them, another chump swoops right in. And she swoons, of course, because the odds are he'll seem like a prince compared to Rex."

When the boat finally eased into the water, Marcy raised her arms victoriously, and we cheered on cue. Then Rex tried to start the outboard. One pull, two pulls. Three, four. "Did he choke the fucker?" Noah wondered. By six, Rex was grumbling. Marcy said something we couldn't hear, then reached around him and yanked the choke out.

The engine belched to life on the next pull, and we applauded again. Rex brooded, but Marcy blew us a kiss off her fingertips, and we groaned as one as they puttered off on their hundred-mile slog to the Pacific.

Later that afternoon, I coaxed Noah into helping me start removing the Joho's keel. I had no more time for self-pity or mixed emotions. The fancy new elliptical rudder had arrived in Bubble Wrap. And Father had called to announce the new keel was on a truck barreling up I-5 from San Diego. "Full speed ahead!" Before hanging up, he told me he'd be down to inspect once everything was attached. "And by then, maybe you'll quit pouting and start enjoying this."

We were trying to loosen the large keel nuts with monkey wrenches when Noah asked, "You've seen my father's billboard, right?"

"No," I lied. "Sure haven't."

"Oh, c'mon!" He pointed at the sign, almost two blocks away yet easy to read. THE END IS NEAR.

"That's his?"

"Of course it's his! And I can't handle it."

"He's probably put them up all over the country, right?"

"So what?" Noah's head jerked backwards twice, his chin popping with each imaginary blow.

"So it's probably not personal," I said.

"It couldn't *be* any more personal. Why else would he pay to put one up right outside his son's boatyard? 'Heed my warning, my sinning son' is what it says. 'You will be left behind!'"

"You're probably—"

"Josh, you don't understand him at all."

Only one of the nuts budged voluntarily. We lubricated the others, then climbed out of the cabin and further braced the hull with more stands.

Ten minutes later, as if there'd been no gap, Noah said, "You know the strange thing about my father?"

"Probably not."

"He wasn't all that bad of a dad."

I nodded.

"Know what I mean?"

"Maybe."

"He's always been crazy to one degree or another, but never mean."

"Uh-huh."

"Until now. But you know, he's buried two wives and hasn't been right since Mom passed. And it's not like I've been helping him see things clearly. I don't even call him on his birthday. Why? Because he embarrasses me. Well, tough shit! Know what I'm saying? Am I still a child? Shouldn't I be embarrassment-proof by now?"

"I'm not."

"But this billboard's downright hostile, Josh."

"Nobody knows he's your dad," I lied, "or that there's one preacher behind all this."

"Wait," he said. "You think I'm *just* embarrassed?"

I packed tools away and stalled, groping for something neutral to say.

"It's not just shame," Noah said. "A tiny part of me is afraid this time he might be right."

"Bullshit." I was tired of playing Switzerland. "What twisted part of you could possibly think that in two months we'll stand around and watch *the believers* ascend?"

"Yeah, yeah, I get that, but he's my father." He thumped his chest with his palm. "And somebody's gonna get it right someday."

When his head started twitching and bobbing again, I escaped into the noisy refuge of power tools, sanding along the top of the keel to expose the seam.

"Mind if I ask a few questions before I measure?" somebody called out.

I turned and saw a woman with a clipboard leaning against a Subaru. After a long beat, I slowly realized she was the sailmaker, then remembered her message that she'd make it to the yard before closing. Dark and boyish, with a black ponytail shooting out the back of her North Sails hat, she was suddenly strolling around the Joho while Noah banged shims into the keel seam.

"Fire away," I said, switching the sander off and following her.

"Why put carbon-fiber sails on such an old boat?"

"To make her go faster."

She hesitated, reading my face. "Right, but if you want a faster boat—to race, presumably—why not go with something lighter with more sail area and get more for your buck?"

"Well, it's a family boat."

Noah kept banging shims.

"As in a family cruiser, or as in nostalgia?"

"As in my family built it."

She looked at the boat, then back at me. "They being?"

"My father and grandpa."

"What's your name again?"

"Josh."

"Last name?"

"Johannssen."

She winced. "Ah, the Bobos. And this is a"—she glanced at her sheet—"a Joho 39. It's been a crazy week." She shook her head and looked at me anew. "So Marcelle's your mother."

"You must be a genealogist," I said, then my phone started buzzing.

"I read her article on the physics of sailing. Do you need to get that?"

I shook my head. It was Number 31—yet another woman who just wanted to be friends. I wanted somebody to adore. "That article flew over most people's heads."

"Including mine," she replied. "But it was exciting to watch somebody even try to break sailing down into math."

"Or confusing and boring."

She grinned. "Well, it sure made me want to know more about your mom."

"Yeah?"

"Any woman who sets out to tell thousands of know-it-all sailors what's really going on—that's what I'd call bravery." She tipped her hat back and pulled a strand of black hair out of her left eye. "You got a ladder to get me on deck?"

Minutes later, flooding with fresh doubts about the sanity of this entire project, I watched her effortlessly hoist herself up the mast as Jack waddled up.

"Big Alex still around?" he asked.

Noah dropped the mini-sledge to his hip. "Wasn't he working on the Valiant?"

"I'll get him." I grabbed Mick first, then we both climbed aboard the forty-footer and found Alex stuck and swearing in the engine compartment, his cell phone inches beyond his reach on the fiber-glass below.

"Why aren't you yelling for help?" I asked.

"Tried to fucking call you and dropped the damn thing," he said between breaths. "Excuse my language."

"You want to be pushed or pulled?" I asked.

"Pulled."

Once we got him free and outside, the boys crowded around.

"Does Jack know?" Alex asked me.

"Pull yourself together," I said. "You look like your dog got run over. Jack can't fire you for being fat as long as you're skinnier than he is."

Alex started to laugh-blubber, and I stepped back too late to dodge his bear hug. "Easy boy," I said as he crushed my ribs. "You've been stuck twice in the past two weeks. That's only once a week."

He released me and bunched his lips, caught again between a laugh and a sob, then hugged Mick even though he hated the kid. Everybody else fell in line. Even Lorraine strolled over and surrendered.

By the time I was back at the Joho, the moon was rising, and Noah and the sailmaker, whose name I'd already forgotten, were gone. With all the shims stabbed into her gut, the boat looked more like an excessively harpooned whale than something my family was getting ready to race.

But what if it actually worked? What if this mad scheme produced some profound reward I didn't even realize was possible? Standing beside her, I imagined the power of new sails and an aggressive keel and rudder with the entire clan aboard, with Father in command and Ruby steering, Bernard on the bow, Mother conjuring helpful observations at exactly the right moment and Grumps informing all of us, as if for the first time, that sailboats are *alive*!

Hours later, I had the boatyard to myself, and all these ailing vessels felt like my very own patients. Sundown and hands cramping, I cleaned up and then went to the lockers and stuffed an acetylene torch and its heavy twin tanks into my backpack. Then I pedaled awkwardly up Fourth to Plum.

THE END IS NEAR.

It seemed so innocuous at first. The end of what? The day? The spring? The legislative session? Yet the billboard grew more ominous and outrageous the longer I stared. Stashing my bike in the alders, I crouched and waited beneath a streetlight that hummed overhead like a massive bug zapper. Once the traffic thinned, I dialed up enough acetylene to light the torch, then kneeled and held the flame half an inch from one of three hollow steel posts. After a minute that felt like ten, the heat finally severed it. Then I cut the next one slightly faster. I was waiting out the intermittent traffic when a man shuffled up with a handwritten cardboard sign that read HUNGRY VET GOD BLESS GO SEAHAWKS! He asked if I had a dollar or a cigarette.

Einstein used to mooch cigarettes, Mother told me, and, in a bind—after his doctor ordered him to quit smoking—he'd peel butts off the sidewalk and fire them up in his pipe. This bum had frizzy hair but wouldn't remind anybody of Einstein.

"No," I said, "but I'll buy you a pack if you help me out here."

He gazed up at the billboard. "You taking it down for the city?"

"Nah, I'm a fed. Will you push those posts backwards while I cut this last leg?"

He laid his sign down. "You're a fed?"

"As much as you're a hungry vet who loves God and the Seahawks." His teeth, I now saw, were perfect.

Two cars passed, then everything was quiet until a brief jangle of falling metal ended with a soft thud from the moist earth. Wrapping the torch in a rag, I tucked it into my pack with the tanks and handed the man a five.

"Hold on here, boss," he said, "this won't cover no pack of Camels."

"Downgrade," I suggested, then pedaled off faster than I'd ridden in years, wondering why I felt so good before realizing all this reminded me of Bernard.

# THE LAND OF EVERYTHING GOES

The very first letter from my fugitive brother arrived in March 2000, festooned with Mexican stamps. The colorful envelope was addressed to *Capt. Joshua Slocum Johannssen (and his family of mystics, carpenters, physicists and tyrants)*. It's embarrassing how much it meant to me that Bernard picked me as the headliner three months after he'd stranded me on the Shilshole gas dock.

*Dear Family of Redundant Consonants,*

*I am still quite alive and have discovered a ridiculously sublime (yes, that's the right word) new home down south. Don't be fooled by that Puerto Vallarta postmark. Even the clumsiest outlaw knows better than to send anything from where he's actually hiding. But yes, I am way down south, near the Sea of Cortez, we'll say. That's right, Grumps. Steinbeck country! So how was my sail down the coast, you ask. Well, I saw bigger waves than I care to witness again anytime soon, but this boat is, like you said, Josh, sturdy and fast, especially upwind. I admit I worried about dying when it really started blowing until I saw an albatross playing in the gusts and waves. It wasn't afraid. So why should I be? But that didn't help much once it got dark. I was finally able to sleep under sail after teaching myself to double reef the main and put up a small jib no matter how calm it was. I've already had to free climb the mast twice.*

*Actually only HAD to climb it once. The second time I was just practicing in big swells, figuring it'd pay off later.*

*Came across a garbage patch fifty miles off northern Cal that took me two days to sail around. Mostly a tangle of trash bags with strangled birds everywhere, and probably the single grossest thing I've ever seen. But now I'm down here, and running from the law has somehow delivered me to some version of heaven. Who knew that huge parts of the Pacific are a soothing turquoise and so warm you don't want to get out? No wonder you old people never took us anywhere! Otherwise we'd have realized you were holding us hostage in that chilly snothole! I've gone from oppressive low clouds to relentless sunshine, from blackberry bogs to coconut trees. From the Land of Stupid Rules and Obnoxious Laws to the Land of Everything Goes! No building codes or insurance companies down here. No seat belt or helmet laws. You should see them beach these fishing boats at half throttle right up alongside hordes of locals and gringos wading in the shallows. No clouds. No lawyers. No worries! Everything's negotiable. Pay what you can. Maybe it'd all feel different if I'd arrived here on American Airlines after a few six-dollar Budweisers. As is, I feel like Leif What a Guy Eriksson discovering America. Such sweet people compared to those pretentious hyper-capitalists you call neighbors and customers. Mexicans smile and say Hola! and Buenos dias! They're looking for a pleasant day, a kind word, ten or twenty pesos and an afternoon nap or maybe a game of dominoes, and then the worst marching band you've ever heard comes blaring up the street off key—usually just a kid on drums with his dad and uncle on trumpet and trombone all dressed like thrift-store Michael Jacksons. When these so-called mariachi bands ambush you at outdoor restaurants, you have to either pay them to play or pay more for them to go away.*

*These people are so refreshingly not into perfection. Or winning. I'm not sure what you'd do down here, Mighty Patriarch, because there's nobody to beat. And Josh, you'd find plenty to fix, though disrepair seems to be encouraged. But Rube, there'd be plenty of losers for you to rescue.*

*And Momma, you'd go nuts over just about everything. It's all so differ-*
*ent! The birds, the bugs, the plants, the water. The sky. Oh my god, the*
*sky! I woke up on deck one night to so many stars it felt like a bowl of*
*bright lights had been lowered onto my skull. And I saw two blue-footed*
*boobies the first day I anchored here. Two! And the butterflies! Mon-*
*archs, sure, but so many others. And these crazy birds, frigates I think*
*they're called, circle above like gears or clockworks. And this moon! It's*
*such a bright bulb women are shy to undress beneath it. (Or so I'm told.)*
*And the sunsets! No offense, but you all barely know what one is really*
*like. From here you can see the curve of the earth. The chachalacas—*
*good name for a rock band, huh?—gather in trees in the town square*
*and go insane every twilight. They chirp it up completely out of tune,*
*screeching like the Bobo truck when you old men are too cheap to buy*
*new brake pads. The ruckus goes on for about an hour before the sun*
*completely sets. Yet it all feels just right. Like maybe instead of watch-*
*ing television or going to church we should all be gathering to cele-*
*brate, at least witness, the rise and fall of the warm orb—or, as Momma*
*would no doubt correct me, the daily rotation of our planet. All I know*
*is that when you see the sun sink into the water every night it makes*
*you a whole lot more aware that we're basically just this enormous*
*water molecule hurtling through space, which is a bit humbling even*
*for me.*

*Next up? Tequila! And hopefully learning how to speak Spanish well*
*enough to make some money and get laid. My apologies for my candor,*
*Mother.*

*Legally still yours,*
*BMJ*

The next letter—for me alone—came almost a month later and was
far more concise.

*Fucking Mexico. You'd think they'd figure out water and sewer by now.*

Then he went on to recount his battles with Montezuma's revenge and his near fight with a narcoleptic bus driver who kept dozing off and the subsequent unrelated ass kicking he received from several Mexicans.

*Can you guess why? That's right. I picked too pretty a girl. There's a parable in there somewhere, isn't there? And she wasn't even all that appealing after she figured out I wasn't rich. So her brothers or cousins jumped me. I bopped two of them, but the third was one of those low-center-of-gravity types. My ribs have felt better and my left ear's torn and swollen, but not to worry, my action-hero good looks remain intact.*

*What's more, I've come to realize I'm still too close to home. Too many pale Northwest tourists down here. If people ask, I say I'm Canadian or Australian. Told one couple I'm Icelandic. How do you like that? But it's just a matter of time till I'll have to shove off. Besides, my imperial guilt's starting to pile up with talk of a Starbucks moving in. And despite its Eden-like qualities, there is no peace here. If it's not the roosters (everybody has at least a dozen) or the mariachis, there's the night pulse of disco—ince-ince-ince-ince—and the salesmen driving through the neighborhood in trucks with loudspeakers urging everybody to buy a pig or a new mattress.*

*And surfing is way harder than it looks.*

*I know what you're thinking: that the fugitive discovers paradise and then is on the run again. That maybe it's not the place that's the problem. That maybe I'm not meant to stay anywhere very long. Or simply that there's something wrong with me? Naaaah. You can throw that shit out.*

*Think it's time to cross the Big One.*

*Stubbornly, BMJ*

# RUBY'S EXIT

My earliest memory is of Ruby coming home from the hospital. I've been told I couldn't possibly recall anything when I was twenty-two months old. Yet there are no images of her looking like a fleshy owl swaddled in Mother's arms other than the ones filed in my frontal cortex. And Mother admits it might have been the exact same day that I jumped from incoherent babbling to Queen's English. So I'm sticking to my story, though my point is that when Ruby left for Africa right out of high school, I hadn't lived without her since my brain started recording life.

Mother and I hardly spoke the entire ride to the airport as Ruby chattered about Africa and family and fate. "You need to move out of the house," she casually informed me.

"I see," I replied. "I've gotta head out into the ocean or go to Africa in order to live for real."

"You could move down the street." She yawned. "You just need to be helping people who don't take you for granted. No offense, Momma."

"I can't be you, Rube," I told her.

"Thank God," she said. "All I'm saying is humans were never meant to stay in the nest this long."

Still, Mother said nothing.

"My sister the anthropologist," I muttered. Then they both endured

my whiny rant about wanting to go to college but not when the Bobos
needed me at the boathouse.

"You're a prince, Josh," Ruby said when I'd finished. "But quit waiting for your life to start."

"More lectures from my little sister," I said, forcing a yawn.

After she passed through security with a smile and a parade wave,
Mother and I stood dazed in the concourse, as if we'd put our hearts
on a plane to Senegal.

"Your sister is an angel."

"Right."

"No, she might actually be one."

"Says the woman who doesn't believe in angels."

"She was four when your granny passed, right?"

I did the math. "Okay."

"Well, remember afterwards how she spent all her time with
Grumps, loving him up?"

"Let's go, Mom."

"During that same stretch," she continued, shrugging my hand off
her arm, "she walked up to this old man at Green Lake and said, 'You
just lost somebody, didn't you?' He looked so astonished. 'You know
what you need to do now?' Ruby told him. 'You need to go get more
love.'"

"Lucky guess," I said. "Most old people have lost somebody recently."

"But she did it three times that I saw, Josh. She sensed whenever
somebody was mourning. Her advice was always the same: 'Go get
more love.' Like there was some magical filling station nearby."
Mother started weeping. "How extraordinary is that?" She cleared
her throat. "And you know how she used to run around with a towel
on her back like she had wings?"

"Like every other kid in the neighborhood." I put my arm around
her ribs and realized how skinny she'd become. "Let's get outta here."

She waited till we were halfway home to admit she'd hit a wall with the million-dollar-fluid-dynamics puzzler but that she was a finalist for an associate professorship at Arizona U. That news stung, though I didn't comment. "Don't tell anybody," she added. "Nothing will probably come of it."

Soon e-mails—void of all apostrophes, though with marginally improved spelling—poured in from Senegal and then Sierra Leone, Liberia, Ghana and Togo.

Ruby started as a kitchen worker, but there was a shortage of nurses, so she helped out.

*Cant call me a nurse, but Im in the room. And Im anticipating what everybody needs. Im told Im good at this. You wouldnt believe the before-and-afters with patients here. Im the greeter many days when they first come onto the ship and I get to look into their eyes. Sometimes they only have one. And just about every day I see people who are given sight! Think about it! They go from being blind or barely able to see to desent vision in 24 hours! Its just basic caturack surgery. They think were gods! Most people Im working with are Christians, the best kind. But science is saving these people. Go Mom! Got a little veggie garden on the tiny patio outside my room. Things practicly grow over night here. Love you all, including you, Bernard, wherever you are. You too Pops. Im in love with life again now that I finally realize just how short and fluky it all is. Please send tomato seeds!—Rubester.*

I kept rereading that part about my younger sister informing us how short life is.

Next e-mail:

*Thanks for the seeds, Josh! I found more just after I wrote—oops!—and lots of people are hitting me up for fresh erbs already. I didnt want to charge but people pay me anyway. Got off shift yesterday and seven coworkers had lined up at my door waiting for erbs or a masage! Word is out on that too. Can you believe it? I just do what I used to do to Grumps and people usually just go to sleep then wake up feeling better. You know Ive got a feel for these things Josh the way I had for the tiller. So Im torn. I want to help everybody, but more than ever I desperately want to be normal. A couple from London is trying to get me to grow pot for them. No thank you.*

Next e-mail:

*Got a boyfriend! An electrician named Phillipe. Yes, thats how its spelled. I double checked. Sounds French I know but he was born in Haiti and his family lives in Canada. BC! Whoop Whoop! And no hes not a mistake or a loser. God how I hate those words. I called home once last week. When Dad answered he sounded excited for ten seconds then handed the phone to Momma. She didnt sound like herself.*

That night, Mother broke the news over dinner. "I'm teaching at the University of Arizona in the fall."

Father assumed she was joking. "Could you imagine me there?" he asked Grumps. "What the hell would I do where there's no water?"

"Who said anything about you?" she asked, retreating to her office.

I took that moment to announce that I was leaving, too, but sooner. Father laughed aggressively. "Where would *you* go?"

"South" was all I could muster before mumbling about starting my own boat-repair business. "I want to see more of the world," I said meekly.

Mother was back in the room now, nodding behind him, silently rooting me on.

"Stick around long enough to finish our September orders," he said, "then we'll discuss your world tour. We need you into the fall. If you want a break after that, we'll work something out."

"I don't, I don't think so," I stammered. "I need a break right now."

"Listen," Father shouted once he finally realized I was serious. "If you want to work somewhere else, let us find you a place to land. But in October or November, not now."

When he saw me packing an hour later, he informed me, from behind the sports page, that I was his most disappointing child. "And there's plenty of competition for that prize!"

Mother stormed into the room before I could respond. "That's what you tell your only child who still somehow manages to look up to you?"

She and Grumps said more in my defense, though I can't recall any of the words flying while I blindly gathered clothes, books and tools. It wasn't until I was mired in freeway traffic that I realized Father probably knew I would've chickened out if his insults hadn't pushed me out the door.

Once again I considered college—Mother promised she'd find the money somewhere—but it felt too late. And I didn't want to borrow anything from anybody. The entirety of my escape plan was to head south and find work. I made it sixty miles, moseyed into Olympia's only boatyard, had a brief chat with Jack and got hired. Then I drove back up, asked Grumps for the Joho 32 he never used but refused to sell no matter how much Father griped about the moorage bills. Powering out through the locks, I turned left.

Most all boaters exiting Seattle turn right and go north to the San Juans and Desolation Sound, to the American and Canadian islands strewn like rocky jewels across the sunniest swath of the inland sea. That's where the billionaires and movie stars go, with seaplanes dipping in and out of coves so the fattest cats don't have to waste time motoring or driving that far. Turn left out of Seattle and you sail south into blue-collar water and often straight into hostile swirling current.

The Tacoma Narrows turns into a raucous river four times a day. The current runs in both directions, but very little of Seattle's money, swagger or ambition squeezes through this tightening throat into the southern waters, where the boats and houses get smaller and older, the bays shallower, the beaches sandier. At the quiet dead end of this melon-green sea lies a boatyard and five marinas.

Shortly after dusk, I coasted into the shabbiest one, then bought myself a slip the next morning and began my new life amid the dead and dying boats of Sunrise Marina.

# DEMOLITION DAY

Boats are sold, traded or auctioned. They're stolen, given away or inherited, sunken, crushed or seized by Nazis.

Einstein's friends knew what object he desired above all others. So for his fiftieth birthday they conspired to buy him a twenty-three-foot wooden sailboat that was built just for him. Hearing of his disdain for engines, the designer raised the cockpit enough to hide a two-cylinder inboard. He kept the mast short so the sails would be small enough for the genius to handle by himself on a lake very near to his summer home outside Berlin. Stoutly built, the boat had a plumb bow, shallow draft and nearly eight feet of beam. Its maple-and-mahogany cabin came outfitted with dishes and silverware, ready to entertain guests. Dazzled by her mammalian curves, Einstein named her *Tümmler* (porpoise). He was in love.

His wife, Elsa, wrote to his little sister that

*Our ship is magnificent; Albert . . . enjoys this sailing happiness very intensively. The [boat] is a gift from very rich friends (15,000 marks!). I write this pretentious remark for you to get an inkling [of ] what [a] proud ship your brother is sailing.*

In another letter, Einstein's son-in-law described him clutching *Tümmler*'s tiller while explaining his latest big ideas.

*He sails the boat with the skill and fearlessness of a child.... The joy with this hobby can be seen in his face, it echoes in his words and in his happy smile.*

Four years later, while he was visiting the United States, the Nazis took over Germany. Opting to stay in America, the Jewish scientist tried to make arrangements to transport *Tümmler* to the Netherlands. Hearing of his plan, the Gestapo seized his boat in June 1933 and put it up for sale with the caveat that it would not be sold to "public enemies."

Heartbroken, Einstein didn't attempt to find a grand replacement for *Tümmler* in the States. By then he understood the temporal nature of boats. So he found himself a simple stubby fifteen-foot catboat he would day-sail in New Jersey and New York for the final decades of his life. He named her *Tinef*—Yiddish for "rubbish"—as if to prove he'd learned his lesson about glorifying even the objects of his passion.

A boat's decline can happen so fast. You feel the barnacles slowing her down and notice that she lists to port no matter how much you redistribute weight below. Then you step back into your life and forget about her for a few months, and everything ages at warp speed. The varnish has begun to peel, the gaskets to leak, the gel coat to blister, the motor mounts to corrode, the mildew to spread—the evidence of your neglect rising like an unsightly rash above the waterline. Yet giving up on her feels like giving up on yourself.

For many boats, Sunrise Marina was hospice. Once every four months or so, it was Demolition Day. I tried not to watch because otherwise I'd want to save them all. Part of it was the marina ethic. We looked out for one another's boats. The other part was my knack or curse for seeing elegant bones beneath the decay. But once the unpaid bills piled up, these unloved orphans would be put up for auction. Yet nobody wanted most of them, not even for free. So before the dock lines snapped and the boats sank to the clam beds, they were towed to the neighboring timber yard, where a tug shoved them ashore and fed them to a crablike bulldozer that grabbed them by the bows, as if settling grudges, and crunched them like beer cans.

The first sailboat to get destroyed on this bright Sunday morning was a Columbia 26 that for months had been leaning against the dock, half full of water. After the sickening sounds of buckling plastic and snapping wood, *Diva*'s mangled corpse was dropped like a mob hit into a dump truck.

I couldn't resist watching the destruction but was distracted by the mysterious new postcard in my pocket. This one—featuring a seemingly embarrassed Indonesian woman in a yellow bikini—had the most cryptic message yet: *515-SS.* That was all. The handwriting was obviously Bernard's, but it took me until right then to settle on its meaning: *May 15 at Shilshole Marina.* Was I supposed to pass this along to Yoshito, too? My heart thumped, my vision blurred.

Next up was a faded red Coronado 27—obscured by a garish orange fungus—that apparently belonged to the lanky woman pacing along the shore beside the dump truck, flapping her arms like an agitated penguin.

"That boat was always good to me," she said when I walked up. "Had her out in a gale a few years ago. She did just fine, even when we bounced off Blakely Rock. I have no complaints. None. She never did wrong by me." Her words caught in her throat. "Wes and I used to sail her together. In fact, he taught me. Then he started drinking like a walrus and—well, we both did. He ran off to Reno, and I took *Lucille* up to Lopez to dry out on the hook. Ever been to Spencer Spit? Best month of my pathetic life. But then, see, my aunt Ruth got sick and there wasn't anybody else. So that's where I've been, in beautiful downtown Yuma. When the SSI ran out, how was I gonna pay moor . . ." She tailed off.

"So you came up just for this?" I surmised. "To see her one more time?"

"Thought I could convince Neil I'm not a complete—" She started to sob, then steadied herself long enough to say "fuckup."

I left her and strolled over to Neil, who was chatting with the dozer man. "I'll take this one," I said.

He scowled at me. "C'mon, Josh, you know the drill. If you wanted her you should've bid."

"I don't want her, but that woman sure does." We watched her pacing, talking to herself.

"You're kidding, right? I gave her nine free months. *Nine.* She's a rummy."

"So?"

He poked at his gums with a toothpick. "I'd have to charge you full moorage if you're planning on fixing her up."

"I know," I said. "Will you?"

"What?"

"Pardon the execution?"

He glanced at the woman again. "You're a softy, Josh. Where ya gonna put her?"

"Not sure yet."

"They won't let you anchor in the—"

"Pardon granted?"

He nodded and spat.

"Thank you, governor."

Unsure exactly what had just happened, the woman followed me to my boat as hers was towed slowly back to the marina. "Here's an anchor," I said, and handed it to her. "And you can borrow that dinghy there if you need it and the engine, too. Just a two-horse, but it starts on the first pull as long as you choke it halfway till it warms up. I'd anchor near Gull Harbor for just shy of a month. Then I'd do the same in Butler Cove and keep rotating and stalling like that for free moorage till November. If you can't get up here to move her, call me and I will."

She looked at the anchor and then up at me, as if I'd just given her life itself.

"Cara," she said, sticking out her free hand.

"Josh," I replied, taking it. Her fingers were cold.

Our boats stick with us. We never completely relinquish ownership. After the war, more than a dozen years since he'd last seen his beloved *Tümmler*, Einstein made one last effort to locate the sailboat of his life. What he discovered was that she'd sold for a tenth of her worth and then had simply vanished.

Cara and I were still chatting about boats and life when a tall Asian man in a charcoal suit began long-striding toward us on the A Dock. Perhaps fearing he was a bill collector, she stopped talking midsentence, curtsied and departed with my anchor.

"*Do not* message Yoshito again," the man said softly but clearly and without preamble upon arriving at my pier. "And give Minke this."

A disposable black cell phone materialized in his surprisingly large palm. Then he slid it into mine as if simply greeting me. "Have him call the number taped to the back when he's ready," he continued in the same robotic unaccented tone. "*Do not* look at it now. Put the phone in your pocket. *Do not* use it for any other call, and dispose of it immediately afterwards."

Then the only man I ever saw on a dock in a tailored suit with a midnight-blue silk pocket square stepped closer to me, smelling of garlic and some citrusy aftershave. He looked down into my eyes, perhaps for comprehension or a glimmer of intelligence.

"Got it," I said, tempted to share that the likely date of Bernard's arrival was exactly sixteen days from now but not willing to gamble that I could get the words out without warbling. He finally blinked, but it wasn't until he turned and strode away that I resumed breathing.

# JUPITER'S MOONS

Unable to reach my father by phone, I borrowed a car and drove up to Seattle only to find him surrounded by pizza boxes and boat drawings, alone and asleep, whimpering in the recliner.

His words, upon waking, were, for him, astonishingly contrite. "Do me a favor. Tell me how I ended up being such a piece of shit that nobody will live with me anymore?"

This landmark question/admission came near midnight on a Sunday in September 2000. Until very recently, our family had clung to such reliable and predictable orbits. We'd had our slight wobbles, yes, but with each of us always drawn toward the others, and with Bobo Jr. exerting the central pull. Yet in the past year, we'd all left him, like Jupiter's moons suddenly liberated from their orbits. Even Grumps had packed his monogrammed suitcase and abandoned the Teardown. Ignoring his son's insults and pleadings, he'd stormed out with his floppy hat and his pants belted high after the first defective-product and personal-injury lawsuit was filed against Johannssen & Sons. (Father's vaunted light and fast Falcon 35 had been dismasted in a mere fifteen knots of wind.) Grumps needed space so badly he'd gone to live with his estranged sister and had taken the Labs with him because he didn't trust his boy to feed them.

In the month since that dramatic departure—even though the two

Bobos continued working in the same boathouse six days a week—
Father had been living by himself for the first time in his life.

Stunned by the sight of his disarray, I had no answer to his startling question before he reworded it. "How'd I become such an asshole
that I'm left all alone here?"

"I'm proud of you," I said finally, noticing the terraced bags beneath
his eyes, "for at least being aware of your role in this situation."

"Ah, backhanded praise from my unambitious son," he said, jerk-
ing himself completely upright, his righteousness returning. "That's
how far I've fallen."

"What makes you so sure I don't have ambitions."

"Your life to date."

"And what do you know about it?"

"Who knows you better than me?"

"Just about everybody, starting with me."

"Perhaps."

"Perhaps what?"

"Perhaps you need a glass of wine."

"I never liked wine. How could you not know that about me? Just
because you had a brief role in my creation doesn't make you the
expert."

"What're we talking about here?"

"How'd you get the silver?" I asked abruptly while he was still off
balance.

"What silver?"

"Grumps said you could've had the gold."

"That's what he said?"

"Yeah, but you never talk about it. Everybody's always been 'Wow
and congrats, you got a medal!' But why not the gold?"

"He screwed me."

"Who?"

"So I covered him."

*"Who?"*

"The Italian, Sorrentino. Fouled me twice but never took a penalty turn. He was in line for the bronze, so I made damn sure he didn't get any clear air. Thought I'd get the gold anyway. I was wrong, but it was worth it."

"Really?"

He paused. "I don't waste time regretting my decisions."

"Why not? You second-guess everybody else."

"Quit cross-examining me!" He waved his hand like he did when he was telling people to go to hell. "You all changed. I'm still the same." He was almost yelling now. "You need to look at yourselves!"

"You're right," I agreed. "You are still the same, and that's the problem. You're incapable of change."

"*You're* jealous," he parried, "because you've got nothing to change *from* or *to*. No plans, no philosophy, no talent."

Blood pinged in my temples, but instead of walking out I cracked a beer and refilled his glass of red. "You get mean when you know you're wrong and somebody calls you on it. But you don't scare me anymore. Why do you always whimper in your sleep anyway?"

He squinted, measuring my question. "I don't *whimper.*"

"Oh yes you do. And always have. Like a dreaming dog. You were doing it just now when I walked in."

He exhaled. "Go pick a fight with somebody who can't squash you like a bug."

I started to rise.

"I'm sorry." He sighed. "That was stupid."

I sat back down. "Did you just say you were sorry?"

"I'm spent, Josh. Will you just look at these drawings with me. Could you do that and quit harassing me?"

He unfurled blueprints of popular boats that had even-thinner construction than the experimental Falcon 35 we'd built for that litigious orthodontist the year before. I studied each drawing with him, picking out the four I thought would best bolster his case that the Falcon was not a risky or reckless design.

"So what's this whimpering about?" I asked again.

He took a sip before leveling his gaze on me. "Maybe it beats screaming."

"But what're you dreaming about?"

"You don't want to know."

"Then why am I asking?"

"It'll only make you think even less of me."

"I doubt it."

He rose with a grunt and refilled his glass. "I was maybe a year older than you are now, hobbling down a steep mountain with my left foot so infected with jungle rot I could hardly feel it," he began, staring out the window. "I've got a rifle digging a hole in my shoulder, and this kid from Mississippi, Bobby Fontaine, won't stop talking. It's just me and him. We were told to go to a lookout and report back. Bobby was one of those high-maintenance talkers who end every sentence with 'you know?' or 'know what I mean?' He needed constant confirmation. So you had to keep saying 'Uh-huh' because otherwise you'd never get to the end of his goddamn stories. And this one was about some Ole Miss receiver who Bobby swore could go pro. So he's describing some of his miraculous catches and keeps turning back to make sure I'm not missing any details. But I've zoned out. I'm walking down a mountain I know I'm gonna have to climb back up. The whole thing felt like punishment. They kept telling us to take the longer, safer route, but to me it just looked like the hardest route, so I talked Bobby into the shorter one. He's still turning back to check that I'm still listening. And then there's a distant pop—like a harmless firecracker—and Bobby's blood and brains are all over me. So I go down on the ground with him, and I can't breathe. It takes me a whole lot longer than it should've to realize I haven't been shot, too.

And my goal at that point is not to kill whoever shot Bobby but to do whatever it takes to not get killed myself. If I don't move, I think maybe I won't die. Finally I do, though, and I put Bobby on my back, as a shield as much as anything, and climb back up the hill and lie about what route we took and where the shots came from," he plowed on, looking directly at me finally, his voice downshifting for the epilogue. "So instead of court-martialing me for disobeying orders and endangering a fellow soldier, they put a medal on me. If I'd just taken the safer route, Bobby might still be around. Or if I'd just kept saying 'Uh-huh,' he wouldn't have spun his head and that bullet would've gone through mine instead, and you, Ruby and Bernard wouldn't exist either. So there could be something in there that cycles through my dreams and makes me whimper a little every now and then."

"Wow," I said. "That's some nasty stuff to try to forget. But it doesn't sound like you did anything anybody else wouldn't have done, right? And don't most war medals feel somewhat undeserved?"

He sighed, then chuckled. "You're underrated. You know that?"

"Only by you."

We stared at each other until I said, "How 'bout you show me these drawings one more time, okay? Could we go back to that?"

He worked his jaw like he wasn't finished chewing something, then forced a smile and ran his hands over the blueprints to flatten them out again.

"Eventually you'll all come back," he told me when I got ready to leave. "And the truth is I'd rather die tomorrow than live another month without your mother." He looked away before mustering a half shout, "You're all coming back!"

Grumps was the first, though only after Father got busted for drunk driving and needed to be collected from the Wallingford police station. Given that he now needed to chauffeur the jailbird everywhere anyway, Grumps moved back in and unpacked his little monogrammed suitcase. Then he returned to his recliner to reread *East of*

*Eden* and watch *Mary Tyler Moore* reruns, the witty dialogue of which he often delivered before the actors. They ate nothing but frozen food—pizza, burritos and TV dinners—until Mother returned from Tucson four months later.

She'd spent most of her time there peering through enormous telescopes and avoiding grading papers. "I wasn't much better than my laziest students," she admitted. "I'm embarrassed by that, but I guess you never get too old to let yourself down."

Ballard High gladly hired her back, though. And for a spell Mother and the Bobos were pleasantly reunited, the three of them treating one another like precious new roommates.

# THE SHIP OF MIRACLES

Eventually even Ruby returned for seven days of fund-raisers in September 2002. She looked pretty much the same but moved and spoke like someone who'd done and seen things the rest of us hadn't. And she was onstage before we had a chance to get used to her again.

Grumps had coaxed the yacht club into hosting her first presentation during a preseason schmooze for local racers, though even powerboaters flocked to see the Johannssen kid who'd tacked away from the Olympics to go help poor Africans. The girl known for her sailing magic, as the shortcut mythology went, was now on the ship of miracles. She napped most of the drive up from the airport. And I worried for her when we rolled into the jammed parking lot, though she just glanced at the overflow mob and yawned.

While our club wasn't the swankiest, it had its fair share of pomp and sexism and old-growth fir paneling, and it felt increasingly exclusive, or maybe I just started noticing the bigger boats and the brighter bling. What I knew for sure was that the dues sparked monthly arguments at the Teardown. Grumps called our membership a business investment. Father argued they'd hire us to build their boats anyway. Regardless, we all felt like outsiders by now, particularly Grumps, who looked like a living artifact from Seattle's wooden-boat days as he made the rounds shaking hands. Wealthy new members were as foreign to him as the bitter *craft* beers now on tap. Rainier wasn't even offered anymore. The last strong link we'd had was Ruby, back when all the members were giddy to see the club's initials next to the winner's name.

With her late flight, she hadn't had a moment to change, yet her long black dress seemed like part of the show, with its pattern of intertwined giraffe necks. Given a microphone and a murmuring audience, Ruby started calmly, as if she'd adopted Mother's professorial style, carefully explaining the mission and daily regimen of Mercy Ships. Yet the theatrical Ruby soon resurfaced when she began milking stories and speaking louder as her presentation took on the rhythm of a sermon.

She discussed Africa's rampant problems, such as benign tumors and excessive tooth enamel that Western medicine had long since alleviated with routine procedures. Then she talked about all the blind children whose sight they'd restored.

"It's my favorite part of the job, playing with these kids. I sit in a room with them afterwards and help them get used to not being blind. Then I pull out a big purple balloon and we bat it around." She flashed pictures of herself with the children.

A woman behind me grumbled that she'd assumed Ruby would be talking about sailing.

After explaining how the ships were funded by donations, and how everybody on board was unpaid and working for the honor, Ruby closed with one final story. "I've seen more disfigured people than you could imagine," she said. "And to be honest, it was hard to look at them at first, but once you connect with two or three, it gets easy. Eventually you look them all in the eye and see only the people inside. And some you'll never forget. Like Kortolo."

She flashed two images and waited a few beats, sipping water, studying the crowd's recoils and *oh my god*s. The cantaloupe-sized growth on the woman's jaw was so large it was crushing her windpipe and distorting her entire face. Only her right eye was visible. One couple rose and shuffled out of the room. Then another.

"Kortolo was so disfigured," Ruby said softly, "that her husband banished her from their home. By the time we docked in Togo, she'd been living in the woods and came out only at night. It took desperation and a huge leap of faith," she said, her volume rising, "for her to stand in line in the morning light to see if these white doctors on the fancy big ship could help her."

She quieted again. "The line was maybe a hundred yards long that day, filled with crippled and disfigured people. Keep in mind that most of their relatives and neighbors consider these ailments curses, not medical problems. So just being here was an act of courage. Yet Kortolo stood out even in this crowd."

The screen turned from old-fashioned slides to modern video that showed hundreds of Africans standing three or four deep along a gangplank and the grassy shoreline, like fans waiting to get into a concert. The yacht clubbers generated only a faint hubbub until the footage closed in on the mounting commotion near the back of the line where somebody was being passed overhead from hand to hand toward the front. The camera followed this progression as the body finally came to a stop and was placed on its two feet.

Kortolo.

The lens zoomed in on her twisted hippo face, then on my sister's red hair—as if the video had suddenly gone from black and white to color. Ruby took Kortolo's hand and led her onto the ship.

People gasped and muttered. Another couple walked out. Then Ruby flashed photos of Kortolo after multiple surgeries. Suddenly she had a face that was easy to look at: scarred along the left side, yes, but otherwise appealing with a brand-new titanium jaw. When the lights flipped on, even some men dabbed their eyes. (Grumps's face was in his hands.)

"During the ship's five-month stay in Togo," Ruby said, double checking her numbers as never before, "we removed two hundred and eighty-one tumors and seven hundred and ninety-four blind patients were given sight. I'm honored to be part of this, and I'm asking you to join me in being part of it, too."

Mother and the rest of the Johannssens stood, except for Father, until Grumps reached down and coaxed him to his feet. Others were applauding, but there was also an agitated murmur as some sailors retreated to the open bar by the wall of framed photos of former commodores in white hats and snug jackets with epaulets and gold pins. Ruby fielded polite questions about the countries she'd seen, though much of the crowd had stopped listening by the time a tall, graying man in front said, "We all appreciate you coming here, Ruby. Sounds like gratifying work. But could you spend just a minute or two reflecting on your racing days and how your life might have been different if you'd finished that Olympic quali?"

Ruby's left eyebrow twitched. "I don't think about that at all. I came here tonight to talk about Mercy Ships."

"Well, I get that," the man responded, loudly enough to kill the background jabber, "but most of us here tonight are sailors. So we assumed you'd talk a bit about racing, seeing as how you did it at such a high level. Some of us hoped maybe you'd enlighten us as to why you did what you did a couple years ago."

She stared at him as if translating his English into a more familiar language. "I don't reconsider my decision that day, if that's what you're asking," she said to a suddenly rapt crowd. "I'm fine with how things played out. Even back then I never thought about sailing, except when I was doing it. Now I don't think about it at all. I think about helping people who desperately need it. And I'm happy to talk more about that."

There weren't any more questions, and the donations were stingy enough to incite Grumps to terminate our membership the following month.

Ruby did five other presentations—at three churches and two schools—during the week she was home. I was her driver, because she still didn't have a license, so we had plenty of time together. Yet for the first time ever, she felt distant, like she was in a hurry to be someplace else and discussing something else. Even simple conversations turned challenging, as if she'd lost the ability to feign interest in our mundane dreams and concerns.

In public, though, most of her talks were electric, reigniting speculation and rumors of what, exactly, was so special about the Johannssen girl. But at home she refused to perform and barely participated. When old boyfriends appeared at the door, she didn't give any of them much more than a hug or a hello.

While Father kept quiet during most of her visit, on the last day he informed her, after biting an apple so aggressively it cracked like axed kindling, that her presentations reminded him of tent revivals. "You sure as hell turned into quite the little con woman," he said. "I'll give you that."

"Let's be honest, Dad," she said, rising from the couch. "You haven't given me anything in years. Plus, giving isn't really your thing, is it?"

Mother and I gawked at them both as Ruby floated out of the room like it was an offhand exchange.

A couple days before, she had told Grumps he should quit drinking while his liver still functioned. She'd also listened impatiently to Mother share her fascination with nineteenth-century fluid-dynamics equations that are still used daily in the modern world.

"I can see why that interests you, but why does it *excite* you?" Ruby asked. "What has math contributed to psychology or philosophy or even biology? And physics basically just talks about the stage on which the human drama plays out, right?"

Mother blushed as if she'd been slapped. "Trying to understand the physical universe," she said through clenched teeth, "has always been the paramount human drama."

During that visit, I was again reminded that Ruby still couldn't execute fourth-grade math in her head or find her way home from downtown. But she unlocked Grumps's neck, raised thousands of dollars and provided another inexplicable Ruby moment to add to the collection.

The two Bobos were watching a *Get Smart* rerun from their dueling recliners when Grumps turned up the volume for one of his favorite scenes.

"Would you please turn that down?" Ruby asked from the couch, where she was sprawled out with her eyes closed.

"What'd she say?" Grumps asked.

"Turn it down," I said.

"What the hell?" Father demanded. "Go to bed if you need some quiet."

"I don't want to move," she said, later explaining that she'd been battling *a PMS migraine*. "Just turn it down."

"What's she saying?" Father asked.

"Please!" Ruby urged loudly enough for everybody to hear—right before the television blinked off along with the lights.

Mother waddled out of her office in her robe. "My computer," she mumbled. "What just happened?" She looked outside. "Everybody else still has power."

A second later the lights flickered back on, and Father started to reach for the clicker, but Grumps beat him to it and shook his head. After Mother retreated to her office, I turned off the living room lights, and we all sat quietly in the dark listening to the refrigerator hum and pop, wondering what the hell had just happened.

On the drive to the airport, Ruby interrupted one of my boatyard stories to inform me that I needed to stop observing and start acting.

"What makes you think you can say things like that?" I asked.

"You should do more work for people who need it but can't pay for it," she told me. "Give some of your expertise away instead of just soaking people who can afford you."

"I think you're turning into Dad," I told her. "You insult people, then claim you're just being honest."

She thought about that and said, "Point taken."

"I keep it simple," I said, suddenly bent on explaining myself. "I fix what's in front of my face. Then I move on to the next broken thing and try to fix that, too."

She closed her eyes and asked me to tell her a story about our childhood. "Something you, me and Bernard did, something I've forgotten."

That part was easy. Ruby had always been so entirely in the moment that no lobe of her brain had ever stored much. So I took a breath and shared the first memory that popped up.

"The three of us biked to the lake when you were nine. Bernard wouldn't let us wear helmets. And he invented some weird decathlon with events that all involved throwing or hitting rocks. He'd won everything, of course, by the time we got to the skipping. There was this dark-peach sunset under way that was tinting the entire sky. And that's when you, on your final try, skipped a rock the size of a poker chip so many times that we lost count after twenty-three."

"No, not one of those," she pleaded, her eyes still closed. "Tell me a story where I was totally normal."

A couple hours later, when I returned to the Teardown, Mother looked up and then showed me what she'd just typed on the screen:

*Introduction: We prove the existence of an immortal classical solution to the Navier-Stokes equations under the hypothesis of Statement A or D. Our methods are new, and with a solution starting as a limit of P-viscosity immortal solutions have been proved by the author.*

I stared at the words, diagrams and equations, hoping for any scrap of it to make sense as my body temperature kept rising. Lured by the million-dollar prize, fluid dynamicists had been using computers and dyes and every imaginable mathematical contortion to try and solve this problem. But my disheveled Swiss-immigrant rooftop astronomer was beating them to the correct answer? It had been a long time since she'd won teacher of the year. Former students no longer visited her every summer. What were the chances that she alone could take the chaos out of chaos?

I read the introduction a second time and told her it sounded really complicated but also convincing.

Later that night, she showed it to her physics pal at the university, who took forty-three minutes to spot two fatal flaws. Grumps later told me that she didn't speak to anybody for three days, which explained why she didn't return my calls from Olympia.

# A CLEAR VISION

~~~

"This is ridiculous," Mick whined, after his crowbar broke off another rotten plank, exposing more old ribs, rusted screws and black mold. "This shitbox ain't worth saving."

It was the first Saturday of May—three weeks before Swiftsure and just fifty days till doomsday—with three of us prying brittle planks off Grady Rollins's dilapidated yacht while the liveaboards sipped coffee and watched us work.

"They actually get solid," I said, tapping the hull with the backside of my crowbar, "once you get a few feet below the deck."

"Fantastic," Mick said, "but why not do all this in the yard?"

"Nobody will haul her out unless she's insured. And nobody will insure her till the repairs are done. So?"

"C'mon, Josh," Noah said moments later. "I hate to give Mick any credit, but he's right. This boat's fried, done, kaput."

"Probably," I said.

"Then how's this making any sense?" Mick asked.

"Since when does sense factor into boating?"

"What're you charging him for this, anyway?" Mick now wondered.

"What's that matter?"

"Oh, I see. Don't worry my little head over how much you're getting paid."

"I'm not."

"Not what?"

"Getting paid."

"Oh, that's brilliant, Josh. Floating credit is your new business model?"

"No, I'm just not charging him."

"You said you'd pay my rate!"

"I will."

"Wait one motherfucking minute," Noah said. "You're not getting paid?"

I sighed. "I like the guy."

"Man crush?" Noah asked. "You fancy the cut of his Wranglers?"

"I like the way he thinks, okay? His dreams aren't limited by his wallet."

Noah laughed. "Sounds like any other daydreamer to me."

"That's what they said about Einstein."

"Who?" Noah asked.

"Einstein," I said.

"No, who *said* it about him?"

"I'd bill Einstein, too," Mick let us know.

"You're both getting paid," I said, "so let's just do this."

"What's Mr. Big Dreams plan to do with this thing, anyhow?" Mick asked.

"Live on it," I said.

"Seems to me I heard Grady say he's gonna die on it," added Noah, who at my suggestion had bought a powerless powerboat on C Dock and moved into Sunrise. Its lack of an engine—one less diesel to work on—delighted him. But his father's countdown to Judgment Day was taking its toll.

The END IS NEAR billboard had gone right back up the next day, as if my blowtorch escapade were all in my head. Now all the late-night comedians were feasting on his father, and Noah's head-twitching side effect had added a shoulder shiver.

"Will you guys just look at something?" I asked.

My original plan was to hire the boys to help me put the new keel on the Joho this weekend, but it still hadn't arrived on Friday, inciting more phone rage from Father. So I dragged them over to the Grady project instead, and they followed me aboard now.

"Actually, this thing must've been pretty cool once," Noah admitted.

"Yeah, back when it didn't stink," Mick added.

"Check this out," I said, carefully parting Grady's old yachting magazine to its centerfold and laying it flat on a small teak table. "That's what she used to look like."

Mick whistled through his front teeth. "Same type of boat?"

"No, you are standing inside the exact boat that you're looking at right there."

His eyes widened, and Noah glanced around, grinning.

"Grady wants to put a piano in here," I said, pointing across the salon.

Noah laughed. "Like I said, he's bonkers. What's he do for a day job anyway?"

"I don't really know. Sells stuff, travels a ton, mostly back and forth to Texas, I think."

"So you're working for free on a hopeless yacht owned by some dreamer you barely know," Mick said.

"That's right."

Noah sighed. "You'd like him, too. Everybody likes Grady Rollins."

"Well, congratulations," Mick said. "The man is likable."

"He's on his ham radio whenever he's around," I said, "connecting with strangers at all hours. He's good at it, too. It's like he's got this clear vision of what he's doing on earth."

Mick groaned. "You call this a vision?"

"Yeah," Noah said. "And what, exactly, is yours, Mick, beyond a willing piece of ass and a pint of Pabst?"

"You say that like it's a bad thing."

I opened my wallet and handed eight twenties to Mick, then began counting out the same for Noah.

But he just stared at the bills. "If you're not getting paid, neither am I, especially if there's some sort of sainthood to be had here."

"Fuck sainthood," Mick said, folding and pocketing his pile. "I don't work for free. I've got a life to get back to."

Noah snorted. "What would you otherwise be doing today?"

"I don't know. Laundry, cloud monitoring, bug counting, air guitar." Mick looked at us, eye to eye, then back again. "Well, for fuck's sake. Now I'm the dick because I won't work for nothing."

"Well put," Noah said.

Mick wagged his head, chewed his lip, then slapped the money back on to the table. "I'd rather starve than give you guys some imaginary higher ceiling."

"*Calling,*" Noah corrected him as we scrambled back onto the dock. "Higher calling."

"How about a dating story," Mick said, bending over to grab a Sawzall. "If you ain't paying, you could at least entertain."

"Number Thirty-Two looked a little too muscular," I began. "Know what I mean? Like a Latvian bobsledder or something."

"How'm I supposed to picture that?" Mick asked.

"Use what little imagination you have," Noah suggested. "Continue, Josh."

"I didn't think that much of it, but by the second drink I noticed she had a froggy voice and a bisected chin. She also had a switch-hitting name—Kerry with a *K*. I thought we were going sailing, but we hadn't left the dock yet, and she was already getting aggressive. So I found myself panicking, trying to get a good look at her Adam's apple. Then she proved her womanhood, and I woke up with bruises."

Noah nodded. "Everybody needs at least one psychobitch girlfriend to keep everything in perspective."

"Aren't they all psychobitches?" Mick asked.

"No, but the ones attracted to you probably are," Noah clarified.

Mick hesitated. "I'd really appreciate it if the shit you flipped wasn't true."

"Sorry," Noah said, "but I flip so much your way some of it's bound to be."

"Is that an apology?" Mick asked me.

"My mother says it's hard not to go at least a little mad if you sleep with somebody who's crazy," I told them. "She has an equation for it: lust times bipolarity equals doom divided by regret."

That was a conversation killer until Mick glanced up and asked, "So then what sort of woman are you looking for anyway, Josh?"

"Wish I knew. Maybe somebody who gets prettier the longer you look at her. Or somebody with no more ego or self-doubt than a bear in the woods."

"So that's your ideal?" Noah asked, pulling off his protective glasses to get a better bead on me. "A female bear?"

"I thought *I* had weird taste," Mick said.

Hours later, Noah announced, "I hate to admit it, but this work actually feels pretty damn good. Like we're doing disaster relief in Haiti or something. Wouldn't you agree, Saint Micholas?"

Mick grunted, flicked his cigarette into the water, then picked up his Sawzall again and walked over to the increasingly exposed bow. "My old lady's got a stand-up in the basement."

"A comedian?" Noah asked.

"A piano!"

"Then you mean an *upright*."

"She's got some arthritis," Mick continued, "so it never gets played. But it still works and she could probably be talked out of it."

"Is it any good?" Noah asked.

"How good's it gotta be! It's a freaking free piano, okay? That Sinclair girl played 'Frère Jacques' on it when she was dating my brother years ago. Sounded perfect."

"Grady wants a baby grand," I had to tell him. "I doubt he'd settle for an upright."


Later that night, cooking a burger on the barbecue cantilevered off my stern, I was enjoying an uninterrupted half hour to myself when a man in new Levi's, a dress shirt and surfer hair wandered up. "The argument could be made," he said, "that this is your family's prettiest design."

"Who's arguing?" I asked.

"I mean it's slow compared to other Johos but saltier and sturdier and easier on the eyes," he said, still smiling like a monkey. "Smells like dinner."

I finally stood up. "What do you need?" I asked, assuming he was the new charming liveaboard I'd heard about.

"Just looking to chat about your brother for a minute," he said. "My name's Ed." Then, as if an afterthought, he fished a bright white business card from his breast pocket.

*Edward C. Blackmun*
*Special Agent*
*U.S. Fish and Wildlife*

"People call me Ed the Fed." He smiled again, then asked, "You heard from Bernard recently?"

"I'm sorry," I said, once I found my voice, "but I'm in the middle of making a burger here."

"Of course! I can wait."

I opened the grill, flipped the meat and lowered the lid, then dropped down into the cabin to gather the bun, mustard, tomato slices and my thoughts.

"No cheese?" he asked after I lunged back on deck, giving me that gummy smile.

"I think you're wasting your time," I said. "I haven't seen Bernard in years."

"Ah," he said, "well played. But I asked if you'd *heard* from him."

"How about we start over," I said, "and you tell me what you're doing here instead of acting like we're beer buddies."

He laughed. "Fair enough! But—who knows?—we might become friends. See, I'm here to help your brother. We know he smuggles. Could've arrested him long ago, but we're more interested in the people he sells to and the lowlifes above them. If he helps us out a little, he can sail back free and clear into whatever sunset he chooses."

Smelling the burger burning, I lifted the lid again and slid the blackened patty onto the bun.

"Perfect," the man said. "I love it a bit charred, don't you? So have you heard from him?"

"He's never been good at staying in touch." I stacked tomatoes on the meat, wondering just how much this man—and, by extension, the federal government—already knew about me and my family.

"You're smart," he said. "You don't answer questions, but you don't lie either. And you know I wouldn't be here if I wasn't sure you'd heard from him. When you see him, give him my card and advise him, as his wise younger brother, that he should talk to me before he does *anything* else." He showed off his pink gums again, then said, "Enjoy that burger, Joshua."

# MOTHER WAVELETS

The Teardown was tilting more than ever. The mighty Bobos could design boats that flew through air and water at extreme angles without leaking or buckling (with several exceptions), yet neither had ever felt compelled to lift a finger to prevent the slo-mo tumble of their one and only domicile down a blackberry hill into the Ship Canal. By May 6, 2012, you didn't need to be a building inspector to notice the southbound lean. Plasterboard corners were ajar by an inch or more around beams and posts. Walking from the living room to the kitchen was an uphill slog.

I snuck in quietly enough to not wake our second batch of Labs—Hubble and Magellan—or the snoring Bobos, my two simple goals for this late mission being to assess Mother's mental health and to avoid any insults or demands from my father.

I'd borrowed Noah's car hours after Ed the Fed ruined my dinner and Mother called to tell me she'd had a breakthrough. Flipping through old notebooks of abandoned ideas, she'd found a *way back in.*

"To what?" I'd asked.

"Navier-Stokes!" Her giggle sounded addled or insane, maybe both. She cleared her throat and whispered into the phone, "It's still unsolved, Josh! I'm gonna put this out there. I mean, when it's ready. Not yet, no, but soon. I think this may be the one. Yes, yes. I really do!"

I hesitated, unsure what to say that wouldn't sound doubtful. I told her to hold on, that I'd be there later that night.

I found her at her desk, bug-eyed and braless in mismatched plaid pajamas. Two walls were covered with whiteboards and graph paper, elaborate equations moving clockwise around the room like mathematical graffiti or some frenetic musical score with her slanting letters and numbers adding to the sense of dizzying motion. Her pupils were so dilated that her eyes looked like buttons, and her words were crazily rushed.

"Wavelets!" she hissed, as if the word alone would ring everybody's bells. "That's my way back in. Mini-wavelets! What do you think?"

What I thought was that the Navier-Stokes problem was a cruel unsolvable riddle designed to torment my mother. What I said to her was "I don't know wavelets from whippets. So—"

"At the center of wavelet theory," she interrupted me, "is the mother wavelet, which spawns all other wavelets through scaling and translation." She pointed at the equation above her desk: NVSK=EQ. "That right there gives me the algorithm for determining all the wavelet coefficients! Oh Josh, the subconscious is so fascinating. Once a mathematical mind has a clear notion of a problem, it keeps working on it whether you realize it or not."

After I kissed the crown of her head, she leaned back and peered at me over her glasses to get a better read of my face, her expression skidding from hopeful to desperate.

"Einstein never took a day off," she said abruptly. "Even at the end, he was still working on everything that interested him. And when he died, his chalkboard was full of incomplete equations."

My stomach fell. After our last chat, I'd found an online crackpot index that differentiated between real scientists and wackos. One warning sign: a preoccupation with the world's greatest unsolved problems. Another: endless speculation about Einstein's final theories in progress. In this pale light, I saw the gleam of a full-blown loon in my mother's face. I saw Grady Rollins and his piano.

"I've been reading about Einstein a bit myself," I told her gently, "and I'm kind of surprised you've never mentioned what a bastard he could be."

I then recited details of how cruel he'd supposedly been to his first wife, demanding that she keep his office tidy, stay silent whenever he requested and never expect any intimacy whatsoever. "After she divorced his cranky ass," I said, "he married his first cousin and supposedly fooled around on her and never much cared for his own three kids, one of whom went crazy." I took a breath. "All of which seems to contradict this grand stereotype you keep rolling out."

She looked amused. "Are people good or bad, Josh? He was a gift to mankind. And not just for reframing our universe. He advocated for Jews and blacks. He condemned McCarthyism when most everybody cowered. He was such a humanist that J. Edgar Hoover tapped his phone. What better badge of honor? If Einstein was an ass, we need so many more. Besides, I've never claimed he was a great man. I said he was brilliant. Now, quit changing the subject and tell me what you think."

I wanted to let her know that it appeared that her firstborn was at last sailing home. But how could I disclose this good news without mentioning that a federal agent wanted to turn Bernard into a snitch, and all of our phones, mailboxes and e-mails were probably being monitored? I stalled, pretending to be fascinated by an EKG-like drawing of this so-called mother wavelet. What could I say to my own mother? I remembered how hard she crashed the last time she thought she'd solved it. But this late at night, I stared woozily at her string of equations and thought, My God, maybe, just maybe . . .

"You know," I said, her face still radiantly expectant, "I'm sorry but I really don't know what to make of any of this. But I can honestly tell you that it looks both beautiful and brave."

# THE TRICKSTER AND THE WHALES

During the years that followed Bernard's and Ruby's departures, I read their postcards and e-mails with palpitating anticipation, knowing either of them might say or do something inspiring, foolish or revelatory at any moment. Both seemingly had the potential to either change the world or vanish from it.

*Ive been thinking about what you said about how you just try to fix whats in front of you and not overcomplicate what it all amounts to,*

Ruby wrote me soon after she returned to her ship in 2002.

*Thats so healthy but I cant live like that. I dont resent or regret but I do get the sense we got fooled. What are you gonna give when you grow up? Were we ever asked that? We gave our family everything for so long. Im giving myself to as many different people as I can now while I walk this earth in hopes that it adds up to something bigger than the parts. I dont think Ill be coming back home. Its not personal. We have to make choices or we amount to so little, right? At least thats my fear, that all this hope and energy and emotion is no more than a tornado inside me that only I feel. But this boat is full of people who feel like that. Some have worked on this ship for 25 years. I dont know that Ill ever get off again. Today I hope not. Our time is so short. Ruby*

There it was again. My little sister letting me know we were running out of time. Then came a long letter from Bernard which hinted he was headed farther south, the days getting longer and the toilet water spinning counterclockwise. But he also said:

*I think of the family a lot. Believe it or not, I miss Captain Asshole and think of him more often than I'd care to admit, though I guess I just did. I measure people by him. Know what I mean? I wonder what he would make of this boat or that man or this transaction. And I see the science of the sea and sky through Mother's eyes, and the mysterious and inexplicable underbelly of everything through Ruby's. And I try to view it all through your nonjudgmental lens as well, my brother. Always admired how you take it all in without needing to provoke or seduce. Damn, all this Hinano is making me soft. Oops. A clue! I better shut up. Funny, I can't recall Slocum or Moitessier going all melancholy and sentimental. Maybe they cut those parts out of their books. Or maybe they were built of harder stones. Or just lying sacks of shit.*

*I'm making a shaky living of sorts moving merchandise from one place to another. But I can assure you this is the life for me. The freedom I felt on top of mountains is tripled out here. From where I'm sitting, life on land looks like self-inflicted captivity. I drop in on humanity when the time feels right. I showered, shaved and put on my one clean shirt last night. These native ladies kept calling me James Bond. Can you believe it? In case you're curious, my record remains intact. Haven't paid for sex yet!*

Ruby's next letters shared her increasing discomfort with her reputation on the ship as a healer. She stopped giving massages, but word had spread in Ghana that they should ask for the redhead in the room when their procedures were done. She liked to hold hands, and some Africans speculated the real healing occurred in the redhead's hands.

*Wierd things continue to happen when I have migranes, Josh. And I have no explanation beyond coincadince. How would I know if Im special? How could anybody know what it feels like to be anybody else? If Gods coming thru me it isnt at my request. Nor have I heard HER voice. I still dont pray, at least not on perpose and never aloud. I havent asked for any of this. There is a couple here who kept calling me Saint Ruby. I finally told them I dont even really believe in God. That went straight to the chaplin who came to talk to me. I told him I dont dislike religon but that my mothers probably my only spiritual adviser and shes a scientist. Isnt this terrific? The one area of life I know so little about is right in my face now. And the chaplins a talker. He worries me. But if I just sing along arent I a fraud? I didnt ask for any of this did I?*

Meanwhile Bernard's postcards and letters to the boatyard piled up. One in early 2003 ended like this:

*The Pacific is my home now. From my bunk I hear the humpbacks conversing. I live among them now. And my nose is getting so good I can smell land five miles away. When the air pressure drops my sinuses drain and I know a storm is afoot hours before it shows up. There are scary moments but you don't have to be Leif Eriksson to survive out here. I passed one of those avocado-green houseboats that were so popular in the '70s. This one was full of hungry stoners who asked me, in all seriousness, "Which way to California, man?"*

*Sounds weird to say it, Josh, but the Rubester is a regular in my dreams. Some nights she's just laughing at me but usually she's the trickster. A few nights ago, she flew alongside while I was under sail. Or maybe it was an albatross with her face. Regardless, she tried to play it straight but when she saw my reaction she started laughing. I don't want to know what a shrink would make of that. And I won't say it aloud, Josh, but maybe she is closer to God. I know that's not kosher specula-*

*tion in an agnostic household, especially coming from me, but maybe. Perhaps sailing brings us all closer! Though something close to nothing is still nothing, eh? But in this spirit of full disclosure, I will admit I'm increasingly of the opinion that if there are any gods, they must all be whales.*

# NAKED BELIEVERS

Arriving in a wooden crate on a flatbed truck, the black keel looked like the dorsal fin of a killer whale with a small torpedo welded to its narrow tip. In the midday glare, sitting next to this old and tired Joho 39, Father's design gamble looked like a preposterous upgrade incapable of its desired effect, like a boob job on an old lady.

With the Swiftsure race just nineteen days away, I bribed the boys with beer to help me with the keel transplant after work. We crowbarred and sledgehammered the old keel until it finally let go of the hull and fell noisily into the shuddering arms of a forklift while the boat swung overhead like a fresh amputee.

We cleaned and sanded the Joho bottom before measuring the exact location for the bolts sticking out of the top of the new keel. After filling the old holes, we drilled new ones with an inch-and-a-half bit. Then Tommy gently lowered the boat toward the studs, double checking the alignment before raising her again. After reboring two holes, I broke out the case of 3M 5200 I'd been warming in Jack's office for days and passed out Uzi-like pneumatic glue guns. Then we slathered the marine world's strongest adhesive to both the hull bottom and the keel bolts. With Tommy manning the lift, four of us helped guide the big boat down onto the threaded studs. Then Mick and I crawled inside the boat and down into the bilge and evenly tightened eight nuts the size of hockey pucks. Afterwards we stood around outside the boat, killed some beers and marveled at how bizarre the end result looked.

My gut told me that messing with the old design would ruin its delicate balance. But given ideal conditions, the remodeled boat also might dramatically outperform its former self. This new L-shaped keel, though nearly a half ton lighter, sank a full foot and a half deeper, with most of its mass stored in the lead bulb at the bottom. According to Father's calculations, swapping keels and rudders reduced weight by almost 10 percent without decreasing righting force, a reasonable, if unusual, upgrade as long as you told race handicappers exactly what you'd done so they could adjust the boat's rating. Father assured me again that he'd be taking care of all that. In the meantime, he insisted, keep a skirt around her till she splashes.

Number 33, I told the boys, talked me into the Procession of the Species Parade. "She went as a praying mantis on stilts," I said. "You wouldn't think an insect could be flirty, but, man, did she work the crowd."

"Don't you have any normal dates?" Mick wondered.

"What was your costume?" Noah asked.

"She found me a sea turtle outfit. So I was sliding along on a dolly beneath a claustrophobic plastic shell with bad eyeholes."

"That had to suck," Leo observed.

"The more I watched her," I said, "the less I liked her. To be fair, I wasn't her dream date either. She'd agreed to go out because I was *geographically desirable* and overlooked that I lived on a boat and my hands would never be clean again in this lifetime, as she put it, while I overlooked that twenty-seven of her last twenty-nine paintings were self-portraits. The only feedback she gave me on our one dazzling sail together was that it was a *fashion disaster.* I was through with her before the end of the parade, though she'd probably dumped me blocks earlier, seeing as how she went out drinking immediately afterwards with a muscle-bound zebra."

"Is that all you got?" Noah asked.

"One more. Number Thirty-Four was one of those skinny-jeans high-heel types you worry is gonna slip right through the dock slats, snap an ankle and drown. She definitely didn't want to sail. She got motion sickness from everything—driving, flying, yawning. You name it. She wouldn't go to a movie theater without taking Dramamine. So we got loaded, and it was warm, but that didn't completely explain why she stripped to her bra and stretched out on a bunk, ankles crossed, with a premixed store-bought margarita balanced high on her chest and began telling me about her two ex-husbands and about the odd things her most recent *disaster dates* would say and request. If I fell for her even briefly, I knew her next date would hear all about me."

Then I relived—but didn't share—our last conversation.

"Humans weren't meant to be monogamous," she told me.

"I am," I said.

"You and me, we're not marrying types," she insisted. "We're misfits."

"I'm not," I said.

"How many dates have you had in the past six months?" she asked.

"Thirty-four."

Her laugh sounded like a seal barking.

"This probably isn't a great idea," I told her. "I mean, given how far apart we live and how all I've got for you to visit is this boat."

"You kidding me?" she said. "I love this stinky boat! You want to get rid of me you're gonna have to drag me out by my hair."

I sat there, studying her dark mane. It was thick enough.

What I also didn't tell the boys is that I was one bad date away from disproving my mother's equation for romance. So I was getting extremely picky about whom to ask out next. I'd study their photos in hopes of reading their minds and mulled over and over again their backstories and platitudes, their interests and disqualifiers. Yet the closer I looked, the better I understood that Mother's math wasn't the problem. I was the weak link in her equation, the unreliable variable. My inability to discern what I wanted invited chaos into her otherwise-sound equation. So did my cowardice. How much of myself had I shared since Kirsten found me so easy to replace? Last time I saw her, she was pregnant and happy, fondling avocados at QFC.

"Hey, Noah," Mick said while grabbing another beer, "that your father on the radio?"

"Yes," he snapped as we all listened intently to the creaky old voice.

"I'm not the authority. The Bible is the authority. There are numbers in the Bible for a reason. And they tell us things. They inform us."

"Is somebody interviewing him?" Mick asked.

"It's just him," Noah said softly, shaking his head. "He's got a talk show."

"Animals were loaded onto the ark in 4990 B.C.," droned the old man, "a number I arrived at years ago from looking at carbon dating, tree rings and other data. You need to realize the seven days spent loading the ark were actually seven thousand *years*. So add that to 4991 B.C. and you get 2011 A.D. I added one more year because there is no Year One in the Bible. And all that points to *this* being the year of the Rapture."

Mick and Big Alex burst out laughing.

"Thought he wasn't on the air here," I said gently.

"He wasn't!" Noah barked.

"Maybe it's just some old dude that sounds like him," Alex added cheerfully.

"No!" Noah said, his neck stiffening as his head started to twitch. "And I can't . . ."

"What?"

"Deal with it. I can't . . . deal—"

"Relax," I said. "I've got this."

The boat owner with the loud radio was halfway up an aluminum ladder, taping off teak rails. When I asked if I could change the station, he shook his seagull-white beard.

"This is a secular yard," I improvised. "No religious programming allowed."

"Excuse me?"

"Please," I said, "either let me turn it off or change the station."

"When I'm through listening I might," he said, adhering another uneven foot of blue tape to his pocked hull. "Then again I might just tell you to go fuck yourself."

"Hey, it's my friend's father, okay?"

"Who is?"

"That crazy preacher you're listening to!" I pointed at Noah. "It's his father."

"Big deal," he said. "Free country, last I checked."

"Check again," I said, and yanked the plug from the socket.

Stomping back, steam lifting off me, I heard two more radios tune into Grandpa Doomsday. I kept walking, noting the radio I'd just unplugged was back on again and even louder.

Noah's head swung low like he was talking himself out of something. "Don't worry 'bout it," he told me. "I can't keep hiding from him. And it's not like he's some monster. Only thing he's ever read is the King James. He's on his fifth or sixth copy. If people could just see him holding that Bible all scotch-taped together they'd see how harmless he is. And aren't we supposed to look out for our parents when they start losing it?"

"To a point," I said.

"But seriously, what if, like I said before, he's actually sort of right this time?"

"Kinda like you give a monkey enough tries and eventually he'll type *The Grapes of Wrath*?"

"No, more like every party's gotta end."

"Yet the penguins come back, year after year," I said in my own voice-over.

"You're a decent human, Josh. You know that?"

In the awkward quiet that followed, we heard his father calmly articulate what was going to happen in exactly forty-seven days:

"The true believers will ascend suddenly, leaving everything behind, even their clothes. All told, about two percent of the people will go up."

Noah and I stood there looking upward, picturing the ascent of the naked believers as sunlight blazed through clouds and sped toward our eyeballs at precisely 671 million miles per hour.

My father surprised me by showing up at the boatyard that night. He said he might, but in my dozen years in Olympia, he'd made the hour-long drive only twice, both to try to bully me into returning to work with him and Grumps. So it startled me to see him actually wheel up, spring out of the truck and march toward me and the Joho, his right arm swinging in front of his hulking frame like a speed skater. As he neared, I heard him panting and noticed he was wearing Mother's old glasses. They looked silly on his big head, but he'd worn them for driving ever since he'd lost his last pair three years ago.

"What do you think?" I asked while he stomped around the boat, crouching low, cocking his head, rising onto his toes, lining up the rudder with the keel.

"Yes, yes, yes!" he suddenly shouted, optimism and red wine bursting from his pores. "Great work! Great, great! Doesn't it look *great*?"

"It looks," I said slowly, "like a gamble."

"That's what we do, Josh!" He was so excited he looked sunburned. "We take chances!"

Bounding to the truck and back, he returned with Mother's little camera and started flashing.

"Taking pics for the handicappers?" I asked.

"That's right," he said, snapping more photos.

"Because if you don't tell them everything," I said as casually as I could, "your reputation could be ruined. You know that, right?" This was hard to say on an empty stomach, but I kept going. "You could be blackballed."

He horselaughed. "Yes, yes, I'll tell the bastards what they need to know. But my reputation? Are you serious? I'm trying to keep the family business alive here! When we were winning, we turned away orders, Josh. Right now it's so much worse than your grandfather even knows. All we need is a little buzz." He ran both his palms all along the starboard waterline as if performing some sort of faith healing. "How'd you get it so smooth?" He was beaming again. "It's you and me, Josh. It's our turn!"

Bug-eyed and gaping, my father looked maniacal, but I still indulged the possibility that between his derring-do and my practicality we'd slapped together a boat that could add something to the Johannssen legacy, though most likely a prelude to disaster. Instead of sharing that thought, I said, "Bernard might be coming home sometime in the next week or so."

His head spun so fast I heard cartilage pop in his flabby neck. "What'd you say?"

"You heard me. He's apparently passing through town."

"He called?"

"Just a confusing postcard. Probably all bullshit anyway," I back-pedaled. "And even if he shows, I highly doubt he could be talked into racing with us. So don't go there."

It was too late. The image of Bernard, this boat and a full family crew at Swiftsure throbbed in his temples as if the future was right in front of us and we weren't just two grown men walking around a cheap old freakish sailboat in a closed boatyard on a moonless spring evening.

# THE PIRATE AND HIS BUTTERFLIES

The first time Bernard returned from sea it was late 2004, when a hailstorm blew him into Seattle on a thirty-four-foot New Zealand sloop I'd never heard of.

The *buyers* he asked me to meet at the gate of the marina looked like bad guys in a Bond flick, one of them tiny and shiny bald in a charcoal suit, the other a tall grizzly in a tricolored polo. "Top of the morning!" the little guy said in a slightly British accent, though he could pass for Spanish and it was midafternoon. He introduced himself as Antonio and his looming sidekick as Hector, neither of which sounded plausible. *Antonio* chattered about weather and airplanes and what he kept calling *Americana* the whole stroll up the frosty dock while sweat bubbled on his sidekick's lunar forehead despite the chill.

I expected to find Bernard in the cockpit again, where he'd been sitting like a hologram when I'd shown up twenty minutes earlier. Without warning, my brother had finally come home! "Meet me on the Bell Harbor guest dock in two hours," he'd said into my phone before hanging up. It'd been five years and three days since he'd left. Ten months since his last postcard. Yet here he was. Alive!

From three docks away, I'd spotted him hunched over a mug of steaming tea. As I closed in, he began to resemble a weather-whipped version of his former self, his skin multiple shades of red and brown above his beard and across his brow, where bangs no longer tumbled.

His chest was a few sizes thicker, his eyes a lighter sun-bleached blue and spoked with wrinkles whether he was smiling or not. I was too excited to speak sensibly. My first words were "So what's the plan?"

His squint and shrug said far more than I just had. "To finish this tea," he said, "and hang out with my brother."

"You miss voting?" I then inexplicably asked. Followed by "What kind of auxiliary you got in this thing?"

He waved me aboard, then stepped past my trembling hand and hugged me tight without spilling his tea.

Even when we'd shared a room I'd never known his inner world, but he'd gone from difficult to read to impossible. All he'd tell me about *the buyers* was that when they came below, I should be quiet and very alert. "The less you know the better," he said with an oddly raucous laugh as if he'd been alone so long he'd lost all sense of appropriate volume. But it was hard for me to assess anything. Just watching him in person, shifting his weight and moving his hands, was thrilling.

I escorted the dubious duo to his boat, where we stepped aboard and descended into the gloomy cabin. Bernard was waiting there in the shadows, amid the mild stink of laundry and urine and some faint rancid odor I couldn't identify.

"Never understood the attraction of boats," Antonio said with a forced chuckle as we settled around the drop-leaf table with Hector hovering against the hatch steps, the only place he could fit, his water-melon skull eclipsing all daylight. "Now, a car," the little man continued brightly, "*that* I can understand. Something like a Jaguar"—he gave it three pompous syllables—"offers efficiency and elegance. A boat is someone else's naughty daughter. Perhaps I take her for a ride—ha-ha-ha!—but I certainly don't want to own her!"

He translated his aside to the lummox in Spanish as Bernard flicked more lights on, and my eyes registered, with amazement, his sentimental indulgences. I'd sent him dozens of photos, yet he'd tacked the same shot of Ruby in the exact spot on his boat where I'd put it on mine, to the left of the navigation table—her hair a flame crowded by disfigured black faces. He'd also posted the same photo of Ruby *levitating* between us on the dock. I watched the giant's slitted eyes crawl over every surface.

Bernard didn't shake their hands or even say hello. He flipped on a bright battery-powered lamp, slid it to the middle of the table, then pulled a shallow Tupperware bin from beneath the V-berth and put it next to the lamp. "Knock yourself out," he said.

"Plenty of time for all that, my good man. What we are establishing here is the beginning of a long and fruitful partnership."

Bernard popped a false smile of his own. "I'm sorry. Can I offer either of you gentlemen a cocktail?" Then he turned to the big guy. "*¿Te apetece un cóctel, caballero?*"

"Sure!" said Antonio. "We'd love one, wouldn't we, Hector? How refreshing. A bilingual American!"

Again, the big guy showed no sign of hearing, much less comprehending.

Bernard poured spiced rum into four plastic glasses. The little man raised his for a toast, but Bernard was already opening the Tupperware. Inside were sealed plastic pouches, and I recognized the bitter stink of dead insects—supermodel butterflies in this case, as big as my hand, with forked tails and velvety black wings.

"Ahhh," Antonio purred. "Swallowtails." He pulled a thin round magnifying glass the size of a silver dollar from an inner suit pocket. "You mind?"

"Dig in," Bernard said, his skin twitching below his right eye.

The little man began studying the wings, one by one, then the tails, each butterfly absorbing thirty excruciating seconds of scrutiny, as if this were a high-stakes diamond transaction. "I was assured you had Grade A, amigo," he said without looking up.

"I wish you'd pick one accent and stick with it," Bernard told him. "These are all Grade A."

It occurred to me that our only exit was blocked by the enormous mute.

"Well, my good man, perhaps one or two are," Antonio conceded. "Surely you have more?"

"Take another look, Pedro."

"Perhaps you should, captain. These six here are all Grade B or lower." He offered Bernard his magnifying glass and, when he wouldn't take it, laid it on the table and made a steeple with his fingers. "I'm sorry, but we are interested only in Grade As, my good man."

"I'm sorry, too." Bernard shrugged. "Because I don't barter."

"Surely you have more, no?"

Bernard bunched his lips and glanced at me, then turned to the bow and retrieved two more containers.

The little man looked at the bugs more quickly this time. "We were told you might have a queen or two as well? Weren't we, Hector?"

The big man didn't blink.

Bernard laughed too loudly again. "*Ornithoptera alexandrae?* Me?"

Now I knew he was bluffing. He'd written me an entire letter about the *queens* of Papua New Guinea.

"Perhaps we should all have another shot," he suggested.

He filled his glass, then passed the rum as Antonio razzed Hector in Spanglish for not having touched the first drink yet.

Then Bernard pulled a flat metal case from behind his head and opened it to display two green, black and yellow butterflies with wings the size of Ping-Pong paddles.

"You caught these alive, yes?" asked the little man, leaning in closer with his lens.

"Of course."

"And terminated them in what manner?"

"The proper one."

"You can see where colors bled near the body, no?"

"Nonsense."

"Surely you know that to guarantee no smearing they have to be slowly asphyxiated in a kill jar."

"Take another look," Bernard encouraged him, "now that the rum has cleared your head."

"Ha, no, my good friend. What I know is what I see."

"Me too," Bernard said, and then to me: "You know how you collect stories? Let's see how true this one rings: While making the rounds, I've been warned about this unusual duo that strong-arms sellers. Probably completely different guys. Some other chatty bald dwarf with a funny accent and some other silent Sasquatch. Yet the similarities are why I asked you to be packing today. Just to be on the safe side, see?" He turned to the mute. "Now I strongly suggest you resist reaching for whatever's digging a hole in your backside there, Mr. Munster. Have you ever seen *Butch Cassidy and the Sundance Kid*? No? Well, Butch is a talker played by Paul Newman, who looked something like me, though not quite as handsome. And Sundance, well, he was the quiet one played by Redford, who unfortunately—for my narrative purposes—bears no resemblance to my brother. But he was a quick draw, see, with one catch," he was saying now, "he had to be moving to shoot accurately. And that's the other difference between them, because my brother's never needed to move. He's just as fast and accurate if he's running or sitting as still as a barn owl."

Their eyes swiveled between the two of us while my heart slammed. Still, I managed to raise my left eyebrow, not nearly as dramatically as Ruby could, but still easily my most intimidating gesture.

*"Pow,"* Bernard said.

Antonio flinched, but the big guy just continued to perspire. If this dragged on much longer, he'd melt.

Bernard laughed, then whispered, "If you secretly want those queens or swallowtails, the price has just gone up."

"Oh, come now," Antonio said, though his lips had gone dry and smacked with his words. "You've misread us entirely! Let's have another shot, my good man."

"Get off my boat." Bernard's eyes flipped to Bigfoot, who'd started to move forward.

"Please!" the little man implored, raising his palms. "Most of your butterflies are beautiful. Some are rough, perhaps, but overall quite lovely."

"I was gonna give you all the swallowtails for six and let you walk with the queens for four," Bernard said calmly, "but now it's fifteen for the package."

"Come now. We don't—"

"Get off."

"Business and spite rarely mix, my good man."

"One more *good man* and my *good brother* is gonna start shooting."

"We'll take ten thousand," I mumbled.

Bernard's eyes swiveled between them and me. My mouth tasted metallic. I stuck my left hand in my right armpit to hide its spontaneous quiver. Less than a minute later, my brother was counting fifties into ten stacks of twenty.

Then the two men filed out with the butterflies, Antonio commenting pleasantly on the fickle weather and the nagging twinge in his knee. "Aging," he said cheerfully, "is such a curious adventure."

Afterwards, Bernard handed me a mug of water. I hadn't moved or spoken. I sipped half of it, my pulse still fluttering, then dumped the rest over my head and let the water roll down my face and into my shirt.

"I'm sorry," he said. "Bit more intense than expected, but I've seen a lot worse." He pointed to a scar on his neck I hadn't noticed, then pulled up his shirt to reveal a discoloration below his ribs and an arcing pencil-thin seam near his left nipple. "He was right, you know? Those swallowtails *were* Bs not As, but he can sell them as As, and he knew I knew. And, like he said, the queens weren't asphyxiated, but they were definitely As." At that point, my brother pushed three stacks of fifties toward me.

Finally, I relocated my voice and made a point of not looking at the money. "You kill and bag rare butterflies, then illegally sell them to thugs? That's what you *do*?"

"Slow down, prosecutor. For starters, the queens were playing possum on the bow. What was I supposed to do, not put a net over them when they're worth a thousand bucks each? The swallowtails? I caught half of them, but they're not truly endangered or they wouldn't have swarmed me in the hills near Manila, right? Practically flew in my mouth!"

"Sounds to me like some flew up your ass."

"There he is! Brother Josh coming back to life! Okay, if it makes you feel better, I'll admit I don't like dealing butterflies. But they're bugs, all right? Bugs that happen to be gorgeous and only live for a month or two if they're lucky. In this scenario their beauty endures on the walls of twisted rich bastards. Listen, there's people out there poaching beautiful, big-brained whales, but you want me to worry about these garish bugs?"

He pushed the stacks of bills closer to me. "C'mon, Josh, you know I owe you. Besides, you more than earned the bonus. But it wasn't as dangerous as it seemed. They knew other people knew they were here. A couple levels above them is a cat named Yoshito. Nobody wants to piss him off. So you see, I'm just a daring pawn in a much-bigger game." He puffed his chest. "Or perhaps a gallant knight."

"You're a fucking pirate is what you are."

He brayed yet again. "Man, it's fantastic to see you."

I told him his felony charges were so old they'd be dropped or plea-bargained to nothing if he turned himself in.

"You still don't get it," he said. "This isn't my home anymore, or even my country. I'm not turning myself in to a court I don't respect. And to be honest, I've only just begun."

"Begun what?"

He stared at me for what felt like a long time, then said, "Please do that with your eyebrow again."

Instead, I gave him the shorthand version of the family update: Mother's escalating obsession with unsolvable problems; the two Bobos settling on the Falcon 35 lawsuit for more than they could afford; Ruby no longer returning letters or e-mails since she'd left Mercy Ships to deliver vaccines to Nigerian villages.

After a long pause during which neither of us could summon a word, he said, "How would you go about scuttling big boats?"

"You mean sink them?"

"I think the verb *scuttle* is more socially acceptable."

I took a breath and started trying to fit the fifties into my pockets. "The first thing you want to do is disable the bilge alarm," I began.

After we had dinner that night, he surprised the resident Johannssens, who couldn't stop gawking at him. He tossed Grumps a brick of Cubans and even shook Father's hand before scooping Mother into a twirling hug. Then he hoisted Grumps, too, cradling him like a child. "You're shrinking, old man!"

When he poked his head into Mother's office, he saw all the equations on her walls and then big-eyed me as if I were responsible for the mounting madness. He didn't give us any of the answers we wanted. He stayed at the Teardown for an hour and thirty-five minutes and told me he'd exit the harbor before dawn.

Leading the news later that next morning was the discovery that a $1.8-million yacht belonging to the owner of a Bellevue mall had sunk at the dock in Lake Union.

Inside an envelope nailed to the pier was a typewritten note, the press would later divulge, that proclaimed:

*This is the end of the world as you know it. Better warn your greedy friends.*

# THE VERY BEST MOMENT

For the final touches, I paid full price for Lorraine to paint the Joho's bottom baby butt smooth and for Noah to balance the mast and rigging before Tommy lowered our Frankensteined boat into the calm bay for the last launch of the day.

The sailmaker showed up just then, waddling down the ramp with a jib bag twice her size followed by Mick carrying the even-larger new mainsail.

"There's no wind," I warned her.

"Up to you," she said, heaving the jib over the lifelines onto the bow. "But I'd rather sail in nothing than drive back home in that traffic."

The two Bobos arrived five minutes later in matching floppies and midconversation about something that made them both look ill. "Sorry we missed the launch," Father bellowed as he thundered down the ramp, though I knew he hadn't wanted my grandfather to see *Freya III*—as I'd renamed her—out of the water.

Without Ruby to straighten him with her odd little massages, Grumps looked like a tree left out in too many storms: his hips and shoulders increasingly misaligned, his feet and knees at different angles, one leg bowed and the other straight and stiff. Even his mustache was catawampus.

We motored out with the Bobos crawling all over the decks as if they'd never seen this model before while I slogged through small talk with the sailmaker about how long she'd been at North Sails and what other projects she was working on. Then she pulled worn sailing gloves from her pocket, fed the new slugs into the mast and gave me the thumbs-up to hoist the crinkly new see-through, charcoal-colored mainsail. We raised the massive jib of the same fancy material until the two sails hung side by side like brand-new wings. With the Bobos alternately interrupting, she described the desired draft and camber of the sails in different winds, of which there was currently not a whisper.

"They're beauts," Grumps said. "Gotta admit that. We'll see whether they live up to the hype and the price, but they sure look fantastic."

"Oh, they'll sail better than they look, Mr. Johannssen," she said. "But as you're well aware, people still have to know what they're doing. I've made similar sails for some racers who come back complaining they're still in the back of the pack. So I go out with 'em and stand on the bow and want to shout, How can you blame *these sails*? They're the best thing you've got going for you!"

An unexpected puff temporarily filled ours. The fabric tugged and the boat moved—scooted, actually—like a much-lighter vessel. The Bobos smiled but remained oddly quiet, almost sheepish, not wanting to jinx anything by yapping about it. Then another gentle gust, and the sailmaker's eyes widened as the boat accelerated, one pupil veering toward the center as if she were slightly cross- or lazy-eyed, and giving me a second look. What was she? Hispanic or Asian or Native American or East Indian or biracial or maybe just bronzed from looking up at so many sails?

"Isn't this right here the very best moment?" she said. "You know, when the boat first starts to go. When you go from a dead calm and suddenly get a little wind and you realize *this* is gonna happen. And that sound when the boat starts hissing through the water, like a whale exhaling or the sigh of some benevolent god." She laughed. "I'm sorry, sailing makes me ramble at the mouth. But I don't care if I'm racing or it's a slow or fast boat, when it first grabs and goes, that, for me, beats everything."

I avoided looking at the Bobos, who I knew were giving me Bambi eyes, and instead glanced at her ringless fingers, my pulse racing at the absence of diamonds. I pretended to be distracted by some submerged marine life only I could see so as to conceal how appealing she seemed to me.

When she went forward to study the sails from the bow, I finally noticed the dozen Stars tacking out toward the racecourse. I'd been so preoccupied with getting the Joho into the water, I'd forgotten it was race day.

"Quite the sight," she said, returning to the cockpit.

"What?" I asked.

"All those old race boats," she said. "I'm a little weird, I guess, but to me . . ." She spun to look at me at the exact instant I'd swung forward for better footing, and our heads nearly collided. There was nothing boyish about her this close up, with dark eyes shaped like pumpkin seeds and a slight curl to her upper lip, as if bracing for impact. "To me," she repeated, without backing up, "that right there—with all of them clumped together—that is what I call beauty."

I pulled back and looked away, not wanting to foul the moment with my own voice or expression.

My grandfather picked that instant to pull a small flask from his vest pocket.

"Oh Jesus," Father said.

Grumps poured a capful and shouted, "Poseidon, my favorite almighty, please bless this vessel—we have rechristened *Freya Three*— and make her so fast the dolphins are jealous." He tossed the shot overboard, then patted his pockets, frisking himself until he found a cigar and beamed at her. "We've got the whole family racing this year at Swiftsure, except for Josh's brother, who's still at sea."

Father winked at me as Grumps poured another shot and offered the cap around. Both of us turned him down, but the sailmaker took it in a single swallow and started laughing, an uninhibited and voluminous sound for such a small contained woman, a miracle of proportions, really, like hearing all the music that can come out of a tiny sparrow. Grumps looked at me now, wiggling his hedgehog eyebrows as her laughter traveled across the water.

"What did you say your name was again?" he asked.

"I didn't," she said, "but it's Sue."

He chewed on that, lit his cigar, and blew some smoke. "But what's your full name? I bet it's got more rhythm to it than just Sue."

She chuckled. "Well, it's actually Sunita Banerjee."

"I knew it!" he cried. "Sunita!"

She looked at me, as if it were my turn to speak. Waiting for my heart to stop skidding, I silently handed her the wheel and started counting the beats until Grumps would tell her that a sailboat is alive.

"Oh, yes!" she responded triumphantly. "It *definitely* is!"

Then Grumps stared at me again, and after a slow, deep swallow of rum, said, "Can you believe Ruby actually called me?" He beamed like a gambler on a life-changing roll. "Our little gal called me right out of the big blue sky and started this ball rolling! How 'bout them apples?" he asked, his voice climbing. "The Rubester wants to go *sailing*!"

# ENORMOUS PUMPKINS

One of the very few calls I ever received from my sister came in the fall of 2009. "Come on up, Josh," she'd urged me. "I want to show you something. But you gotta come in the next couple weeks or it'll be too late."

Originally, I figured this would be a spontaneous and long overdue family adventure into the wilds of British Columbia to see the elusive Ruby, but then learned Canadian border guards wouldn't admit Americans with DUIs. This ruled out both Bobos, since Grumps had got his first the year before, driving home from the boathouse with a Rainier between his knees. And Mother bailed at the last minute for some *critical project* she couldn't suspend or explain—at least not well enough for me to understand.

Since her one grand fund-raising trip home, Ruby had come back just once, in 2006, a visit as awkward as it was wonderful, with none of her stories normal or verifiable, such as one about a wealthy Nigerian gangster, in a leopard-skin hat, who'd asked the Red Cross exactly whom he should talk to about purchasing her.

So driving solo to what sounded like her latest make-believe venue in early September left me fearing my deficiencies would be all the more obvious without other Johannssens to divert her attention.

She'd given me the name of her farm, but her directions were useless, largely because she still didn't drive and had no sense of direction, leaving me to bang around Pemberton for more than an hour until I found a narrow road skirting the Ryan River and curling up onto a lush plateau with a series of farms called Twinbrook or Mockingbird and then, finally, Do-Right Organics.

Gravel soon faded to soft dirt split by bunchgrass and flanked by overgrown bushes and vines still reaching for one last jolt of seasonal heat as a succession of handwritten signs popped up like flash cards ten yards apart. DO RIGHT! . . . EAT SMART! . . . LIVE BETTER! . . . LOVE LONGER!

Eventually, the driveway broadened into a lumpy field where five weary buildings were cluttered with rusty equipment and dented trucks and raggedly dressed young men and women milling around a fruit-and-vegetable stand under a patchwork of fluttering tarps. I heard clucking and then saw white fluffballs of baby chickens before a shack door swung shut. The backdrop for all this was orderly rows of what looked like raspberry vines and a vegetable garden the size of an Olympic swimming pool with pumpkins so large and orange they could probably be seen from space. Two men were packing zucchini, tomatoes and onions into crates behind the vegetable stand where a creatively pierced woman with a neck tattoo—EPIPHANY—was counting colorful money.

"We're closed, but what ya need, hon?" she asked, eyes down, her lips moving as she flipped through the bills.

"One of everything."

She glanced up. "Everything?"

"Actually, I'm just looking for one Ruby Johannssen."

She studied me, then went back to her bookkeeping. "Get in line," she said.

"She here?"

"She doesn't do drop-ins."

"What do you mean?"

"Gotta get on her schedule, hon."

"Ruby's my sister," I said.

"Mine too," she replied, counting fives now.

"That's strange. You'd think I'd remember you around the house."

She studied me again, then laughed until the hobos stopped packing fruit to gawk at me.

"Claims he's Ruby's brother," she announced.

One of the men thrust a filthy palm at me. "Glad to know you."

Others surrounded me.

"Ruby," I said. "She around?"

"She's everywhere," said a pigtailed woman with eyes so far apart she'd be hard to surprise. She stepped forward and hugged me as Epiphany hollered, "Ruby!"

Everybody went so strangely quiet that I said, "It's been a long day, but are those pumpkins abnormally gigantic?"

This struck them as hilarious. "Your sister," Wide-Eyes told me, "grows the world's biggest pumpkins."

"The biggest *everything*," the hobo added.

I nodded skeptically. "Those are hers?"

"The biggest ones are."

"Got her own special fertilizer," someone volunteered.

"Yeah," Epiphany said. "It's called Mozart."

"Mozart?"

"On a loop. Just loud enough for the pumpkins to hear."

"Third and Fifth Symphonies," Wide-Eyes added.

Hearing a familiar mock scream, I turned and saw my sister sprinting down a raspberry row, sun-reddened arms wheeling overhead, swimming through air. She never had learned how not to run like a five-year-old. My memory goes hazy here, but I know she tackled me and then whisked me away by the hand, her complexion, the squeeze of her grip and her muscled shoulders all exuding strength and health as if, like her pumpkins, she was thriving well beyond the norm, though I also noticed the splinted finger and swollen knuckles and the long scar on the inside of her left forearm.

She immediately bombarded me with effusive and unreliable stories about the glorious people who worked there.

"Where do they all live?"

"Right here for the most part."

"They pay rent?"

"They help out."

"Of course," I said. "You give the lodging away."

"This isn't a country club, if that's what you're asking. Some of these people are ex-cons or former addicts, but all of them love growing healthy food."

"Where's Phillipe?"

She squinted. "No idea. Left two or three years ago with some gal from one of the Carolinas. Actually, I'm not sure which gal or which Carolina."

"I'm sorry."

"Don't be. He wasn't who I'd hoped he was, but he got me here. And I've got new boyfriends and girlfriends." She laughed. "I love it when you don't know what to believe. To be honest, they're probably all pretenders, too. I attract 'em, right? This sweet cowboy sold me a tractor last month, then stole it back. Can't prove it, but that's what happened."

"I'm told you grow the biggest pumpkins in the solar system," I said.

"Just the *province*. We won first place for gourds last year. Gonna be bigger this year, but I won't let 'em enter again. Last thing we need is more attention."

I shook my head. "Good luck with that. But how do you explain it—even to yourself? Why are you—only you—always doing things that attract attention?"

She shook her head and sighed. "What I love about this place is it isn't about me at all. It'd be so much easier if I believed the same things others do. Then maybe we could have a conversation about mythology or reincarnation or whatever. Guess I just believe in intuition and luck more than most people. But nobody wants to hear that. They want it to be something *more*."

"Intuition and luck can't explain you," I said.

"No?" She smiled. "Sailing's training, intuition and luck, right? And it's not hard to tell which seeds will grow best or how to locate someone's inflammation and to poke around till you figure out how to unlock it. You've got a lopsided walk, by the way. Favoring your left side."

An hour later, she laid me out on her dining room table, touched the middle of my back with two fingers of her uninjured hand and made a slow circular motion, then did the same behind my knees. And that's the last thing I remembered before she woke me.

"C'mon, snoozy, I've got something to show you."

She had me drive a rusty Ford to a treed corner of the vast property that sloped toward the river with vegetation so rampant and outsized it was intoxicating just to drive through.

Wanting answers to the same old questions, I began with "Why don't you ever visit or write or at least call?"

She looked confused. "I don't think in terms of when I last saw you or talked to you. You know I'm no good with phones or time. Days feel like hours to me. Somebody wants to see me? Come visit! Do we really need to watch reruns together to be a family?"

"But you don't even ask about everybody."

"We haven't got there yet."

Then I hit her with updates: how Mother was still consumed with inscrutable math, how the Bobos were facing another product-liability lawsuit, how Grumps had two recent fainting episodes that involved tiny strokes, how nobody had heard from Bernard in almost three years, and how I kept dreaming that he was dead.

"We'd know if he was," she mumbled. "That's so sad about Grumps."

"Call him! He adores you."

"It's mutual, but when I call or go home I'm that little kid again who knows where the wind's coming from. I don't want to live all that over and over. I feel best when I forget I'm even here. That's what I like about hospice work."

Reeling, I asked, "What is that, exactly?"

She smiled. "You help people deal with dying, Josh."

"I know what it is. I mean, what do you *do*?"

"I read and sing to some. I help others rethink and revise their lives. They've helped me realize that I've never been all that comfortable with mine."

Smells of grass and rotting fish greeted us as we stepped outside the truck, my door rubbing steel on steel both opening and closing. The air was so still and clear I could see freshly hatched bugs flying over my head like stunt pilots. Then I noticed a shallow pond no bigger than a pool table and twitching with activity. When we got closer, I recognized the color and reek of spawning salmon. She put a finger to her lips, grabbed my arm and pulled me away to where the bluff overlooked a ditch, narrow enough to step across, and a sluggish river below. I spotted some motion in the creek, then the occasional wiggle and leap of a red-and-silver fish the size of my thigh that was lunging against the current and up the hillside.

Maybe it was the mini-massage and the nap, but I couldn't find words that fit what I was seeing.

"This is the only river access we have," she told me, "so I decided to try to create our own little salmon run. Why not, huh? The creek's been pesticide-free for over twenty years, and there's already a natural pond in the middle here. We dropped in a few hundred babies—they call 'em fry, right?—during my first fall here three years ago. I didn't know then that it ran almost dry in August, and figured it was another crazy long shot anyway. But then starting a couple weeks ago they started returning, and we're using the carcasses for fertilizer. But we're not showing all this to anybody. It's our little secret. Otherwise, it'll be a circus, and we'll get regulated and sanctioned and God knows what. But we're definitely gonna need a bigger pond." She looked around, straddled the ditch with one foot on either side and then laughed at my astonishment. "I knew you'd get it, Josh! I knew you'd love this!"

I looked down the slope as this sparkling ten-pound salmon muscled up through grassy, ankle-deep water, all determination and instinct, culminating its journey into the Pacific and back up this tiny, trickling creek with GPS like precision and a few final thrusts toward its origin.

# A LESSON IN BOATBUILDING

When Grumps came shuffling up A Dock cradling a six-pack of Rainier tallboys two Saturdays before Swiftsure, he didn't generate any more double takes than any other codger until he stopped at Grady's semi-dismantled yacht and unleashed his showy falsetto. "Goddamnit, Joshua, you're a sucker for hopeless projects."

Pretty quickly, the liveaboards figured out who he was. "Grandpa Johannssen!" Rem bellowed from his yawl on B Dock. "We've heard so much about you!"

"Well, it's high time somebody has. I so rarely get the fanfare I deserve." He smiled at everybody beneath his push-broom mustache. "Looks like we've got an old-fashioned planking party on our hands."

When I'd wondered aloud if his steam box was still around, I hadn't expected him to crawl into his rusty truck and drive it on down. Yet here he was, and seeing him now made me question all the fretting over his mortality. With his Gilligan hat and the dirty fleece vest he'd worn daily for the past decade, he looked more like a man entering his seventies than one spiraling into his late eighties.

"Well, what the hell are we waiting for?" he asked. "Let's unload the truck."

Mick and I grabbed the narrow twelve-foot-long pine box that'd been dangling over the tailgate the whole jaunt down the freeway. Noah carried the old kerosene tank, while Lorraine packed a cart with the stove, propane tank, hose and car jack. Rem followed us back and forth, hauling sawhorses and openly speculating on how much he'd get paid for this. "Least a beer, you'd think, wouldn't you?"

As we set up, the liveaboards kept firing questions. This normally incurious ensemble suddenly wanted to know all about planking, as if there might be something critical to be learned. So Grumps explained:

"We're softening wood so we can bend it to the shape we want. And, Poseidon willing, it will stay that way. All we need is what we've got right here, a simple propane camping stove and a tank full of water to boil so we can generate steam. And, see, we've connected a hose from that tank to this steam box, which I outfitted with these three-quarter-inch dowels to keep the planks suspended. We've also got a thermometer drilled into the box here so we know when it hits two-ten and it's ready to go."

Nearly twenty people, including Trent, Georgia, the nudists and the other regulars, were watching by the time the first plank came steaming out of the box. Then, with our thick gloves, Noah, Mick and I carried it over to the exposed port bow and clamped it onto the yacht's solid vertical ribs. "Let's go!" Grumps shouted, simultaneously coaching and narrating, a Rainier in his hand now, given that he'd never heeded any beer restrictions on Saturdays. "Get some screws in her, boys!" Noah and I predrilled the planks, then spun the screws tight, and the hot, moist plank bent into place.

While we caulked the seams, Grumps backhanded his sudsy mustache and responded to every silly boatbuilding query, as if he'd hoped to be asked those exact questions, weaving answers with outtakes and digressions. "I was never any great shakes as a sailor myself," he volunteered after cracking another Rainier. "Thought I was good, but along came Junior. Could see the difference by the time he was eleven. Then, of course, there's my granddaughter. After watching little Ruby, I realized I had only the faintest notion of what it means to sail."

"How 'bout Josh?" Noah asked. "Could he sail worth a shit?"

"Sure, he could!" Grumps fired back. "But he was mortal like me. You know the best thing about a sailboat?"

Oh no, I thought, stepping back. Here he goes.

"The greatest single thing is it hooks you on something you can't really explain to anybody, not even yourself, and that's one damn humbling experience."

Even grumpy Lorraine smiled along. Mick had power-sanded the stern well enough for her to follow him with two coats, even touching up bare sections without once complaining. I saw Grumps checking out her double-fisted style, rolling with her left and brushing the bubbles flat with her right to make it all look sprayed. When he asked how she'd matched the flat-gray hull paint so perfectly, she sucked hard on a Camel, then knocked the long ash into the can, stirred and grinned.

Grady wasn't due back for two days, but that didn't prevent him from ambling up shortly after seven when this spontaneous party had swelled around his yacht and we were just one steam away from entirely replanking the port bow. He stood there with a shiny new bruise below his left eye, looking like a man struggling to catch up with the present. "So what's this all about?"

I stepped forward. He still hadn't seen the bow. "Grady," I said, "meet my grandfather."

"A high honor, sir."

"Well, don't get all carried away, Mr. Grady. I do believe the honor is mine to meet someone these fine people consider deserving of all this labor."

That's when Grady started glancing around and saw the fresh cedar on the bow and lurched backwards like he'd been stung. Noticing activity at the back of his yacht, too, he stepped away, buying time, and found Lorraine standing in a dinghy, a smoldering joint pinched between her lips now, freehanding SHANGRI-LA in gold letters to the stern.

"Don't look!" she cried. "I haven't shaded it yet!"

He turned away and inspected the sky, then covered his face with one hand. "My deal didn't go through, Josh," he said softly, sidling up to me.

"What deal's that?"

"Doesn't mean the next one won't," he continued quietly. "It's just that, I mean, you people are the best, but right now I really can't—"

"This one's on us, Grady."

"No, wait. What?"

Rem started laughing, and Grady tried to join him.

"You're joking, of course," he said. "Sorry, I'm short on sleep. Please, just give me an invoice or the hours and parts or whatever's easiest. Can't pay much of anything till late next week, but I'm good for it. You know I'm good for it," he repeated, as if convincing himself.

"Maybe you can hire us to do something else," I said, "but this phase is our treat. No charge."

Grady started to speak, then turned away from us as though somebody had just hailed him from the north.

"The last plank is cooked," Grumps announced. So we secured and caulked it in place as Grady rocked from foot to foot until my grandfather shuffled up beside him and said, just loudly enough for me to hear, "Boats embody dreams like nothing else, don't they?"

After we cleaned up, Rem pulled out his Weber and the nudists (clothed tonight) brought a dozen frozen burgers, and Georgia, the former nun, provided bottles of red and bags of Doritos while Grumps passed out cigars and shared his repetitive asides about everything he couldn't believe: how he'd outlived his wife by twenty-five years, how pricey everything was getting, how light they were building sailboats these days. "I'm shrinking," he volunteered after another beer. "Every day I wake up a little shorter, but from my vantage everybody else is just getting taller. Like Josh there, still a growing boy as far as I can tell." I then overheard him telling Lorraine how he gets up to pee in the middle of the night and sometimes nothing comes out. When he started sipping his third scotch, I led him back to my slip and down the steps into a thirty-one-year-old boat he'd built and onto a narrow bunk he'd designed.

"As far as floating ghettos go," he said, reclining with a yelp, "I like this one a lot." Then he laughed. "Bernard needs a woman like Lorraine."

"We all do," I said.

"No, *you* need Sunita." Then he yelled her name like a battle cry: "Su-ni-ta!"

"That's enough," I told him. "So, no false teeth to take out or prosthetic limbs to hang up?"

"Your mother's a wonderful woman," he said, "but she may be losing her mind." Then, even more abruptly: "And what the hell did you and your father do to that boat? He's so excited he can't see straight. It's all over his face. More than fancy new sails, that's for damn sure. Can't get a lick of work out of him. The entire world is on hold until that almighty race. He played you like a banjo, didn't he?"

He rolled over and started breathing audibly, in perfect cadence, before I could respond.

# CATS IN SPACE

As the planking party rolled into darkness, the liveaboards sheepishly told me, one by one, about the projects they wished I could help them *think through*. That Samson post or anchor winch they wanted mounted to the bow. The installation of an inverter, a new diesel or a composting toilet. Most of them, though, for now, were simply happy to be here.

"Living!" shouted the new stoner on D Dock.

"Life!" Rem hollered back.

"Eating!" Noah pitched in, even louder. "Reading the paper on the toilet in the morning!"

As the sky continued to clear, I mentioned that the space station would be flying directly overhead at 10:37 p.m.

"The what?"

"The International Space Station," Noah told them in his anchorman voice. "Our boy Josh keeps track of these things. It's a research vessel—with astronauts from where?"

"Russia, England and here, mostly," I said. "They go up for six-month shifts."

"And fly directly over us?" Rem asked doubtingly.

"They orbit the earth every ninety minutes," I said. "So yes, sometimes, like tonight, they fly right above us."

"And you know this how?" demanded Trent, who increasingly saw himself as the marina's attorney as well as the resident expert on Frisbee golf, windsurfing and federal drug laws.

"My mother," I said.

"My momma tells me who's got prostate cancer," Rem said. "Who's in *Parade* magazine and what a pound of hamburger costs nowadays."

"They do research up there," I said.

"Sounds like bullshit to me," Trent countered. "So like what do you claim they're studying up there?"

"Like how to build a spaceship," I said, "that can tour the galaxy. That sort of thing."

"C'mon."

"They learn all sorts of stuff we can't figure out down here," I explained, "because of all the gravity bearing down on us."

"Like what?" Trent demanded. "Let's hear it."

"Like what meds might work on osteoporosis," I guessed. "That sort of thing."

"So they got lab mice up there?" Grady asked, looking straight up.

"They got a mice problem is what they got," I said.

"What do you mean?" Trent objected.

"Their lab mice escaped and made babies in the ductwork," I told him.

"No fucking way."

"So they sent up cats," I added.

"That's complete bullshit!" Trent exclaimed.

"It's true," Noah said. "They sent up three bloodthirsty cats. NPR had a program on it."

"You don't listen to NPR," Trent said. "You just listen to your doomsday daddy."

"Two calicos and one Siamese," Noah added, ignoring the allegation, which was true. Since moving into the marina, Noah had listened to his father nonstop. When he wasn't tuning in on his boat radio, he was moping around with headphones.

"Think about it," I said. "It's low gravity, right? So the cat-and-mouse, chase-and-kill scenes are all in slow motion."

More people turned to listen.

"All true," Noah said. "They selected the best mousers in the country, just like they pick the best astronauts. Trials and everything."

"*Very* low gravity up there," I said. "God knows how the litter box works."

And there they all were, crouched and slouched on a rotting dock, stargazing and contemplating floating cat turds, when a familiar young woman materialized, though nobody recognized her till her teeth flashed beneath the dock light.

"Marcy!" Mick blurted.

Everybody was suddenly manic with happiness to see her, though we kept peering behind her for signs of Rex. As chaos resumed, I pulled her aside and asked what had happened.

"When we got out of the strait," she said, "I was celebrating. Finally! You know? The Pacific! The swells were maybe five feet at most, but coming right at us. And it was getting dark. Rex had talked about that boat being just fine in ten- or twenty-footers. 'Bring 'em on!' he'd been saying for weeks. Then, once it got dark and one broke over the bow, he started shouting that our boat was *way* too small."

"Was he seasick?"

"No, but his voice sounded funny. 'I'm a little scared, too,' I told him, 'but we can handle this.' 'I'm not scared!' he yelled back. 'But I'm not stupid either!' Then he gave me hell for rushing him into this. Just because I was going blind didn't mean he had to die, too."

"You're going blind?"

The tears behind her thick glasses made her big eyes look even larger. She took a breath and said softly, "There aren't many happy endings if macular degeneration gets you when you're young. But for now I can still see." She raised a fist in mock celebration. "So we made it back to Port Angeles, left the boat there and hitched down here."

"So what's the new plan?"

"We're taking a *break* from each other," she said. "He's driving home to St. Louis, and I just really want to find someone who'll head back out with me and not freak out."

"In your boat," I said, "I'd probably lose it, too."

"But you could fix anything that broke, and you wouldn't yell at me the second things got hairy." Her chest rose with a deep breath, and then she stepped forward and hugged me.

There are moments when you feel opportunity rising like one of those homemade hot-air balloons made out of garbage bags and candles.

"Josh!" Noah yelled. "Is that it?"

Looking up, without releasing Marcy, I spotted it instantly by the size and speed of the moving dot of light, so I raised a thumb.

"There she is, ladies and gentlemen," Noah said. "Your International Space Station."

"That's a *plane*," Trent insisted.

"No, it's a satellite," Georgia argued.

"The army base sends up crazy, teched-out shit all the time," Rem offered. "Could be one of those fake UFOs they throw up there to fuck with us."

"No," I said as Marcy released me to hug Lorraine. "That's definitely the station. Looks like it's going about the speed of a fast plane, but it's actually flying two hundred and twenty miles above us and ripping along at about seventeen thousand miles an hour."

"He makes this stuff up as he goes," Trent accused.

"Like I said, my mother's into space."

"Mine's into reality TV," Mick said. "*Bitchy Housewives of Wherever.* Just loves that shit."

I shouted to Grady, "Call 'em on your ham."

"Who?" he yelled back.

I pointed up. "Nothing but air between us. Call the space station!"

"Whiskey Zero Sugar Victor callin' the space station," Grady shouted into his radio seconds later. "Whiskey Zero Sugar Victor tryin' to reach the International Space Station. Do you read? Over."

"His accent is confusing them," Noah speculated. "They think they're flying over Oklahoma."

Grady tried again. But the fast dot was gone, and everybody ran out of commentary and conspiracy theories as Marcy and Lorraine strolled off the dock together. Then Noah and I endured a few more maintenance requests and drunken lies till only the two of us were left drinking water and watching the sky. I hadn't seen him this relaxed in weeks. He asked about my dates.

"Haven't had any online in a while," I explained. "I tried to go old-school yesterday, you know, to just ask somebody out—in *person*."

"How'd that go?"

"Poorly."

I admitted that I'd become so accustomed to the online-dating ritual—exchanging Q-and-A e-mails before graduating to phone chats and coffees or dinners—that I didn't know how to call Sunita Banerjee on the phone and just ask her out. I didn't even know if she had a boyfriend. She wasn't on Facebook or online period from what I could tell. Finally, I'd driven to Seattle and visited the North Sails loft under the pretense of grabbing the spinnaker we'd had her repair, pretending not to have heard Father had already picked it up.

When I finally spotted her, she was just a torso next to a sewing machine sticking out of a hole in the glossy pine floor that made the vast loft look like it might double as a dance studio. At first, I didn't recognize her, because she wasn't wearing a hat, and her black hair was all over her shoulders.

After my bogus spinnaker story, I blurted out an interest in buying a new genoa for my own boat, which wasn't a complete lie, seeing as how every self-respecting sailor is always contemplating jib upgrades. "Maybe you could come out with me sometime," I mumbled, "and give me a little advice on which sails to fix or replace, that sort of thing."

She studied me, as if speed-reading my face, her left pupil straying slightly. "Is this work or social?" she asked. "Because I've got a young daughter, and no family in the area." She took a breath. "What I'm saying is I don't go out just for something to do, if that's what you're looking for. So are you asking for headsail advice, or are you asking me out on a sailing *date*?"

"Work," I said, panicking. "I'd really like to know what you think."

"Maybe," she said, then looked down at the Dacron jib she was repairing. "I might be able to combine it with another trip down there for another job."

"Sure," I said. "Perfect."

"But not this month." She sounded almost stern now.

"Cool," I said.

"We're buried," she added, looking directly up at me again. "And I don't have much time for any out-of-town work. Not with a four-year-old."

"Awesome," I said.

"What's awesome?"

"Four-year-olds."

She half smiled and retreated to her world of fabric and physics and invisible forces.

Noah rubbed his forehead. "You told her *four-year-olds* are *awesome*?"

"I know, I know. But my only somewhat-steady girlfriend left me after I told her I wasn't crazy about kids. It took her all of a month to find some guy who was. So now I tell everybody that I *love* kids so much I'm considering opening my own day-care center."

On that pathetic note, we headed down the dock to our respective bunks. I got a few hours of anxious dreams before I brewed coffee and tried to stir Grumps, still dressed in the same fraying shirt he'd worn to the planking party.

"I can't lose you," I said, surprised to hear my fears aloud after three nudges failed to wake him.

"How the hell're you gonna do that?" he asked without opening his eyes. "'Scuse me, anybody seen my grandpa? Seem to have misplaced the old fart.' Maybe what I need is a dog collar that says: MY NAME IS BOBO SR. I LIKE CANADA GEESE, RAINIER BEER AND PRETTY SAIL-BOATS. IF FOUND, CALL JOSH."

"All right," I said. "Cork it."

His eyes finally opened and attempted to focus, then closed again. "If I ever get to that embarrassing point where I can't speak or wipe myself, when everybody says to just pull the goddamn plug, remember that I'm not everybody. Don't think you're doing me any favors by tossing me into Lake Union with a forty-pound Danforth around my neck. Okeydoke? I want every last day I can get my aching hands on. And then I want an Icelandic burial. I've told your father all this, but he never listens. Nothing fancy. Just roll me up in a blanket and drop me in a crevasse, preferably on Rainier, but Baker would do. That way, I'll be preserved forever, mustache and all. It's a vanity, I'll admit."

"Yeah, yeah, sure. You got it. Meanwhile, what is it you *want* for breakfast?"

"Funny," he said, then sat up with a yelp and a groan. I handed him his trifocals. He set them aside and blew his nose, one nostril at a time. "Nothing tells you exactly how old you are like mornings," he said cheerfully. "Swiftsure, Josh! And we've got a family dinner the Saturday before, right? Ruby swears she'll be there, too." He rotated his trunk with a groan, stretching his shoulders. "It all makes me want to yodel."

"Please don't," I said, but it was too late.

# ALMOST NORMAL

I'd arrived early, expecting signs of anticipation: meat marinating, a vacuumed floor, a tidied bathroom. Instead, it was as if they'd forgotten or didn't believe anything unusual was about to happen because it looked like yet another humdrum Saturday afternoon at the Teardown, the tables and counters littered with newspapers, spindled sailboat drawings and coffee mugs, and the scratch-worn floors with tumbleweeds of black dog hair. Not until the Labs started yipping did the Bobos look up from an *All in the Family* rerun. Grumps held up a finger for me to wait while Archie called his idealistic son-in-law a meathead. Then they laughed all over themselves. The only actual sign of preparation was Father's freshly dyed hair. I grabbed the remote and muted the commercial.

"What's he doing?" Father asked, stopping his toenail clipping long enough to click the sound back on in time to catch the Jack in the Box punch line. Meanwhile, Grumps marveled at the sight of me, tugging on his mustache, deep into his second Rainier, a brittle *Cannery Row* paperback open in his lap. Neither had showered or put on a clean shirt, opened a window or washed a single dish.

"You do remember that Ruby—and possibly even Bernard—are coming to dinner, right?"

"Wow!" Grumps sat upright. "Wouldn't that be something?"

"Can't wait." Father snorted. "Mary Poppins and the Easter Bunny joining us, too?"

I found Mother squinting at the computer in mismatched pajamas. She nodded when I reminded her about dinner, then held up a palm to let me know now wasn't the time to talk.

"Might want to get dressed," I whispered.

Without another word, I began vacuuming, probably the first time the machine had been plugged in since I'd last been here. For so long, Mother did everything when we weren't looking, but for more than a decade now she'd been in her own world, quite distant from this one with its toilet rings and frayed towels and sheets we'd worn thin in the nineties. The house had remained a museum of family nostalgia and dated electronics. Out of oblivion, defiance or frugality, they'd never owned a DVD or even a CD player, much less a smartphone, and still played the same half-dozen jazz albums on the hi-fi. Mother's old Compaq and Internet connection was their lone link to the modern age.

Father scowled at the noise I was making and turned the volume up again as Grumps hunched closer to the old Zenith. Deciding to attack the bathroom now, I pulled the plug on the vacuum and watched dust twirl around them in trapezoids of slanted sunlight. I was carrying the bulging bag outside when this utterly strange yet oddly familiar couple rounded the blackberries, arm in arm.

He wore an Old Testament beard, she a green beret. Their movements grew increasingly kindred as she handed her sack to him, broke free and ran toward me with an operatic shout of "Jooooooshuaaa!"

I dropped the bag and waited to be crushed while her homeless-looking sidekick strode up, leading with his head and shoulders. "Little brother." His voice had somehow deepened yet again. Ruby swung her arms around the both of us, and for a few seconds we hung awkwardly on to one another.

Bernard had called from a pay phone two nights before, and I'd hinted at the dinner plans, but to actually see him was still staggering.

"They don't believe you guys are really coming," I said.

Then Ruby and I spoke at once, neither of us hearing what the other one said. My eyes couldn't focus, and my breathing was audible as my brother rubbed his palms together like a man trying to get warm around a fire.

"So they're all here?" Ruby asked.

"Where else could they possibly be?" I resisted asking where her hair had gone and why she was so skinny. "Brace yourselves," I told them.

As I shoved the squeaky front door open, I saw the Teardown through their eyes. It'd been six years since Ruby visited, eight for Bernard. The dogs went berserk, and the two Bobos couldn't have looked more alarmed if we were masked burglars. Then Mother emerged from her office, fully dressed with a cheerful smear of lipstick.

I gave a circus bow. "Allow me the honor of presenting Mary Poppins and the Easter Bunny."

"Well, look at you drop-jaws," Ruby finally said, bounding over to give Grumps a noisy kiss, and then Mother and finally Father, while Bernard remained stapled to the floor.

"Oh, for Christ's sake." Father rose hesitantly toward him. "For a second there, I thought you must be Ruby's Latest Mistake."

This brought oxygen and laughter to everybody except Bernard, who remained silent and hidden behind the beard, which looked even larger indoors, cascading to his sternum like a wool scarf.

"Speak!" Father demanded. "Let us know you're you!"

"Ease, hike, trim," my brother mumbled, the beard turning him into a ventriloquist. "Boat speed, boat speed, boat speed."

Over the chuckles, Ruby said, "I found him walking up Eleventh."

"You walked here?" Dad asked, still seated in his recliner.

Bernard nodded.

"Should've called!"

"No phone."

"So where the hell you been?"

Bernard looked at each of us, everything but his eyes still concealed behind that beard. "Out in the world," he said softly.

We waited for more, but that was it until Ruby chipped in, "See any flying fish?"

"Yes."

"Any land on your boat?"

"Yes."

"You eat any live?"

"Just one." The beard twitched. He might have grinned.

"Well, well," Father began, then tailed off or second-guessed his choice of words while Mother came closer, as glassy-eyed as Grumps, and grabbed one of Bernard's chapped hands, pulling him down so she could kiss his sunburned cheek. At last he shook hands with the Bobos and dropped to the floor so the Labs could climb over him and try to lick his face.

"And what about Miss Ruby here?" Grumps asked, crouching toward her from his chair. "How'd you get so thin, sweetie? Any hair under there?"

She pulled off her beret and shook her imaginary mane, buzz-cut short along the rounded contours of her small skull.

"Will the surprises never end?" Father asked. "Why would you possibly—"

"Less wind resistance," she said. "I'm all about aerodynamics these days. Why'd you dye yours blue?"

"What's she even talking about?" he asked us.

Hubble's tail knocked Grumps's Rainier out of his hand and onto the floor.

"Want one?" I asked Bernard, loping toward the paper towels and the fridge.

"I like you in short hair," Mother told her. "It draws even more attention to your beauty."

Ruby fluttered her eyelashes and spun her face toward an imaginary bank of cameras before floating into the kitchen with her fresh vegetables.

The family that had filled this house with so much jabber for so many years was suddenly speechless. I followed Bernard's eyes to the three half-hull models of the Joho 26, 32 and 39 above the never-used fireplace. Then I tailed him into our old bedroom doorway, Grumps's room now, though he hadn't changed anything, as if still just visiting, because there were the same bunk beds and posters and Bernard's handwritten three-word manifesto when he was nineteen: EVEREST WITHOUT OXYGEN!

"Everything looks smaller." He cleared his throat. "So much smaller."

Slinking downstairs, we peeked into our parents' bedroom, where we'd probably been conceived, and where they'd definitely slept beside each other on the same flattened queen mattress every day—minus Mother's Arizona sabbatical—since 1975. Here the Teardown tilt was at its most visible, like a fun-house mirror or an Escher drawing, the headboard angling down and away toward the single-pane window, blackberries peeping over the sill. Father's side was almost a foot below Mother's, making it easy to imagine her eventually rolling down and smothering him midsnore, while the entire house, like an unlatched suitcase, spilled the contents of our lives down the hill.

"Did you find Yoshito for me?" Bernard asked.

"Uh-huh."

"When? Where?"

I showed him the disposable phone. "Call the number on the back when you're ready to meet him."

"I don't want you feeling awkward again," he said, pocketing the phone.

"Too late." I handed him the special agent's card and gave him an abbreviated version of our conversation.

Bernard's expression didn't change, as if he was used to dealing with much worse than this. "If he really knew anything, he wouldn't have risked talking to you."

"But if they're listening to my calls," I whispered, "they may know you're here right now."

"I doubt it." Then he matter-of-factly pulled the phone back out, glanced at the number and started dialing.

"What the hell?" I closed the door behind us. "You're calling him now?"

He shrugged, then said what sounded like *"Ko-knee-che-wa"* into the phone and fired off several terse sentences of Japanese, before turning to me. "You've got a car?"

"Yes, but—"

Then he held a finger to his lips and finished his phone chat with another blast of gibberish before hanging up and telling me, "Ten tonight. And yes, he knows about the fed, but he's not worried. And, by the way, I won't be needing a new boat."

"Now you tell—"

Ruby burst through the door. "Hey! You can't strand me with them."

We sat at the table like rusty actors returning to a familiar set and script, and dinner felt almost normal for an exhilarating half hour, passing around the same old spaghetti and Ruby's colorful salad. We played our old roles, for the most part: Father running things; Momma filling gaps with relevant info and facts; Ruby spinning stories, true and false; Bernard calling bullshit piece by piece with just his eyes; Grumps relentlessly positive, his wristwatch alarm ringing every ten minutes.

"He can't hear it," Mother whispered.

"But we can," I said.

Ruby asked me about the boatyard, which led Grumps to reenact our planking exercise and Mother to ask about her farm.

"It's getting too popular," Ruby said. "We get a half-dozen applicants a day. Some are friends and relatives of my crew. Others just heard about it. I finally got talked into charging for tours."

"Are there tours of other farms up there?" Mother asked.

"Not really."

"Then why yours?"

"The gourds, mostly."

"Really?"

"Who pays money to look at squash?" Father asked.

"Nobody ever listens to me!" I cried. "She grows the largest pumpkins in the universe!"

"The province," Ruby said.

"How much you charge?" Father wanted to know.

"For a tour, ten bucks Canadian."

"My sister the capitalist," Bernard said.

"The word is *philanthropist,*" I said. "The money goes to some homeless foundation, right?"

"For crying out loud," Father said. "You get a salary?"

"Just room and board, like everybody else."

"But it's your farm?"

"It's our farm."

"It's hers," I said. "Plus she's got her own salmon run, but you probably forgot that, too."

Grumps kept asking if he could get anybody wine or beer, with everybody saying yes except Ruby, who never once had a drink with us in this house. I watched the old man scrutinize everybody, then shake his head. "I've lost control of time," he said.

The sharp double rap on the door tripped the two-dog alarm and jolted us all and especially Bernard, who sprang from his seat—his left elbow swinging high enough to flash his armpit holster—and slipped into the bathroom in one swoop.

Ruby followed the dogs to the door and greeted the shrinking Mrs. Trowbridge, our nosy neighbor.

"What a surprise!" she exclaimed, though it clearly wasn't. "It's just been so long since I've seen you, Ruby!" Her eyes scanned the faces and counted the plates before she apologized profusely for interrupting dinner and left with a confused expression.

"You're still a fugitive?" Father began as Bernard rejoined us, and I cleared the table.

"Far as I know." Bernard took his seat with a wider stance, his hips parallel to the door.

"Let's just beat this damn thing once and for all!" Father said.

"They'll dismiss all that crap in a heartbeat!" Grumps added cheerfully. "There's a statute of limitations, right? Nobody cares anymore!"

"They'll dismiss the son of a bitch!" Father pounded the table twice. The dogs yipped, thinking somebody else was at the door.

"What if they don't?" Bernard asked. "Those statutes don't apply to people who run from charges."

Father leaned toward him. "Can't spend your life hiding from the Betsy Trowbridges of this world. If you've got to do a little time, then do it! You've proved you can do just about anything, by God. You can—"

"For once," Bernard snapped, "try *thinking* instead of just *pushing*."

Even the dogs looked chastened. Grumps took this opportunity to switch from Rainier to rum.

"Can't you imagine," my brother continued, his voice gaining clarity and momentum, "that perhaps someone who feels a need to climb the tallest mountains and sail the largest oceans might dread the idea of spending *any* time in a cage?"

Given how little he'd spoken, this sounded like the Gettysburg Address. But there was more.

"'I am a citizen of the most beautiful nation on earth. A nation whose laws are harsh yet simple, a nation that never cheats, which is immense and without borders, where life is lived in the present. In this limitless nation, the nation of wind, light and peace, there is no other ruler besides the sea.'"

"Moitessier," I said into the silence that followed.

"*Who?*" Father feigned ignorance, then smiled begrudgingly. "Lord, how I hate that romantic son of a bitch."

"Getting you into Canada would be easy," Ruby said softly.

"Yes!" Father pounced. "Ruby will get you across, and the rest of us'll meet you in Victoria on Friday!"

"C'mon, Bernard," Ruby whispered. "Swiftsure! Nothing but family on board. No Betsy Trowbridges. No cops. Just tell us you're in. Say the words. It'll make you feel so good!"

The silence now was even longer. "I'm out," he said. "I can't. I won't."

There was just enough give in his voice, though, for Ruby to start rattling off exactly how fantastic Swiftsure was going to be this year, throwing out fake odds about old boats like ours with state-of-the-art sails winning in erratic conditions like those forecasted. "How could we possibly lose with Leif Eriksson himself on board?" she cried, pointing at Bernard. "Please tell me I'm not the only one who sees the resemblance!" She grabbed the photo of the Ballard statue off the wall and held it next to his head. They looked nothing alike. "Finally!" she shouted. "All the proof we'll ever need to establish our direct lineage to the great Icelandic sailing hero himself!"

Father drummed his fingers on the table, the wine lowering his patience, before turning to Bernard. "So how you been making it anyway?"

"Creatively."

"I bet, but legally or illegally?"

Bernard threw back his beer. "You don't want to know."

"Oh, but I do."

"I sell butterflies," Bernard told him, "and sink boats."

"For Christ's sake," Father said.

"I'm just so happy we're all here," Grumps said, tearing up again. "Even if it's just for right now."

"Have we adequately thanked Odin and Thor for this reunion?" Mother asked.

"Don't forget Poseidon!" Ruby added, grabbing Grumps's shot, tossing its brass-colored contents over her shoulder and splashing the Labs, who stood up to shake.

"C'mon Bernard!" she goaded. "Tell us some sea stories!"

"Already talked more tonight," he said after a pause, "than I have in the entire past month."

"Can I tell your stories then?"

His head bobbed, and she took it as a yes.

"So Bernard," she asked herself, looking over her left shoulder, "were you ever serenaded by dolphins out there?"

"Almost every day," she replied in her best Bernard mumble over her right shoulder. "They'd come out during lunch and dance in front of the bow, then hop up on their tail fins and salute me."

"See any giant squid out there?"

"Tons of 'em, Oprah. Can I call you O? Off the coast of Japan, their tentacles were waving like bamboo in the wind."

"Oh, come now, Bernard, did you see the Loch Ness Monster, too?"

"Nice try, O. She's a freshwater creature."

"You've been gone for years. Why didn't you go all the way around the world?"

"Got lost in the Pacific, girlfriend."

"Did you look into the eye of a whale?" Ruby asked her brother.

"Several," he said.

"Did any of them speak to you?"

"Yes, but I'm still learning their language."

Mother asked if he'd seen any northern lights as Grumps headed uphill to get more rum. Before Bernard could respond, Father said, "Can I tell you what I've seen? I've seen pants falling off my old man."

"Got no butt to hold 'em up anymore," Grumps hollered back.

"You'd make one unsatisfying meal for a grizzly," Mother commented.

We looked at her, in disbelief, awaiting an explanation.

"Bears go for the buttocks first," she said.

"Kinda like that sports broadcaster?" Ruby asked. "What was he called?"

"Albert!" Grumps laughed himself off balance. "Marv Albert: the butt biter!"

After we'd all collected ourselves, Mother felt compelled to make the case that we weren't any weirder than most families. "We're just more extraordinary," she said, leaning into the table toward us. "And we remain close even when we're far apart."

"And we are all going to Swiftsure!" Grumps shouted after his watch alarm sounded yet again.

"Let me see that." Ruby slid the watch off his wrist and passed it to me. Then she kissed the back of his hand, which got him misty and Bernard laughing. I clicked to the alarm settings, turned them all off and gave Grumps his watch back.

Then, all of a sudden, the familiarity evaporated, and we seemed more like strangers, our changes and differences rising like welts in the fading light, though perhaps I was sensing what was coming, not what was right in front of me. My eyes scoured Bernard for more scars, tattoos or any other hints as to what he'd been up to, while I worried that too much air had left Ruby's balloon.

Desperate for normalcy, I flipped on the hi-fi and put on *The Best of Dizzy Gillespie* for the two Bobos while we youngsters lay on the floor with the dogs, well out of earshot. Ruby told us that her hospice work had got a little depressing and she now was balancing that with holding preemies at the hospital once a week. "Some of them are the size of potatoes," she said. "When they stop crying it feels like a compliment. You both really need to experience it."

Eager to change the subject, I said, "There's a Star racer who's been sailing in Olympia for three years in hopes you'll show up. He's had a crush since you raced Lasers against him in your teens."

"Clark Thompson?" she asked.

"No."

"Lenny Hurst? Brock Jensen? Tom O'Brien?"

"Mario Seville," I said.

She scrunched her nose. "The name's familiar."

In an hour, we'd all scatter again, but for now, we were on the floor, the three of us, with the familiar sounds and odors, scratching the dogs while the Bobos discussed Swiftsure logistics and Mother drifted back toward her office as if tugged by some unseen force.

Following instructions, Bernard and I checked our mirrors compulsively for any suspicious headlights tailing us before parking Noah's car behind a desolate bar along Aurora. Then we strode down two alleys until we located a staircase that spiraled up to a one-bedroom condo above a renovated garage where we found some muted reality show playing on the massive screen behind the head of a fiftyish Asian man with a bleached smile.

The two of them spoke for several incomprehensible and disconcerting minutes before Bernard pulled Tupperware from his backpack and set it on the granite counter of the kitchen island. "Your brother Japanese very impressive," Yoshito told me, between glances at huge dead butterflies. "Most people know sentence or two—how to say thank you, how to get sake."

He waved aside Bernard's offer to open more containers and then handed him stacks of bills, which my brother, in turn, didn't bother to count before dropping them in his pack. After another flamboyant exchange of Japanese and a final round of smiling handshakes, we exited.

The encounter was so much less stressful than I'd expected, I almost fainted from relief. I was carelessly switching lanes and thinking about Ruby on her long drive home, when I noticed the reds and blues spinning directly behind me.

"Oh, shit!" Braking gently, I began to pull over.

"You're not speeding," Bernard said calmly. "You haven't done anything wrong."

Before I whimpered to a full stop on the shoulder, the squad car screamed past in pursuit of somebody else.

My brother laughed. "You're not very good at this, are you?"

Merging timidly into the slow lane, I listened to him deconstruct the Yoshito encounter. "We made fifty percent more than we would have if we'd dealt with his underlings because I've been courting his ass ever since I heard that he respects white men who speak fluent Japanese. So we have Rosetta Stone to thank for this."

He dumped the money into his lap. "You good with ten percent?"

"Fifteen," I rasped.

"Standing up for yourself, I love it. But ten is generous."

"Why didn't he examine your butterflies?" I asked, still overheating but my voice returning.

"He's betting I won't screw him if he doesn't screw me—a potential miscalculation on his part because I won't ever sell butterflies again. See, I've landed myself a real job, Josh—well, kind of real."

"Oh yeah? Drug running? Espionage?"

"Can't talk about it other than to say it's down in the Southern Ocean and begins on June twenty-fourth."

"That's the day the world ends," I told him. "My friend's preacher father says that's when all the believers will ascend."

"Well," my brother said, "how's that for perfect timing."

# OUR WOBBLING PLANET

~~~~~~

There's no Las Vegas line on the exact doomsday date yet, but Noah's father is far from the only person to speculate on it—just more willing and eager to get specific.

Shakers predicted the world would be over in 1792. The American farmer William Miller settled on dates in 1843 and 1844. Jehovah's Witnesses picked several years between 1914 and 1994. Various kooks and zealots have used numerology and algorithms and other methods to select actual days. Most recently, millions of pessimists rallied around a misinterpretation of a Mayan calendar that indicated we were running out of time.

Just about every religion and mythology has a story about this. All yarns need endings, preferably action-filled Hollywood crescendos that tie everything off with one last battle between the righteous and the wicked. Christians still insist that Jesus's return to earth will be the Armageddon finale, and 41 percent of Americans think this will happen before 2040. Hindus see the beginning of the end similarly, with Vishnu descending atop a white horse. One Buddhist prophecy foresees stages of deterioration until seven suns suddenly appear in the sky and the earth is consumed in flame.

Icelandic mythology has a single ominous word for the end days: Ragnarok. Just about every Norse myth references it. Yet there wasn't the convenience of an actual *date*. So Vikings prepared daily, never knowing when the battle was about to come and set the seas ablaze. Their only hint was that Ragnarok would be preceded by a specific series of events, starting with three straight winters without summers in between, when men would go mad, start mauling one another and have incest with their siblings. Then, at the very end, the moon and sun would exit stage left, and all the land would sink into the ocean. (Floods are wildly popular in end stories, as are earthquakes, tsunamis and volcanic eruptions, which helps explain why people get so pious during natural disasters.)

Scientists have their own theories. Fans of the Big Rip argue that an expanding universe will eventually pull *everything* apart—stars and planets and even atoms. Believers of the Big Freeze imagine the expanding universe will grow too cold to support life anywhere. The Big Crunch reverses these equations and claims that a massive collision will produce Big Bang II, the Sequel. But all these scenarios are millions of years off, and no astronomer would dare predict a doomsmillennium much less a doomsday.

Less-scientific apocalyptics warn about Nibiru, the rogue Planet X, that's supposedly on a collision course with earth. That this calamity was predicted by a woman who claimed she received e-mails from aliens hasn't discouraged her believers; but let me assure you that if Nibiru was flying toward us, my mother would've already seen it as easily as you'd spot a moose in a bowling alley. Along these lines, Einstein allegedly muttered something like "If the bee disappears from the surface of the earth, man will have no more than four years to live." Sorry, Albert, but that doesn't sound very scientific to me.

So here's my take on the end: seeing as how this planet's rotation is slowing, perhaps we'll eventually become a fixed sphere, like our moon, with one side in the light and the other forever dark and cold.

There's also the possibility that the 23.5-degree tilt of our axis could increase over time. And this alarms me because I know exactly what a 23.5-degree tilt feels like. Too damn much! It's time to put more people on the top rail or fly smaller sails. Mars twirls along at a 25-degree tilt, Saturn at 27 and Neptune at an even 30. Perhaps they were all more hospitable in their younger, less-tilted heydays.

Given that the only reason there's life on earth is because of the attractive pull of a star 93 million miles away, and seeing as how our nearly unsustainable tilt combined with our planet's chubby midsection makes us like a spinning top that's starting to stagger, how could we possibly believe all this will never end?

It's a wonder we're still here at all.

# THE PILGRIMAGE

Given dreary predictions of light winds, it was invigorating to see snapping burgees and choppy water as we powered out to our corner of the world.

As we exited Victoria Harbour alongside a hundred and fifty other sailboats, Father blathered about weather and current and crew roles, a variation of his prerace stump speech we'd heard and mocked so many times. Mother and Bobo Sr. would handle spinnaker-pole adjustments and monitor instruments. Bernard would run the bow with my help. Father and I would muscle the winches. Ruby or whoever was closest would manage the main. We'd take shifts steering—except Mother and Grumps. If it blew hard, we'd wish we had more crew, but this was going to be a Johannssen affair.

Granted, I hadn't seen the entire family in the morning glare for years, but they sure looked like impostors. Eagle-eyed Ruby wore glasses? Mother's jowls had drooped overnight? Father's belly had doubled in size? Yet Bernard, behind his Zeus beard and Ray Charles sunglasses, wore the most beguiling disguise of all. I couldn't find my brother in that face no matter how long I stared. (He'd slid through customs with a New Zealand passport declaring he was Charles E. Chapman from Wellington.) Only Grumps, slouching beneath his British driving cap like an old jockey, looked anything like himself.

Everywhere I looked people were taking photos and movies of the exiting procession, with countless cameras and phones seemingly pointed at us. This wasn't, in fact, my imagination. We were on the front of *Victoria's Times Colonist* the next morning with Father at the helm and Ruby at the center of the picture, looking worried. *Seattle skipper Robert Johannssen Jr., his daughter Ruby and crew* read the caption.

Before we raised a sail, Father went through his normal neurotic rituals, steering the bow directly into the wind, then slowing down, stopping and running it hard in reverse, hoping to knock off any kelp or detritus still clinging to the keel. If anything was truly hanging off the boat, he'd know it immediately, but he was equally good at imagining drag. "Feel anything?" he asked. "No," we comforted him. "All clear." Yet he did it all over again, hard into the wind, and then full speed in reverse. "Feel anything?"

Temporarily satisfied, he let us raise the sails and traverse the starting line in the escalating boil of wind, waves, boat wake and current slop, periodically pointing *Freya III* straight into the breeze and letting the sails flog in order to triple check exactly where the wind was coming from in relation to the starting line.

"Heading?" he asked.

"Two-seventy," I told him.

"Two-sixty-five," Mother said seconds later.

"So which is it?" he demanded. It scarcely mattered. We'd gauge the wind direction at least twice again, but our captain found solace in repetition.

There were just eight knots of wind, the instruments told us, though it felt like twice that in the prestart mosh pit with so many near collisions and so much adrenaline-slinging between jittery skippers. Months of logistics, maintenance and daydreaming were all fused into this start, which likely meant very little in a 122-mile race, yet in this crucible felt like the most critical juncture of our lives.

More than three hundred boats and two thousand sailors used to gather for Swiftsure back before iPhones and Xbox distracted humanity. Twenty years ago, the race felt like a mythical rite of passage, a religious pilgrimage or a migratory phenomenon for which people of all ages geeked up to sail out into the abyss.

By the time we reunited, it was still the region's premier race even if the number of boats had been cut in half. And little Victoria was overrun yet again.

Though just sixty miles from both Seattle and Vancouver, Victoria dresses itself up like a quaint British city. Maybe the manicured gardens and afternoon tea came with being named after the United Kingdom's chubby monarch. Buzzkill Vicky—she wore black more often than Johnny Cash—never even set foot in Canada, much less her namesake city. But that didn't discourage Canucks from celebrating Victoria Day every May, which Ruby suggested was almost as ridiculous as Columbus Day in the States. Their national holiday usually fell on the Monday of the Swiftsure weekend near the end of May, so the dueling festivities invariably clashed, with the international marina boozefest spilling across the street toward the ivy-ensconced Empress Hotel, which strived to preserve its dignity by overpricing its serving of tea and crumpets at fifty-nine bucks.

Still, plenty of welcoming venues were bursting with wind-burned patrons boasting they'd sailed this race twenty-three straight times and had seen all anybody could possibly see. (When it came to measuring your Northwest sailing penis, your number of Swiftsures was right up there with how many ocean miles you'd sailed.) Engineers, doctors and lawyers had always been well represented, but nowadays the crowd was starting to look like a VFW happy hour. There was a limp and groan to this gang, though cocktails temporarily rewound the clock, and the lies piled up with the empties. *Went from blowing thirty to fifty all of a sudden and masts started dropping like palm trees in a hurricane. So we had two choices, turn and run or douse. Instead we took a third option, and did nothing. The forestay snapped first, and it sounded like a thirty-aught-six.*

Every story got topped, if not by veiny retreads, then by boyish software designers and other hotshot upstarts in pricey Gill jackets and polarized sunglasses (even indoors), strutting the same clubby jocularity that had always made me feel like my family had pledged the wrong frat. *She looks like a blonde, sure, but does the carpet match the drapes?* Everybody swapping stories of heroic nonchalance, using that rapid gunslinging sailor lingo that had never moved me. The only Johannssen who'd ever felt at home here was my father, who drew swarms and murmurs. People wanted a handshake or a word, even if they thought he was nuts.

Hobbling back to the marina on the eve of the race, Grumps had yammered about whether Ruby would actually show up, the possibility still too dreamy to get any traction in his mind. The beers exaggerated his unstable gait to the point Bernard and I spotted him on either side. Meanwhile, Father was bantering with Canadian and American racers who'd tailed us to the marina to see our boat, some of them covering their mouths to muzzle their amusement at the sight of our faded and bedraggled old Joho surrounded by gleaming new rigs half its weight and ten times its price.

"I hear voices below!" Grumps gushed. "She here already?"

"You actually racing this old girl tomorrow, Bobo?" an older man asked. "Nothing wrong with nostalgia, but have you seen the sleds you're up against?"

"Oh, we'll see," Father toyed. "At the rate things are going, we might not even make it to the start."

"Huh. So you and the family are just up here for the sightseeing."

"That's right. Might go to that wax museum or check out the flowers."

Then the hatch slid open. "You win, Momma. They weren't too drunk to find the boat."

"Ruby!" Grumps cried.

Her name and secondhand lore reverberated through the drunks on the dock as she sprang from the cabin and hugged her grandfather, rocking him side to side.

Once the rivals stumbled off we settled in below, with Ruby and Mother giggling like kids who couldn't look at each other without busting up and Father—like old times—blaming "somebody" for forgetting his toiletries.

After sleeping so lightly it felt more like waiting, I began my rounds at dawn, lashing a line to the boom to help prevent unintentional jibes. Then the smaller stuff, from cotter rings to shackle blocks and barber haulers. Hoisting myself to the bottom spreaders, I switched out a dead lightbulb and continued up to the top of the mast to replace the broken cups on the anemometer. There I lingered, watching the yellow sunrise and the hopeful boats below until my harnessed legs began to numb and Father appeared on deck. I hung on a bit longer, knowing if the two of us were alone I'd confront him about the handicap rating I'd seen listed for us in the prerace blotter.

Swiftsure doesn't begin with a horn or a gun but a cannon.

There were three separate starts, with the largest and fastest boats engaged in the first one. Then, twenty minutes later, came ours, with a few dozen boats between thirty and fifty feet jockeying for position in the roiling water.

If Father had to be stuck in a single place and time, he'd probably choose this one, marauding back and forth with thirty seconds to go, bullying everybody with his nimble boat handling and domineering voice, heads swiveling at his every bark.

With twenty seconds left, the fleet condensed with skippers hunting for gaps to dart into in hopes of creating space and finding unobstructed wind. We surged forward precariously close to the massive Coast Guard ship, which was serving as the left end of the starting line, and once our bow overlapped the stern of a Beneteau 50 in front of us, Father bawled, "Gotta gimme room!" and its skipper yielded more space than he needed to, guaranteeing us clear air and the inside track, the cannon thundering overhead the instant we crossed the line.

Temporarily deafened, we engaged in the necessary sail-sculpting adjustments, with Father calling the trims. *"Give me a little vang . . . Yes . . . More! . . . Okay . . .* No backstay yet! *Keep the sails full, the draft aft, a little less jib halyard."*

"Thank you, Odin, for that start!" Grumps shouted, throwing his gloved hands up near his head, followed by Bernard's Tarzan howl. Father grinned, his eyes scanning sails and water, crouched next to the low rail so he could study the jib—stripped to a T-shirt in forty-five degrees, his belly ballooning the cotton, unshaven, hungover and thrilled, no hat, sunglasses or sunscreen, as usual, his hair, I noticed for the first time, thinning, his eyes bright and his hands light on the wheel, a hopeful blush in his cheeks. For now, we all shared it, quietly appreciating the remarkable pace with which the old Joho slashed through the turmoil toward smoother water.

Forty minutes later, we were still moving as well as anyone in our class and gaining on larger boats that had started twenty minutes earlier. "Eight knots!" Grumps cried, scanning the instruments. "Eight-point-three knots upwind!"

Everybody but Father and I looked surprised. Mother was particularly puzzled. "These boats can't do eight knots upwind, can they? When was the knotmeter last calibrated?"

"Let it go, Marcelle," Father said.

Prone on the bow, Ruby watched the slot between the sails and said absolutely nothing, which meant everything was perfect, the foils curved like raptor wings for maximum velocity. Even Mother looked excited, silver bangs blowing across her inquisitive eyes.

With the wind shifting ten degrees to the south, boats began tacking toward the Canadian shore. "Let's make sure it's a header before we go," Father said.

"Everybody's already gone," Bernard noticed soon after.

"The lemmings aren't always right," Father told him.

"Correctomundo!" Grumps chirped.

"We might still go outside Race Rocks anyway," Father added.

"More adverse current out there for the next hour or two," Bernard pointed out.

Father waited long enough for it to seem like his idea, then said, "Prepare to tack."

"You see *Wild Rumpus*?" I asked.

"Yes," he said, "I got it." His quick eyes bounced from our sails to the water to the boats crowded around us. "Everybody ready for a great tack? Hard alee!"

We tacked flawlessly. That's not saying a whole lot, but the jib was released exactly when it wanted to go, then snapped to attention on the other side in synch with the mainsail before being gradually yet aggressively squeezed into the starboard winch, minimizing the lull when we weren't going full speed, all of this transpiring during an eighty-five-degree pivot through the eye of the wind with the boat settling onto its opposite rail and its preferred fifteen-degree upwind tilt for control and speed while heading directly at *Wild Rumpus*'s brand-new cockpit.

"Starboard!" shouted its alarmed captain.

"Hold your course!" Father bellowed, estimating angles and speeds to the intersection of the two vessels as we passed six feet behind this half-million-dollar forty-five-footer without forcing it to alter course or us to perform a penalty circle.

The entire twelve-man crew, half of them draped over the rail in matching *Wild Rumpus* hats, gaped at our drab shorthanded boat and uncoordinated garb—or maybe at their sleek new chariot getting beat straight up, so far, by an old clunker. Or possibly—as word spread—they were gawking at the rarefied sighting of the legendary Ruby Johannssen. Regardless, they *were* staring, which was what inspired Bernard to make loud monkey noises followed by Ruby's seal barks and Father shouting, "That's enough!"

We rode the lifts toward the shore, then tacked when we had to. "Who's ahead of us?" Father asked.

"In our class, nobody," I said. "Everybody ahead of us owes us time."

His smile was so wide that I could see the gold cap on one of his molars. "We're in this thing," he said. Then, louder: "We are in this thing!"

"And Poseidon willing, we'll stay in!" Grumpa seconded.

"What?" Ruby shouted from the bow.

"We're in this goddamn thing!" Bernard relayed.

"Whoop-whoop!"

Mother rolled her eyes but couldn't stop grinning.

For another hour we did nothing but sail together with a teamwork that had long since vanished on land. Once we got past Race Rocks, Father let Ruby steer.

Then the wind died.

# ZEPHYRS AND BROACHES

Ruby would later claim the breeze was dying before she took over but, if so, only subtly. Regardless, within minutes, there was very little wind, then none at all. Without it, the advantage of our perfect start evaporated as the fleet gradually bunched up, lighter boats creeping toward us and the others marooned near the Canadian shore as if trapped in a drying painting.

This sudden lull didn't stop the racing, of course. Everybody kept watch for zephyrs, burning brain cells on theories about when or if to tack and which sails to fly, most of them now hanging superlight jibs called drifters. A few boats hoisted spinnakers, but the only puffs that materialized came right at their bow, inverting the chutes. Soon they were all doused and replaced with drifters. At Father's request, Grumps lit a cigar to reveal the true direction of whatever wind there was, and the smoke went straight up.

Despite the doldrums, we executed every slow-motion tack as if there were real wind and each maneuver might determine the race, with Bernard gently escorting the drifter from side to side like it was made of sacred cloth. Ruby gave the wheel back to Father, and we sat along the rail on the side where the sails hung to help give the boat a favorable go-fast tilt if it happened to move. We hallucinated puffs and wind lines all around us. Then it got worse.

"The current," my brother observed, "is about to push us backwards. We should anchor."

Grumps glanced at the instruments. "There's three hundred and eighteen feet of water beneath us."

"Maybe we should tack back toward the middle," Father said.

"Where the current's strongest?" Bernard asked.

"We don't know that," Father said.

"Sure, we do," Mother corrected him. "And it's going to get even stronger over the next hour. Two-point-three knots at the peak."

He glared at her. "I don't seem to remember you saying much about current."

She shrugged. "Well, the wind wasn't supposed to drop below five knots. That's the surprise, not the current."

"I hate this goddamn race," Father whined. "Every other year the whole thing turns fluky."

"The wind's definitely coming," Grumps said softly. "I just felt something on my face. You feel that?"

"No," Father said. "Why's Ruby so quiet?"

"She's napping on the bow," I told him.

"What's she so goddamned tired about? Where's everybody else, Josh?"

Looking through the binoculars, I rattled off which boat was where and how much time it owed us, or vice versa.

"We're going backwards," Ruby announced upon awakening. We all looked for landmarks, and she was right. Actually, *all* the boats were going backwards. We just happened to be going the wrong way faster than the others.

"We need to anchor *now*," Bernard insisted.

"We're racing," Father said. "Who *else* is anchoring?"

"I see. Now the lemmings *are* right."

"We're still in three hundred feet of water!" Bobo Jr. barked. "Even if it wasn't a stupid idea we don't have that much line."

"For what it's worth," Grumps contributed, "we're going one-point-two knots in the wrong direction."

"Let me tie all the lines together," Bernard grumbled, "and I'll find the fucking bottom."

We eyed the ongoing conflation of the fleet near the rocks, the limp-sailed boats looking like a flock of exhausted swans.

"Jesus H. Christ," Father grumbled.

"We need to get closer to shore to anchor," Bernard insisted as several more boats crawled past us.

"Exactly how're we gonna get there?" Father asked. "We've got no wind or steerage to go anywhere."

Ruby moseyed back to the cockpit and yawned. "Drop the sails. They're pushing us backwards."

Father started to speak, then turned to Mother.

She bunched her lips, bobbed her head and said, "In these conditions, it's all about drag. And there will be less drag without them."

Once Father closed his eyes and nodded, we dropped the sails in unison and waited, studying the instruments, the glassy water, the distant landmarks, the other boats. Almost immediately, we stopped moving backwards in relation to the fleet.

"Speed?" Father requested.

"Half a knot over the ground and still in the wrong direction," Grumps reported cheerfully. "Almost a knot improvement over what we were doing."

"Yay!" Ruby celebrated. "We're going backwards slower!"

Barely heading the wrong direction made us temporarily the most productive boat around, or so it appeared as we passed *Obsession, Ultimatum* and *Bedlam. Delirium*'s crew was the first to copy our tactic. Within fifteen minutes, half of the surrounding boats had dropped their sails. Though by then it was too late, because there was a solo puff that we alone raised our sails in time to catch, allowing us to become the first to experience the thrill of sailing faster than the oncoming current. The wind built steadily and kept our speed at almost three knots for the next hour, good enough for us to dream we'd round the mark by dark. But then it abandoned us again, and more superlights approached our stern before ghosting past us.

"How're they moving over there?" Father demanded. "What the hell are they doing that we're not?"

"They're just lighter," Grumps soothed. "And it's just gonna be fluky out here till it's not. Wind's coming."

"Really?" his son asked. "Where's it gonna be coming from? Any of those clouds look to be moving to you? See any movement anywhere?"

Mother coughed. "The weather report—"

"I know what the goddamn report said. What about you, Rube? Any brilliant ideas, or you hoping to sneak in another nap?"

"How about you shut your trap for a few minutes?" Bernard suggested. "Let's see if that helps."

"Perfect," Father replied. "Now I'm getting etiquette advice from a fugitive."

"Just relax," Grumps told everybody.

"Losers relax!" Father snapped, then rubbed his nose with his palm and lunged below, where we heard him devouring an entire roll of Ritz crackers.

We ate dinner in shifts, sticking with one-hour rotations at the helm despite no wind whatsoever. *Freya III* sat facing the pumpkin-colored horizon with flaccid sails when the stories began.

Lubricated by almost two weeks on land, Bernard shared remarkably detailed accounts of his travels through the South Pacific and Southeast Asia and told us his new personal heroes had committed their lives to preventing the slaughter of whales. "I might as well let you all in on a dirty secret of life on earth: international whaling laws are not enforced. The one place we truly need policing, there is absolutely none. Plenty of rules but no one to enforce them."

I watched Father silently reading the sails and water and instruments while gorging on a bowl of pasta to give his mouth something to do while Ruby took us for a vicarious ride in a jeep bumping down dirt roads through Nigeria with a team of people handing out boxes of polio and tuberculosis vaccines when they suddenly realize they're completely lost.

"Let's focus on sailing," Father said after he finished eating.

"I'm sorry," Bernard said. "Do we need to talk about you?"

"Hell no, but maybe we could concentrate on what we're doing here. You can tell all the war stories you want later."

"We're drifting, not sailing," Bernard clarified. "Being hypervigilant in light air is ridiculous. In no air, it's insane."

"C'mon, Dad," Ruby coaxed. "We're getting to know each other again. What're you and Grumps building these days?"

He glanced at Bobo Sr., then dodged. "Little of this, little of that."

"Very little," Grumps added, retreating into the cabin.

"Suddenly everybody's interested in the family business," Father said to nobody in particular.

"Chapter Eleven," Mother said.

Father shook his head. "Oh, sweet Jesus."

"You can tell the courts all about it," she fired back, "but you can't tell your kids? Well, they filed one of those Chapter Elevens last week."

"What's that?" Ruby asked.

"A polite way of saying bankruptcy," I said.

"What it is," Bernard clarified, "is a way for corporations to hide from their debts."

"That's enough!" Father snapped, then began coiling lines in the cockpit.

"We got sued again," Grumps said matter-of-factly, reemerging from below with a Rainier, "because we cut too many corners on yet *another* boat I didn't want to build in the first place."

"No, we didn't!" Father said.

"Yes, *you* did," Mother said.

"Was I not far enough under the bus already?" Father asked. "If it's sharing time, why don't you tell the kids about your little talk with the principal?"

She hesitated, looking meekly at each of us. "I've been encouraged to retire."

"What?"

"It's been a hard year. I fell asleep in class several times. I've been preoccupied."

"But she's got it!" Father erupted. "That's the crazy part. She has the solution and just won't turn it in. She's solved a million-dollar problem but won't claim the prize!"

"Because it's still not ready," Mother said sheepishly. "But it's close. Or I hope it's close."

"Listen, you all know I'm not smart enough to know what she's even trying to prove," Father said, coiling another rope into submission. "But I know that if Marcelle thinks she's right, she probably is. Tell 'em who's already looked at it. Tell 'em!"

"A few friends."

"Friends? How 'bout the top fluids guy at the U?"

"He's a fluid dynamicist," she said, "but hardly the top of anything. And just because they didn't find anything wrong doesn't make it right."

"So what's to lose by throwing it out there?" Ruby asked. "If it's wrong, so what?"

"Exactly!" Father said, looking up at us and then back down at the frayed end of rope in his hands. "It's time to claim your reward!"

Mom shook her head. "I'm not motivated by the money."

"Well, we are!" Father cried.

"Says the bankrupt boatbuilder," Bernard mumbled.

"Says the goddamn anarchist," Father retorted, "who sank Doug Applegate's yacht."

"What?" Ruby exclaimed.

"Jesus, Rube, doesn't any news make it to your door?" Father asked. "Applegate docked a seventy-foot stinkpot in Lake Union until it sank the morning after Bernard swung through town about—what was it, Son—eight years ago?"

Everybody stared at my brother, awaiting his denial, but there wasn't one. Grumps gulped more beer as Father said, "An insurance investigator dropped by the boathouse a couple months afterwards to ask when I'd last seen you. So how much you get paid for that one?"

"Gratis." Bernard looked sleepy, almost bored. "Scuttled that bad boy for free."

"My God," Father said.

"It was my pleasure," Bernard added.

"He's joking," Grumps said faintly. "Please tell us you're kidding."

"How'd you do it?" I asked.

"Broke in through a hatch and pulled the bilge fuse. Then I hacksawed a drainage hose below and tied an anchor to that and dropped it into the bilge below the thru-hull. It was simple, and I was careful. Wore gloves."

"Bernard," Mother whispered. "Stop this. It's not true."

"Nobody should own a toy that big," he said plainly, "particularly not a man who kills mass-transit plans so everybody has to drive to *his* mall and pay to park in *his* garages. His boat was an obscenity."

"You've always been wild," Father said, his bloated face shining with anger, "but I never took you for stupid. That *obscenity* was insured. You didn't cost him a nickel!"

Bernard shrugged. "The message was sent."

"What message exactly?" Ruby asked, collecting our dishes.

"That there's a leveling force out in the world when people get too selfish," Bernard said, as if explaining one of Newton's laws.

"And that's how you see yourself?" Ruby asked from down in the galley. "The leveling force?"

"Who the fuck else is gonna do it?" Bernard asked, snatching the frayed line from Father's hand.

"Wow." Grumps groaned. "Don't laws mean anything to you?"

"I play by rules that make sense to *me*." Bernard slipped electrical tape from his coat pocket and wrapped it tightly below the loose strands.

"What do you think, Josh?" Mother asked. "You're in the business of keeping boats afloat. Is it okay for Bernard to sink big yachts?"

Avoiding her eyes, I checked the instruments—still no boat or wind speed—before answering. "I've always admired Bernard's confidence that he's doing the right thing even when he's not."

He laughed, unclipped the blade on his hip and sawed through the taped section of the rope, and the loose ends fell away. "So what is it that wild and crazy Josh is hiding from us all?"

"Just some embarrassing dates, I'm afraid," I said, resenting his tone. "Remember, I'm the unambitious child."

"I don't know," Father said, scanning the water and sails again. "I think dating on the computer says plenty about you."

"Bobo," Mother cautioned.

"What? There's obviously something he likes about how impersonal it is. That's all I'm saying. Less risk of feeling anything, right? You can't piss a computer off. Can't make love to it either, but I guess that's as it should be."

I tried to laugh but felt nauseous. "You don't even know what online dating is."

"I know you don't dive into life." He sounded as if he'd been waiting for years to tell me that. "You don't take risks or tell anybody off or ask anybody out or even try to get a better job."

"Is this an intervention?" I asked, hoping somebody would rescue me.

Bernard pulled out a lighter and burned the freshly cut end of the rope until it melted into a unified tip.

"I'd argue," Ruby said slowly, "that Josh is the most ambitious member of our family."

Father laughed.

"He's the one," she continued, "who's always seen the best in each of us, especially in *you*." She made a gun out of her thumb and forefinger and pointed it at him. "And he's also the one who thinks he can fix whatever's broken even though he knows it'll just break again. He's our confider and accomplice, and probably does the same stuff for a whole lot of other people. He tries, against crazy odds, to keep everything and everybody intact. That's *his* ambition. It's just so different from yours that you're blind to it."

Everybody stared, awaiting my response to the most generous assessment of my life anybody could ever offer. Then they started yapping simultaneously about the size of whatever footprint, if any, I was leaving on the planet. I watched but didn't listen.

For so long I'd defined myself as so much smaller than these people. Sitting there, finally seeing them all together again, it was obvious they were neither giants nor immortals. I looked at Ruby's bulging collarbones again, the thin stubble over her ears, and finally realized that her impetus for one last Swiftsure wasn't because Grumps was getting feeble.

"Oh, Ruby," I said, stopping all conversation. "When'd you get diagnosed?"

"What'd he say?" Grumps asked. "What's he talking about?"

Ruby's eyes took a long time to find mine.

"How bad is it?" I tried to say more but couldn't.

Mother's hands started fluttering like caged birds. Father sat down and stood and sat again as if his flat cushion had turned into a sharp stone. Bernard looked straight up and swore inaudibly. Then Grumps said, "I'm lost, utterly lost."

"How bad is what?" Ruby asked. As convincing as her embellishments often were, she'd always been a lousy actor.

"Ruby?" Mother said, her face pale and pinched. "What's Josh talking about?"

"Wind," Ruby said, looking past us. "We've got a puff coming on the starboard quarter beam. Let's ease the sails, nice and slow, while Bernard prepares the spinnaker, and then we'll squeeze 'em all in just a hair and head up twenty degrees when it gets here."

We gently spun into action, as if the art of exquisite light-air sailing could suspend time and consequence. Ruby took the wheel, and Bernard glided forward to attach the halyard and get the chute ready while Father and I quietly adjusted the sails. Mother sat frozen, staring up at Ruby, as the boat mercifully began to move.

"I'm through the worst part," my sister finally volunteered, her fingers trembling slightly on the wheel. "If the chemo and radiation don't knock it out, I'll have to spend the rest of my days with just one booby." She palmed her left breast. "So yes, I've got it, but look what it's up against!" She clenched both fists and snarled. Then everyone listened to her answer Mother's questions as if they were prepping for an oncology test, until Father elbowed into the discussion to see if he could bully some slacker Canadian doctors or insurance fat cats into healing his little girl.

By the time we'd rounded the mark, it was past midnight, and the wind and waves were building behind us.

"I'm sorry, Daddy," Ruby said.

How many years had it been? Yet we all knew exactly what she was talking about.

"I did do it partly to hurt you, which was cruel considering everything you'd hoped to gain from it."

Father played a flashlight over the main, then the jib, assessing their shapes. "Hard to tell if that was an apology or an insult," he said. Then, after a few long beats, he asked, "You kids remember our trip to Bend?"

"Of course," Bernard said. "Our one and only family vacation not on a sailboat?"

"I don't," Ruby said.

"Well, you were four, maybe five, and you and I woke up early and went for a drive while everybody else slept in. We rolled through town with the windows down and the sunshine pouring in until this song came on the radio, and it was just me and my gorgeous smiling daughter driving around on this perfect brand-new day. You know I can never remember songs, but this one stuck with me because it was about this woman named Madam Joy who turned everybody's head because she was so damn happy. I still think about it because it was right then I realized you'd grow up, turn everybody's head and walk out of our lives. So how bad is it really, Rube?"

She recoiled the mainsheet. "It's starting to blow," she said. "Let's just sail."

I heard Mother and Grumps sniffling as the wind and swells continued to build. All the shuddering, whistling and snapping of spare halyards and loose shackles meant it was already gusting harder than forecasted. The waves got louder, sighing and snorting behind us, chasing us like bulls. With Ruby's touch on the wheel, the Joho rode the swells well enough and veered upwind through the troughs for speed and control, then turned directly downwind for fast and efficient surfing. The boat lights astern began to fade and those in front brightened.

"Eleven knots!" Grumps announced brightly as we dropped down the face of one wave, displaced foam fanning high on both sides of the cockpit.

Father stood on the high side with the flashlight so he could better monitor and tame the rambunctious spinnaker. Bernard worked the vang, which along with the line in my hand helped control the boom and the mainsail as the wind continued to build.

"Ease!" Ruby shouted, and the three of us simultaneously let out a little slack, reducing the pressure on the sails and curbing *Freya III*'s desire to tip wildly and swing up toward the wind. As we improved the rhythm of this tactic, she'd yell "Trim!" right before the boat stabilized, and then we'd tighten the sails and vang and accelerate again, carving a serpentine path through the waves.

"Twelve-point-five knots!" Grumps rejoiced.

As well as Ruby was steering, we were clearly going too fast for this boat in these conditions, surfing out of rhythm and somewhat violently, the bow diving lower into the rollers in front of us. We felt the size of the swells growing in the darkness. Mother was calling out wave patterns behind us but seemed out of synch, too, her information coming too late or not at all. Larger and higher funnels of foam hissed past the cockpit.

"Let's drop the chute!" Bernard yelled.

"We're fine!" Father shouted back as the silhouette of a new, water-ballasted boat glided past us with such balance and ease that the skipper was sipping coffee from an open cup. Following our own captain's orders, we continued at full tilt with hopes of winning the trophy after all the handicaps were calculated—flooring this old El Camino downhill until the steering wheel started vibrating.

"Twelve-point-eight!" Grumps hollered.

When the end of the boom swung close to the water yet again, Ruby shouted "Ease!" followed soon after by: "I don't have any rudder! Everybody on the stern!" We scrambled back, and she pointed us more directly downwind before the boat started rounding up on its own. "Losing rudder again!" she shouted. "Reduce sail!"

"Thirteen-point-eight!" Grumps cried, no longer enthusiastically.

"Dropping the chute!" Bernard yelled.

"We're fine!" Father insisted after we hit the next wave even lower and water sprayed over the cabin. "Let me have her!"

He took the wheel, and Ruby worked the vang while I tried to trim the spinnaker. We went up and over fifteen knots in such smooth fashion that everything suddenly seemed under control, like when a jet shudders through the sound barrier. Or maybe there was a softening of wave angles, a peaceful aberration that allowed us to go even faster. I'm not sure. But we broke all our Joho 39 speed records for about ten minutes, as if all the gravity, torque, force and will that constitutes my family was grounded in the math and physics that sent this old boat crashing ahead on this razor's edge.

Grumps looked at me and screamed, "What exactly did you do to this thing?" Then there was a slight wiggle in the mainsail, like it was reconsidering everything and no longer on our side.

"Ease!" Father howled, fighting the wheel, but we kept turning up toward the wind, spinning on the keel until we were sideways in the biggest trough yet. And that's where and when the boom and spinnaker, and finally the top of the mast, slapped the water.

"Grab on to something!" Bernard yelled. "Hold on!"

Going from record speed to a standstill in several seconds was enough to hurl us around like crash-test dummies as icy water gushed into the cockpit. Amid the chaos, I reached too late to stop Grumps from launching to the low side as all the Johannssen moxie and hubris were abruptly reduced to this swamped wreckage.

I looked wildly about in the dark to make sure we were all still aboard. Ruby was the hardest to find. She'd flown forward, farther than Grumps, and his body was blocking my view of her. Neither of them, I slowly realized, was moving.

"Get the spinnaker down!" Father shouted from behind the wheel, trying to steer a boat on its side that couldn't respond. A swell rose underneath and lifted us up like an offering, or a sacrifice, before dropping us back down into another trough while Mother and I crossed quickly to the low side.

Ruby said she'd knocked her head but felt fine, and Grumps said he might've whacked his knees. We couldn't tell how badly hurt either of them was or if they even knew. The water on our legs was breathtakingly cold. By the time the next large swell arrived, the keel had started to do its job, righting us enough to stop the sea from pouring in. But the wind pressing against the sails still kept us nearly pinned to the water.

"Lower the spinnaker already!" Father yelled again.

"It's stuck!" Bernard screamed back from the bow.

"Release the halyard!"

"I did!"

"Pull on the damn chute!"

"I did! I am!"

I scrambled forward to help, but the halyard was too jammed and the spinnaker continued filling and flapping in the water. My brother growled and then climbed the mast until he stood atop the spinnaker pole. From there he grabbed the halyard and whipped it back and forth over his head, trying to free it above. He kept at it while arguing with Father about whether he shouldn't just cut the fucking thing, then it finally sprang loose, and I was able to pull in some of the sail before the wind blasted it again and jerked me briefly off the deck. Father now had Ruby steer, then wedged himself into the cabin opening and told me to feed him the wet sail; this way, if it tried to fill again, it would have to pry him out of there like a cork. We didn't need to test those physics, though, because the wind dipped enough for him to stuff the spinnaker below, and Ruby nimbly steered us back on top of a swell with just the mainsail flying.

We had no idea how many boats passed us while we flailed in the dark. The fact we were even still in any race at all felt irrelevant and absurd. Yet we were off and running before the wind again—five knots, seven, nine—with Father back at the helm as the rest of us assessed the damage.

Ruby was cold and chattering but making sense. Mother inspected her head with a flashlight and found no wounds. But after checking both of Grumps's legs, she gasped at how quickly his right knee was swelling. Dropping into the rolling cabin, she reemerged with towels, blankets and dry clothes. I helped her pry Grumps's pants off and strap what ice we had left to his knee, which was approaching the size of his head. Mother handed him the rum bottle, and I bundled him in blankets, slung a harness over him and clipped him to the lifelines.

Everybody but Father took turns swapping out wet shoes and clothes as the cockpit finished draining.

"Should we fly the chute again?" Father asked once we were all on deck.

"Nooo!" came the crew's reply.

"Well, we need some kind of headsail," he responded reasonably, and Bernard went forward to raise a small jib.

"So, Josh," Grumps said after another long silence in the rolling dark, "tell me what you did to this boat."

When I finished explaining, I told him he'd have to ask Father what the race handicappers knew about the alterations.

"They know enough," he mumbled. "You saw our rating."

"It should've been at least eight points lower," I said. "You didn't tell them about the rudder or the keel, one or the other."

Waiting for a response, Grumps shook his head sadly. "Well, that's pathetic. You, of all people, Junior, never needed to cheat to win a sailboat race." Then he chuckled. "But who knows? Maybe the rating was spot-on after all. She's obviously a crazy horse downwind, huh? We proved that. But I gotta admit she sailed upwind like a scalded cat! Now go get dry and warm, and let Ruby steer for a while so we've at least got a shot in hell at finishing strong."

"Gladly," Father said, and stepped aside. Five minutes later, Ruby asked Bernard to please raise the spinnaker again.

Daybreak showed us ahead of *Wild Rumpus* and *Delirium,* both of them owing us time. So we let ourselves get excited, but then the wind died, then shifted, and we trudged through the worst of the adverse current and had to jibe twice before crawling over the finish line behind them both. Hope still flashed in Father's eyes until we spotted *Obsession* and *Bedlam,* to whom *we* owed time, dropping sails up ahead as we powered silently back into Victoria.

This was the part I hadn't imagined, the aftermath. Ruby, Bernard and I folded, packed and stored the sails exactly how we'd been trained to. Next we scrubbed the decks while Mother made six sandwiches, each one tailored to our individual preferences. At the tumultuous race dock, she asked for ice, a wheelchair and a taxi. Amid the commotion of other boats arriving and tying up, Bernard and I carried Grumps up to a bench. This was when my brother disclosed that he'd be flying out of Victoria shortly.

"Where to?" Mother asked.

"I'll let you know when I can," he said.

"What about your boat?" I asked.

"Already sold her."

Now Father shook his head. "Will the mysteries ever end?"

"I hope so," Bernard said, "but I don't know when." He hugged Mother after she started crying, which sent Grumps into sobs on the bench until he was comforted by Ruby.

"Oh, Jesus," Father pleaded. "Can we hold this thing together for just a few more minutes?"

Too tired or deflated to respond, the rest of us waited silently for the wheelchair. Or if we did say anything, I've forgotten the words. If I'd known this was the last time the six of us would all be together, I would've remembered every last note. But what I'm left with are just the main chords: Ruby pretending she'd see us again in no time; Bernard acting as if he were returning to some noble battle; Mother ruminating on our volatile family chemistry; Grumps nostalgic for the moment that just elapsed; Father taking every departure personally.

Bernard left first, slinging his bag over his shoulder and sticking out his palm. Father pulled him close and said, "Thanks for sailing with us." Then Mother and Grumps exited for the high-speed ferry to Seattle, and Ruby vanished on a slow one to Vancouver. Finally, Father and I pushed off and motored homeward out of the harbor. He insisted on taking turns napping and watching out for logs, but as it played out he slept and I steered the entire seven hours back to Seattle.

# THE MISSING HEART

〜〜〜〜

It must have been a puzzling sight, two men in coveralls sitting on overturned buckets behind a baby grand piano on a concrete raft propelled by a small Johnson outboard puttering through Sunrise Marina. Then, no doubt, even more baffling to watch them sidle up to an old, impossibly long yacht that could be seen as leaning toward either renovation or demolition. Only a sharp observer would've noticed the thirty-foot crane parked right in front of *Shangri-la* and subsequently connected the dots.

"So what really happened?" Noah asked me as Mick swung the crane arm over the raft.

"What do you mean?"

"Well, you seem all messed up from your family-weekend thing. You guys win or what?"

"Oh, hell no."

We slid padded straps, lined with fresh wax paper, under the soundboard and between the legs and looped all four ends over the crane hook.

"Then why was it so *epic*?" Noah wanted to know. "That's the only word I've got out of you so far. I mean it was just a race, right?"

"Hard to explain."

"Try."

"Okay, for starters, my family never does anything in moderation. And if you factored in the racing handicaps—and that's another story—maybe we were leading the whole thing before the shit hit the fan. But right when we were going our fastest is when we broached."

"How did that happen? I thought you guys are, like, expert sailors."

"Physics, Noah. Too much sail area up for that boat in those conditions. The whole thing was crazy. The redesign, our small crew . . . every piece of it."

We pulled the black tarp off the salon roof we'd already sawed open. Then I climbed down inside as Mick eased the piano off the raft.

"But it wasn't the sailing that was so epic," I shouted over the drone of the crane. "It's what was said."

"Like what?"

"Like everything, like my sister's got cancer."

"Oh, man." He looked down at me, veins angling like fault lines across his forehead. "You mean Ruby?"

"The one and only."

Mick didn't like the alignment and set the piano back down and tried again from a lower angle.

"Hey," I shouted to Noah as the piano slowly descended toward our guiding hands. "How many days till the Rapture, anyway?"

"Very funny." He sanded his cheek stubble with the back of his glove. "Twenty-six," he shouted back. "Part of me keeps worrying that delusions of grandeur are genetic."

I nodded. "What would your father think about you doing all this for Grady?"

"He wouldn't get it."

"Neither would mine."

We waited as Mick carefully maneuvered the crane, delicately lowering the 1943 eighty-eight-key Baldwin baby grand into this tired old yacht as if returning its long-lost heart.

# THE STUPID BITCH

Mother liked to remind us that Einstein was a nobody, a peculiar twenty-six-year-old patent-office clerk with a pregnant girlfriend, when he changed the world. And the pantheon of scientists didn't immediately embrace his daring ideas about gravity, energy and light, either, with years passing while they made the rounds and he climbed the rungs.

The reaction to Mother's brainstorm was, by contrast, almost instantaneous.

Three weeks after we returned from Swiftsure, she posted her solution to the Navier-Stokes problem on a Cornell University website where scientists shared theories and findings.

Her paper sat unnoticed for all of thirty-six hours before *Nature* magazine bannered her assertions in its online edition.

*Perhaps one of the greatest mathematical mysteries of all time has been solved by a high school physics teacher in Washington State named Marcelle Johannssen. If deemed accurate, this former state teacher of the year could be in line for a $1 million prize from the Clay Mathematics Institute. The problem involves the 19th century Navier-Stokes equations, which are at the heart of many fluid-mechanics calculations. Her solution is currently being examined by Dartmouth physics professor Wilson George, who has scrutinized three prior papers claiming to have* *also solved the old riddle. In those earlier cases, Mr. George found flaws within a few hours. He has looked at Ms. Johannssen's paper considerably longer, he said, and at press time had yet to find any problems with her mini-wavelet approach to expanding our understanding of the equations. However, Mr. George cautioned that to be deemed worthy of the prize, Ms. Johannssen's solution would have to withstand up to two years of scrutiny.*

That one paragraph drove the science bloggers into hysteria mode, with the nerd buzz rising loud enough to send the hyperventilating local media to the Teardown.

Her voice shaking, Mother called me for advice when the first TV truck wheeled up. I told her to be her humble self and to say something like "Time will tell if I'm right, but I've given it years of thought and at the moment this is my best shot." I should've encouraged her to tell them to go the hell away until it was confirmed.

The interviews were predictably light on the science before badgering her about what she'd do with the cash. She was interested in the solution, she said, not the prize, though admitted she'd accept the million if it was offered. But what would she buy? "I've got a relative with some potentially large medical bills, and I'd sure enjoy a larger telescope." Despite her stress and insomnia, she looked and sounded astonishingly good on TV. Grumps and Father were guardedly ecstatic, like lotto winners waiting to see the door-sized check.

The Dartmouth prof with interchangeable names called the following morning for a brief conversation. Mother thanked him and removed her paper from the Cornell website, stating only that a serious flaw had been discovered and she needed to determine whether it could be overcome.

Then the shitstorm kicked in. Who knew an angry, anonymous online mob couldn't wait to sink their boots into her ribs?

*Just another charlatan—the stupid bitch thought she'd solved N-S!*

And there were more cordial, condescending commentaries that cited her lack of formal education:

*I don't mean to be elitist, but more than ever, the most daring advances in mathematics come from people already at the pinnacle of their profession. The era of Swiss patent clerks or curious Seattle housewives making major contributions to our understanding of the universe is clearly over.*

She and I read every comment. So did the Bobos.

Their reaction was to take five days off to build and wire an enclosed and heated cedar-paneled observatory on the Teardown roof. Then Father handed her a doodled gift certificate with a blank check and encouraged her to buy whatever telescope she desired.

# RUNAWAY MARINA

My ideal marina would run like a co-op, where everybody makes their boats available to everybody else. Imagine it. We've got Hobies and Lasers, Stars and Vipers, J/Boats and Beneteaus, C&Cs and Hinckleys; yawls and ketches, sloops and trimarans. All of them used all the time by all of us. Handy people help maintain them for free moorage, beer and tips. It runs like a time-share, but you don't have to fly to Hawaii or Mexico to enjoy them. They're right here. Depending on your mood, you could sail a Santa Cruz on Monday, a sailboard on Tuesday and pop out on some old Thunderbird or Joho on Wednesday. There would be simple tests to qualify for different boats and rotating captains to teach the nuances, but skim past the insurance paranoia and you'd have my dream marina instead of the predictable and prevailing model with one underused and underloved sailboat per person.

The first hint that Sunrise Marina was in for an altogether-unusual Saturday came when the corrugated-tin roof sheltering two C Dock slips blew off. Wind that wasn't supposed to show until after four arrived shortly before noon, with wire and rope halyards pounding the hollow aluminum masts so hard they sounded like huge cowbells. Conversations turned into shoutfests, as the entire marina, humans and inanimates alike, groaned and rattled in the hinge-squeaking, rope-straining, temper-fraying onslaught of gusts and waves until that twenty-foot-by-forty-foot sheet of rusty roofing rattled loose over C-14 and C-16, crashing down onto an old Bayliner and an even-older Tollycraft, which unfortunately belonged to Noah.

For the past three weeks he'd been slogging through his days in the boatyard like a sedated patient, a haunted look settling over him while he listened to his father preach nonstop, as he was doing right before the roof flew off. Mercifully and finally, tomorrow was dooms-day. Survive the weekend, and theoretically he and we could resume our lives as sedentary humans.

Yet Noah was riveted to the countdown. There were no imperson-ations, no mention of penguins, no razzing of the boys. He'd drunk himself out of his tics and twitches. Hungover and zombie faced, he performed his boatyard work with his father's station always playing on his headphones. "You know," he'd muttered the day before, "I'd completely forgotten how much I love the sound of his voice."

Saturday's unexpected windstorm—they called for twenty-five knots, not forty-five—didn't help keep things in perspective. Noah stepped out on deck after the roof slid off his boat and vanished into the murk. He glanced up at the turbulent sky, then retreated back inside to hear his father.

"We are coming to the end of this spectacular drama," the old preacher told his listeners. "Next will come an earthquake that the Bible says will be bigger than anything we've seen. And this quake will then open the graves of every believer who's died during the past thirteen thousand years."

Despite the storm, it was warm enough for Rem to walk around in his boxers and T-shirt, griping about the marina owners being such cheapskates that the goddamn roofs were blowing off, as if this vali-dated every slanderous charge anybody had ever made against them.

The second hint that the day had hopped its rails was when a skinny platinum blond resembling my sister swaggered down the A Dock with her hand atop her head in the gale. It'd been just four weeks since I'd seen her at Swiftsure, yet she looked absolutely foreign all over again.

"Aren't you a pathetic sight!" she said, patting down her wig and exhaling theatrically. "This thing's driving me crazy. Don't look so concerned! I'll be my fashionable self again in no time."

When I hugged her, she felt as thin and light as a bony ten-year-old. "Ouch!" she said, and asked to be put back down.

"What're you doing here?" I asked. "Why are you . . . why didn't you . . . What I mean is I'm just surprised—and *thrilled*—to see you."

"Today's that Star regatta, yes? Races start at three, I seem to recall. You apparently didn't think I'd come or you wouldn't be treating me like some ghost. Why didn't I call? When do I ever call?"

"Look around, Rube," I said, palms up and pivoting. "The races were canceled. It's blowing forty, gusting fifty. We just had a roof torn off."

"Since when do races get scratched because it's windy?" she demanded, mimicking Father's bravado.

"I'm sorry," I said. "This is different."

"Hey," she said, glancing past me, "is that the famous Mario?"

Looking up, I saw him strapping thicker mooring lines to Yvonne's Star.

"Hey, Mario!" she shouted.

He looked over to scowl at whoever was breaking his concentration. But then his eyes and mouth opened wide, and I swear his entire body wobbled, as he strode awkwardly toward us into the wind. I could tell he wanted to run.

"Ruby?" he said when he got close, his face a mix of delight and concern. Then he bowed like Johnny and I did after losing races together—a deep one, as if greeting the queen. "Is that really you?"

She pulled off her wig and rubbed her buzz cut. "I'm afraid so. Recently sold all my locks, though, so I'm kind of between hairdos.

But wow, don't you look fantastic? Larger and more adultish, but great. I came down to sail with my chickenshit brother, who now claims the races were canceled due to wind."

She tilted her head to the side as a gust whistled through the dock, rattling halyards and shaking roofs. "Any chance you'd take me out for a sail, Mario?"

"All I've, why all I've got," he stammered, "is the Star, and it's not really mine. But if you want—"

"Hey, I'm kidding. I don't need to sail," she said flatly, suddenly looking too tired to stand, then turned toward me and admitted, "I also came down to make sure Momma was okay with not solving that problem."

"And what do you think?"

"She's not all right."

Hatches and latches kept clanging. Tarps flew off some boats and wrapped around others. Loosely furled jibs swung out wide and drove boats against the docks. Another roof section flew off near Noah, widening his path to the heavens.

I fried quesadillas in my galley and sorted embellishments from truths as Mario and I listened to my sister rave about how fantastic she felt. She was eating quinoa and raw vegetables and doing this yoga and that Tai Chi. Huge flocks of snow geese had changed their migratory paths to spend a weekend on her farm, she told us. "Woke up and looked out the window, and it was like a foot of snow had fallen. Guess the navigator goose got drunk or lost, or they decided our farm needed some fertilizer. It stinks, sure, but you still have to call that a gift from above, don't you?"

"But is everything in remission," I pressed, "or are you just being positive?"

She squinted. "Didn't I cover that already? Everything looks great—except me. I'm re*cup*erating."

"You're too thin, Rube."

"Chemo doesn't make you hungry, Josh, but I feel like a champ."
She punched the air in front of Mario's nose. Then she wound down,
ate very little and dozed on the bunk through the ensuing pandemo-
nium. Mario sat there watching her sleep. I didn't know how to ask
him to leave.

Rem was the first to notice and ran to my boat. "Josh! Josh! We're
moving, Josh!" Then to everybody: "The marina's moving!"

I knew instantly what he meant because I'd been registering motion
on some new level, something different than the wind and the current lapping against the hull. A look to shore confirmed it. We were
heading out.

Sunrise Marina was theoretically bolted and strapped to the dry
land, and further secured by steel hoops looped over pilings as thick
as telephone poles. But if the shore ties snapped and the pilings were
short or rotting and the tide and waves washed high enough, how
secure was it? Strangely, the storm actually seemed to be weakening
at the moment the marina let go and started floating away.

Most of the liveaboards couldn't hear our warning cries until we
were actually at their boats. The A, B and C Docks were now severed,
along with water and power lines, from the rest of the marina. Some
seventy-two boats, we'd later count, as well as eleven shacks and a
partially roofed dock, were drifting out of the shallows, the floating
docks and smaller piers bending at tortured angles yet moving as one,
like a city block or a crowded trailer park suddenly sliding north. For
many of these boats and owners, it marked their first outing in years.

We continued alerting liveaboards hunkered obliviously below.
Some, like Noah, had been drinking through the storm. I had Georgia, the former nun, and Cara—who'd moved aboard the Coronado 27

I'd rescued from demolition—make sure everybody put on life jackets, and before long we looked like some outward-bound expedition for wayward adults.

I shouted repeatedly for everybody to prepare their anchors. "But do *not* drop them yet!" That didn't keep Trent from misunderstanding and letting his fly and dragging it behind us until it pulled the cleat off his pier. I'd planned on dropping them en masse before we hit the log booms, but when we blew east into deeper water I realized there was a chance we could make it into the next cove and out of the storm's path.

That's when I heard Ruby awaken and ask Mario, "What kind of crazy marina is this?"

After we cleared the logs and rounded the treed peninsula, I had Rem double check that everybody had life jackets on and flashlights handy. "Everybody on C Dock," I shouted, "get ready to drop your anchors!"

Some tossed them over immediately.

"Not yet!" I yelled.

More anchors flew. Little ones, big ones, Danforths, Bruces, Deltas, plows.

I gave up. "Okay! Now!"

People threw anything they figured might stop us. Lunch anchors, grappling hooks, crab pots, fishing lures.

"About sixty feet of scope!" I yelled. "And tie off to sturdy cleats."

The waves calmed. The docks somehow remained intact. Anchors seemed to hold. Grady checked his GPS and checked it again. "We are stationary!" he declared.

We'd come to a stop almost a mile north of our address yet looked like we belonged, as if this were some sort of newfangled mobile marina you could get to only by boat.

I had Rem do a head count. None of the eighteen liveaboards on the three docks was missing except a stoner named Wendell, who'd been washing his laundry and had come back to discover that his boat and dock had vanished.

Calling the Coast Guard, I gave our coordinates and assured them that all residents and visitors were safe and accounted for—including Noah, who still hadn't taken a break from his father's broadcast to step outside and see what was happening.

Checking on Ruby, I was startled to see Mario's arm around her. "Mario works in transportation logistics!" she said, like this was the cutest thing she'd ever heard.

With our runaway marina seemingly secure, the shortest night of the year rolled in as we congregated in front of Grady's *Shangri-la,* seeing as how it was the largest boat and he had the most beer. Cramming aboard, we filled the air with our babbling astonishment while taking turns plinking childish songs on the baby grand.

Ruby, in her dazzling wig, listened vacantly to Rem rattle on about how he deserved more acclaim for noticing our near catastrophe before anyone else. "I mean Paul Revere probably couldn't buy his own drinks after alerting everybody, don't you think?"

I felt guilty for not doting on her, though Mario was giving her constant attention, shadowing her like a bodyguard. And I remembered how even a younger, healthy Ruby wilted at parties when she wasn't the main draw. "You don't want to play a little something?" I finally asked, pointing at the piano.

Her left eyebrow gunned that idea down. "I'm exhausted," she said as Georgia's flawless "Yankee Doodle" elicited polite applause.

At Mother's insistence, Ruby had taken lessons but infuriated her teacher by refusing to learn how to read music. The only time I ever heard her play was in a bank. Why they had a piano, I have no idea, but she sat down and banged out something jazzy and fun before stopping in the middle, insisting that it wasn't a real song and she'd messed it up anyway.

When Georgia broke into "Mary Had a Little Lamb," I made eye contact with Ruby, who shook her head but edged closer to the piano. And after a very slow rendition of "Skip to My Lou," she asked if she could play.

Georgia yielded reluctantly, but soon Ruby's freakishly long fingers were poised over Grady's baby grand as she got acquainted with the keys and pedals.

"What're you gonna play for us?" Georgia asked.

"I don't know songs," Ruby said, finally looking up. "I just plunk around for something that sounds good to me."

Then she banged out several quick, clever rhythms, first with one hand, then both. People stopped chatting. Grady moved closer. With those quick riffs as her foundation, she shifted into a loud, fast and jazzy asymmetrical jag that she later called a variation on the one song she'd taught herself on the Mercy Ship's piano, then she swung back to her initial rhythms. People started wiggling and moving—Mario whooped like we were at a rodeo—and as the sound rose up in this confined space, she returned to what felt like a catchy hook we all recognized but couldn't quite place. By now she was milking the attention, closing her eyes, smiling and rocking from side to side. When she resumed that hook, Cara began to scat. That's right—the dock lush who'd inherited enough money from her recently deceased aunt Ruth to cover her moorage bills was *scatting*. If you'd heard it on the radio it might've sounded all right, a decent voice with a little training, a sense of timing and a nice repertoire of *bumgiddydeedees* and *shoobydobobbies*. But given that she was ripping it in Grady's mildewed fantasy lounge on a wonderfully peculiar night, it was *Ella* good. The best part, though, was watching my sister smiling and rocking so hard that her wig fell off. She kept swinging us back around to that same jazzy hook with Cara's improv piling up on top of it. Nobody else was doing anything but listening and gasping and dancing in place. Resisting the encore calls, Ruby plunked around in hopes of finding another rhythm, misfired several times and then grabbed her wig and rose slowly, her fatigue a lead sweater by now, to acknowledge the applause.

I stole her away to my boat and set her up in my best sleeping bag in the most comfortable bunk. She was groggy the moment she got horizontal. When Mario started telling me for the second time that she was his one and only, I resisted informing him that he'd have to date a billion women to be sure. Then I left him there to watch her sleep.

Returning to *Shangri-la,* I found Rem fishing off B Dock and whistling off tune. Then Georgia leaned over the stern of her big catamaran and dropped a crab pot that somebody had given her years ago. She used sharp cheddar as bait, her theory being that no living creature can resist good cheese. And half an hour before midnight, Noah finally made an appearance.

"Good to see you!" Georgia shouted. "Oh, quit looking so glum. Can't you at least find a little humor in all the doomsday bullshit?"

"What if God's into irony," Cara mused, her voice husky from singing, "and messes with us by sending up the *non*believers?"

"Did you *shave*?" Georgia asked Noah. "Now isn't that presumptuous? You want to be all proper for your ascension, don't you?"

Noah forced a grin. "Hedging my bets," he said, then noticed the nudist couple toweling off after some skinny-dipping. "As the sunlight begins to disappear at the end of their fifth year," he said, reviving, at last, his Morgan Freeman voice-over, "and the warm days begin to cool, they too will climb out of the water. And they will march just as they have done for centuries ever since the emperor penguin decided to stay, to live and love in the harshest place on earth."

Trent didn't laugh along. He still resented Noah calling him a meth head to his face when he hadn't done any meth in nine goddamn months. "Why are you always quoting that sappy movie?" he demanded now. "It's not like it's *Caddyshack* or *Pulp Fiction* or some other classic."

Noah looked away. I was about to defend him when he said, "Because I can't quite get over those penguins, Trent. Minus-eighty degrees, and they still waddle seventy miles across land to try to make a family. Okay? Have you ever even seen it? When the mothers go off to fatten up so they'll be able to feed their unborn babies, the fathers wait with the eggs between their feet for up to a hundred and twenty-five days *without a single meal*. It's love and family and sacrifice. If you think all that is sappy, I pity you. And there's this one scene..." Noah stopped, bunched his lips and took a deep breath. "This one scene where a mother's trying to wake up her dead chick. And she's shrieking a bit and poking at her. And you're invested in both of them by this point. And, ah shit. They're so resilient, those fucking penguins."

Trent turned to me, wiped imaginary tears and lip-synched, *Those fucking penguins.* "Take it easy, Noah," he said. "I'm just saying it's not *The Notebook* or *Schindler's List.*"

From here the drinking snowballed and the head counts got trickier as people retreated to their boats without letting anybody know. Those of us still standing stared up at the clearing sky, which is why I noticed the bright dot flying overhead like a very slow shooting star.

"Grady," I shouted. "The space station again!"

I'd never seen him move so quickly, scrambling across the wheelhouse to his ham radio.

"Whiskey Zero Sugar Victor callin' November Alpha Sierra Sierra."

Turning to me, he said, "I found their call name on the Internet."

"Whiskey Zero Sugar Victor," he repeated into the radio, "come in November Alpha Sierra Sierra."

"Whiskey Zero Sugar Victor," responded a strange voice, "we've got you loud and clear. Welcome aboard the International Space Station."

We cheered.

"November Alpha Sierra Sierra," Grady nearly shouted, "the humble people of the Pacific Northwest salute you and your crew!"

A chuckle crackled through the speaker. "And we, the crew of the International Space Station, salute you as well, sir."

"What should I say?" Grady asked the remaining drunks. "Peace be with you!" he yelled. After no response, he shouted, *"Namaste!"*

When midnight finally arrived, nothing overt happened other than more people slinked off to bed. Eventually, everybody but Noah and I had either surrendered to sleep, drowned or—unbeknownst to us—ascended.

"Mathematically speaking, according to my father, believers should be going up by now," Noah said.

"Maybe just not from our docks," I told him. "We're a small sample. And mathematically speaking, according to my *mother,* I should have found the love of my life by now."

Shortly after daybreak, two tugs showed up and helped tow the marina back to where it belonged. Meanwhile, Grady and I organized boats with working engines to tow the powerless ones to temporary moorages.

By the time I finally got Ruby to shore, she was pleading with me to quit worrying about her. "My doctors are great. I've got so many friends nursing and helping me already, it's absolutely exhausting. I'm gonna be just fine, Josh, better than fine."

"But don't you want some breakfast," I stalled. "You've got such a long drive. Why can't you just hang around more often?"

"C'mon, I'm right here right now. Who just gave you a surprise visit? Who played some halfway decent jazzy piano last night just for you, huh?"

"I love you, Rube."

She laughed. "You think I don't know that by now?"

"I don't think you have any idea."

She gave me a long smile. "Pull yourself together, soldier." Then she left me with her pimp walk, arms swinging behind her, spinning her head back to make sure I was watching. Then my bald sister slid inside a small station wagon with BEAUTIFUL BRITISH COLUMBIA plates (she'd finally got a license, passing the test on her third try) and turned the wrong way out of the marina. I stood waiting until she'd executed a clumsy U-turn and drove back past with a parade wave as Mario pulled out and followed.

# DATE NUMBER 35

Five weeks after the doomsday storm, the boatyard had resumed its seasonal mania with fresh rounds of manifest-destiny couples, naïve ocean goers, delusional captains and feverish boat shoppers. Wait till October, we'd tell them, and the prices will drop with every inch of rain. But no, these people needed boats *now*.

Amazingly, Noah bounced back to his old self after his father's public apology for getting the date wrong *again*. In hindsight, he told the smirking media, he'd miscalculated. What he'd been calling "the end day" was actually the beginning of its six-month prelude; the true ascension would occur on December 24. All of which made him fodder for yet another day's news cycle. Then it all went mercifully quiet, and Noah spoke to him for the first time in five years. "You know," I overheard him say comfortingly, "there was one hell of a storm here that night. Completely unexpected, too."

Lorraine had quit the yard to head out with Marcy in her Catalina 27, at least for an Alaska adventure. We were all delighted that Rex was no longer in the picture. But Lorraine? Are you two *together,* the boys desperately wanted to ask when the two of them said good-bye. We launched *Sophia,* Blaine Stanton's Pearson 36, that same afternoon. He looked more exuberant than ever with his rebuilt heart. There weren't enough hands for him to shake for all the expensive and irrational labor we'd done for him.

Then Sunita the sailmaker surprised me the following evening at Sunrise when she strolled up to let me know she was fitting sails for some old Morgan 36 on G Dock, but that she'd be willing to look at my sail inventory if I was still interested in maybe ordering a new jib. She said she had called me.

"Dropped my phone in the water last Wednesday," I explained, knowing it sounded like a lie, "and haven't replaced it yet." I couldn't look her in the eyes for long. I hadn't broken down all day and didn't want to in front of her.

"I'll pass on the sails for now," I said, my eyes roaming, my heart thumping. "I've gotta help a few liveaboards with some things right now."

Her head bobbed beneath the North Sails hat. Finally, she said, "I'll check back when I've finished up." I shrugged like it was fine either way, but she couldn't have picked a worse day to track me down.

When she next found me, I was upside down inside Cara's lazarette, drilling holes for screws to brace a tiny fuel pump for the diesel heater I'd installed. I could hear her on the pier talking into her phone when I called up to Cara, asking for a screwdriver I'd left in the cockpit.

After finishing that project, I didn't see Sunita anywhere as my liveaboard posse trailed me to Remy's yawl, where he was cursing a new leak behind the engine that kept setting off his bilge alarm. I squeezed my head between the engine and the cockpit until I was far enough back to shine a flashlight on the puddle beneath the shaft seal. I dried everything off a few times and at last located the pinhole leak beading near the shaft.

Resurfacing, I blew my nose and saw Sunita from the back on the far side of the dock, chatting with Cara.

Awaiting bad news, Rem paced in tight circles on the pier. He didn't have the cash to pull the damn boat, he explained, and couldn't sleep with the bilge alarm going off every two hours.

"It's not the seal," I told him. "It's a hairline crack near the shaft log." I grabbed a tub from my bag and mixed up this special epoxy that can cure in water. Breathing poorly, I hastily mixed the adhesive, then dried and slathered the pinhole. It took every inch of my fingertips to work the goo into the right spot. I lay there, head pinging, and waited. The leak actually stopped—for now.

Scraping my scalp climbing out, I dabbed at the blood. Sunita was still there with several liveaboards lurking and muttering, *Hey, Josh, hey, man.*

I indulged every question because only work kept me together these days. But finally she stepped up and said, "Could we talk?"

Following her down the dock out of everybody's earshot, I said, "I'm sorry, but I really don't know when I'll be done here. I've been putting these people off way too long." When she didn't respond, I lost control of my words. "And if for some crazy reason you're the slightest bit interested in me, I really don't have the patience to wait for you to figure out that I'm geographically undesirable, don't own a car, look like a stray dog most of the time, occasionally drink coffee out of Styrofoam cups, might make out with your sister in your dreams and have four goddamn planets in Scorpio."

"Josh."

"Yeah, I'm sorry."

"I love stray dogs and Scorpios." She smiled. "I also like guys who fix other people's problems in their spare time and who are too shy or guarded to just look me in the eye and ask me out."

How's it possible I'd barely noticed her that first time she came into the boatyard? Having been a resident of this planet for thirty-one years, I'd seen thousands of women and witnessed countless forms of beauty. Not immediately noticing hers was like failing to notice that a hummingbird defies the laws of flight.

"Will you go," I began carefully, "and I know this sounds weird, but will you go with me to my sister's funeral a week from Sunday? It's really a wake, is what it is, but I realize that's a very strange first date. And if you—"

"Oh, no," she whispered.

"Oh, yes."

Somebody called her name, probably the irritable podiatrist whose boat she was working on. He shouted "Sunita!" again. She ignored him and, after what seemed like a very long time, finally said, "I'd be honored."

Then she didn't so much hug me as get in between my arms. I was fine until that happened.

## THE IMMORTALITY OF SAILING FAST

There were no ashes.

The sweaty man who ran the Squamish Chapel & Crematorium told me this was a rare occurrence, though not unheard-of, particularly with infants. Sometimes, he explained, the *process* is so efficient and the remains so small there's little or nothing left behind.

Ruby had lost a lot of weight, but she was much bigger than any baby, I said, to which he had no response other than to blink excessively and stutter that there would be no ch-ch-charge.

I didn't know how to make sense of this, or explain it to the family. Had Ruby left no ashes because she wasn't made of carbon and oxygen like the rest of us? Was this just her final believe-it-or-not stunt? Had we collectively imagined her altogether? Or had one of her farm zealots simply stolen the ashes?

There was no Bernard around to investigate. He'd left so abruptly after Swiftsure, mumbling only that he was teaming up with *some people down south,* that we had no way to let him know he was now sisterless. The rest of the family didn't have much to say about the ash mystery, as if they'd expected something inexplicable from Ruby, even now.

"At least they didn't try to pawn off somebody else's ashes," Mother said, then shared a creepy story about a pathologist who'd absconded with Einstein's brain, cut it into two hundred and forty thin slices and stored them in Mason jars for thirty years.

Though Ruby's doctor never returned my calls, his caffeinated nurse told me the only surprise about my sister's passing was that she'd lived so long. Initially, they'd diagnosed it as noninvasive breast cancer, but an April ultrasound showed three large tumors on her liver, too. "We knocked it back as best we could with chemo, radiation and stem cells." The tumors were too large and aggressive for an operation, she explained, and Ruby wasn't a strong candidate for a liver transplant. She handed me an envelope Ruby had asked her to mail once she'd died. "You said you were driving up for the ashes and all, so I thought I'd make certain you got it."

*Dear Family,*

*Sorry I didnt tell the full truth about how sick I was but I didnt fully know yet and theres always been way to much fuss about me. I didnt want to exit like that to. Im not ready for this life to end but in the time Ive had how could anyboddy hope for more? Even though Ive ben gone so long Ive never left any of you and never will. All my love to all of you.*
*Ruby*

The unanswered questions mounted as I drove off. Why wasn't she a *strong candidate* for a transplant? Would her treatment have been better in the States? And the saddest ones: Why had she insisted on battling this without her family? Why hadn't she let her scientist momma and her fix-it brother try to help?

So many people packed into the Sons of Norway Hall it got passout hot. There were friends, sailors, locals of all ages and Canadian farm workers, too, with people dressed in suits, overalls, dresses and cutoffs. Mario Seville was there in all black, sniffling like a widower waiting to be comforted.

Father stood to speak but couldn't stop blubbering about *his Ruby* and sat back down. None of us had ever seen him even tear up before. Then Grumps sang an Icelandic song about fate and coincidence before breaking down himself. Mother started with a dry chronology of Ruby's life before veering off script. "She was extraordinary, oh yes. We all hope to feel glory and make sense of the chaos, don't we? Earthquakes, tsunamis, hurricanes, forest fires, liver cancer. Why Ruby? She never even drank. People lose perspective at moments like these. Yes, Ruby was a miracle. But so are all of you. And so is an earthworm. Let me leave you with a suggestion and a tip: study nature to better understand the gift of your life. The most amazing thing you can ever encounter is what's going on inside of every single cell in your body." She looked at everyone and recoiled, as if shaken by all the intent faces. Steadying herself, she said, "I've always been honored and flattered to be Ruby's mother. And I always will be."

Finally it was my turn. I struggled to explain what it was like to watch her sail, then shared stories that showed her goofy humor because everybody desperately needed to laugh. "Another unusual thing about my sister is that she's always been more vivid in my mind than most people are in person." Then I closed my eyes and described her, really fast and very specifically.

"A thin pink birthmark on the underside of her neck curls up beneath her right jawbone. She has a laugh versatile enough to fit any moment, and a left foot that is a full size bigger than her right, and a belly button that is neither an innie nor an outtie but a flush-decker, and a mole the size of a pencil eraser behind her left ear. Her fingers are almost twice as long as they should be. Her eyes are a pale shade of green that can be found nowhere else. And if you watch closely, her hair color shifts with her moods."

I don't remember much else other than this huge unwashed Canuck lifted me off the floor when I walked from the microphone toward Sunita.

Within a month, our Star fleet would quit racing due to shrinking turnouts, and Mario Seville would never be seen on the bay again. The boatyard boys would unceremoniously scatter as well. Mick got a job near his brother in a Bay Area yard. Big Alex left to work on truck diesels, where he was far less likely to get stuck in engine compartments. Jack, who the boys always speculated was making *a bundle* supervising us, suddenly retired to a trailer park to live off disability. Noah went home to Boring, Oregon, to care for his father after he fell and cracked three vertebrae.

Later that same week I left, too, motoring north out of Sunrise Marina toward Seattle at daybreak. For a full hour I had the planet to myself, my wake fanning out some mysterious message across the glassy inlet, the sky and trees more vivid in reflection than in reality. Then, so swiftly, the mirror faded, and the harsh sun illuminated the humdrum of yet another day, I-5 droning in the background.

Grumps was beyond thrilled when I asked if he'd share his room with me. So I moved back in and slept above him on Bernard's old bunk. I made the Bobos breakfast in the mornings and helped them work on a comfortable and original boat that Grumps had designed for a repeat customer. And on my second weekend home, to my father's disbelief, I jacked up the sagging corners of the Teardown and replaced sections of rotten beams and posts with fresh wood and new joists. Dropped tennis balls no longer rolled toward Olympia.

While the bankruptcy proceedings continued in slow motion, I learned of a potentially exotic windfall in the works. A retired forty-six-year-old tech tycoon had approached Father after Ruby's funeral to give his condolences as well as his phone number, saying he'd be honored if the Bobos would consider trying to design and build him the fastest mono-hulled sailboat in the Northwest in time for the next Swiftsure.

And so began the perfect diversion for our post-Ruby world. Drawings were anchored at the corners with beers and wineglasses after dinner, with me and Mother and even Sunita offering comments and ideas over the Bobos' shoulders.

They were leaning toward a light and narrow carbon-fiber 69-footer (the maximum diagonal length of the boathouse) that would excel in light and erratic winds, with a 100-foot mast and a deep-bulb keel that retracted upward, reducing the draft from 13.5 to 8.5 feet depending on needs and conditions.

Once the preliminary drawings and an estimated $1.9-million price tag were enthusiastically accepted, every family brain cell focused on this exclusively; with Father's *boat speed, boat speed* providing our mantra alongside his vision of a sloop that sailed effortlessly at fifteen knots and left almost no wake. He worked feverishly on all the options, as if this job offered not only solvency but an immortality that came with building the fastest sailboat in these waters.

Grumps insisted on perfect sailing ergonomics, challenging us to make it as comfortable as it was fast. After running fluid-dynamics equations on different hull shapes, Mother advocated a flatter, dinghylike hull with a wider stern. Sunita suggested bigger *wings*—oh, how Father loved to hear her talk about sails—with a wider, more powerful main that would overlap the backstay by three feet. My role was to make sure the rigging, winches, blocks, electronics and plumbing were all as handy, lightweight and durable as possible.

During this creative frenzy, we heard from Bernard for the first time since Swiftsure. His letter to the Teardown came with a clipping from the *Herald Sun* about a *vigilante vessel* ramming and disabling a whaling ship in the Southern Ocean.

*Dear Blood Relatives,*

*I'm not sure why but I'm compelled to tell you what I'm up to even if it violates my own code of secrecy. When I left you all in Victoria I flew to Melbourne where I've teamed up with like-minded people to start a new organization to defend the whales of the Southern Ocean. (We're still arguing over what to call ourselves. But we've incorporated in Canada and we've got a few anonymous sugar daddies backing us for now.) And as you can see from this article we've taken action with a crew of 11 courageous men and women in their 20s and 30s. We're Americans, Australians and Canadians and one New Zealander (me!) aboard this big, fast and very stout trawler.*

*We're going after whalers who violate international moratoriums. Right now, it's the Japanese slaughtering hundreds of minkes in the name of "scientific research." You wouldn't believe the carnage. We tracked their lead boat at night. And when we got close enough, we (I) told them through a megaphone to stop their illegal whaling immediately and leave the area or we would enforce the laws of the International Whaling Commission and incapacitate their vessel. They ran. We followed and found them whaling again two days later. We didn't give them a second warning. We rammed them at 10 knots right in the side. Nobody was hurt but the boat had to be towed away. Well, you can read the article.*

*I must be getting old and soft because I find myself sitting here on deck at nightfall, halfway around the globe, wondering what my family would think of me. That's the danger of seeing you all. What I know for sure is that I've never been more at peace with what I'm doing. To stay on the safe side, everybody down here knows me as Charles Chapman, from Wellington. (Please destroy this letter, Josh.) So the crew calls me Chap or Captain Chapman. That's right. I am running this fucking show. I am the sheriff of these southern seas. How do you like that?*

"Good God!" Father exclaimed. "Just when you think things couldn't get any worse, he gets twice as crazy! What are you smiling about?"

"I like it," Mother said softly.

"You like what? That Bernard's a suicidal egomaniac?"

"No, I like to think that the illegal whalers and poachers of the world have to watch out for my son." She pushed her hair back over her ears. "In fact, I love it."

"Don't be ridiculous."

"I like it, too," Grumps said sheepishly.

"That makes three of us," I said, borrowing Grumps's lighter and walking Bernard's letter to the fireplace.

"Sweet Jesus," Father said.

Bernard's words were still playing in my head when I rolled up to Sunita's green bungalow north of Ballard. Three days before, she'd asked me to move in with her but quickly admitted her one and only reservation: Mia hadn't *warmed up* to me yet. That was an understatement. The chubby four-year-old terrified me ever since I put my hand on her head and she looked up crossly and said, "I don't want two daddies."

But with Mia's father out of town and her one reliable babysitter unavailable, Sunita asked if I'd watch her for a few hours. "Just don't let her watch *Toy Story 3*," she whispered on her way out the door, "or that's all she'll do."

I asked Mia to show me her toys and games, but she didn't want to play with any of them. "C'mon," I said, picking through her closet. "Legos are awesome."

"Legos are dumb," she said.

"You've got great dolls. That's for sure. Look at these!"

"I hate dolls."

I showed her some simple card tricks. They were too complicated. I tried to win her over with ice cream. She wasn't hungry. I did some remarkably convincing impressions of dogs, goats and Canada geese. Still nothing. I flipped through her videos. "You wanna watch *Toy Story 3*?"

"Not really," she said.

"Oh, come on!" I begged. "I love that movie!"

"Okay," she said grumpily.

We giggled on opposite sides of the couch for 103 minutes. "You want to watch it again?" she asked.

"Definitely!" I said. When she scooted closer, I finally started glancing around at my new home.

# NOTHING IS PERMANENT

Einstein's doctor ordered him to quit sailing in his late forties or risk antagonizing the inflamed walls of his heart. He agreed to a salt-free diet but wouldn't give up his hobby. It was part of who he was, and he sailed most of his remaining years while seeking a *simple and beautiful* unifying theory of the laws of the universe. Simultaneously, he also was advocating a world federation of sorts that might help curb the warmongering that usually accompanies nationalism. So yes, as Mother pointed out again recently, Einstein was trying to leave the world not only better understood but also at peace.

Flash forward sixty years to early 2013 and Grumps, too, is ignoring his doctor's advice to stop sailing. His goals and ambitions, though, are modest and shrinking. He hopes to leave his business solvent, his family comfortable, his geese with plenty of stale bread. Mostly, he wishes he could hold on to the memories he feels spilling through his fingers.

He's used a cane ever since Swiftsure but often looks like he needs a walker. His doc insists that if he boats at all, he should putter around in the powerboat that a grateful customer willed to him, yet I still take him sailing if the wind's light enough. When I hand him the tiller, his agility returns in bursts, as if the unsteadiness of a sailboat focuses his joints and inner ear. He doesn't steer as well as he used to, but I just adjust the sails to suit wherever he goes.

And we talk about Ruby.

My parents avoid mentioning her. But when Grumps gets me alone, he asks me to tell Ruby stories, as if he's afraid that otherwise he'll forget her altogether. Most of them sound brand-new to him, no matter how many times he's already heard them.

"On my eleventh birthday," I tell him now, sailing across Lake Union in the fading light, "you guys left us for some Great Lakes regatta. Mother said you were just postponing my party until you got back. I tried not to pout, but Ruby picked up on it and talked Bernard into helping her blow up a couple hundred balloons while I was asleep. So I woke up on my birthday to a room stuffed floor to ceiling with so many balloons I could barely walk."

Grumps smiles and nods.

"Here's another one," I tell him after we tack back toward the marina. "And you might remember this one. We were all headed for the locks on a Friday night for a week in the islands, but our air horn was dead. So we couldn't honk to get them to open the Fremont. We had to keep circling, and Father was yelling up at the bridgeman, pissed that we couldn't get his attention, while the rest of us continued searching for the spare horn. Finally, Ruby said, 'Let's just pretend *we're* the horn!' Mother and I played along. So the three of us counted it down and, in unison, gave one long '*Uhhhhh!*' Followed by a short '*Uh!*' It sounded like bad a cappella. And there was no response. So we did it again, all of us this time, much longer and louder: '*Hoooooooonk! Hoonk!*' Albert and Isaac got excited and started yapping, too. Then the bridgeman tooted the *will-do* retort, and the cars suddenly stopped on both sides, and the little bridge began to lift."

"I do remember that," Grumps says.

"Have you had enough?" I ask him.

"No," he says, though I can see the tears in his whiskers. "One more."

"All right, but then we're dropping the sails and heading in."

"That's fair," he says. "Let's hear the last one."

"It's early fall," I tell him, "and the three of us are bicycling down to Golden Gardens to catch the sunset. Ruby's idea, of course. And once we're on the beach, she and I hop from log to log to see how far we can get without ever stepping on the sand. Bernard thinks that's stupid and starts throwing rocks. Little ones for distance, at first, then larger ones, until finally he's hurling boulders, spinning and grunting like a discus thrower, heaving them high out over the water. He's going for maximum splash. That's when I start whining that summer's over and the days are getting shorter and our guinea pig, Rufus, just keeled over and that one of my favorite teachers, Miss Winters, just died in a car crash. And Ruby says, 'Oh, Josh, it's like a play: you gotta see everything while it's onstage because after that it's gone.' Even Bernard stops throwing rocks to hear what she'll say next. I think she was ten at the time, maybe eleven. 'Look around!' she says, and twirls like a gymnast with her big hands out wide. 'The trees, the birds, the dogs, the houses, the people. Nothing is permanent!' And she's smiling. That's what gets me. She's *delighted*."

# THANKS

To Norman Franzen, my inspiring math guru, and to Suzanne White Brahmia, my friend in physics.

To David Elliott, Norm Smit, Genny Tulloch and Mike O'Brien for sailing insights. To Lenny Mason, Jeff Shurtz and Neil Falkenberg for boatyard wisdom.

To Chuck and Dee Robinson for the writing getaway. And to my insightful early readers, including Jess Walter, Grace Lynch, Cindy O'Brien, Tom Nelson, Delia and Rich Whitehead.

To my agent and accomplice, Kimberly Witherspoon, and to my editor and friend, Gary Fisketjon.

And, as always, to Denise. Without her faith and humor, these pages would be blank.

## A NOTE ABOUT THE AUTHOR

Jim Lynch is the author of the novels *The Highest Tide, Border Songs* and *Truth Like the Sun,* all of which were performed onstage. His honors include a Pacific Northwest Booksellers Award, an Indies Choice Honor Book Award, a Dashiell Hammett Prize nomination and a Livingston Young Journalist Award for National Reporting. Lynch lives and sails in Olympia, Washington, with his wife, Denise.

## A NOTE ON THE TYPE

This book was set in Legacy Serif. Ronald Arnholm (b. 1939) designed the Legacy family after being inspired by the 1470 edition of *Eusebius* set in the roman type of Nicolas Jenson. This revival type maintains much of the character of the original. Its serifs, stroke weights, and varying curves give Legacy Serif its distinct appearance. It was released by the International Typeface Corporation in 1992.

*Typeset by Scribe, Philadelphia, Pennsylvania*

*Printed and bound by Berryville Graphics, Berryville, Virginia*

*Designed by M. Kristen Bearse*